The Palmer Family in 1943

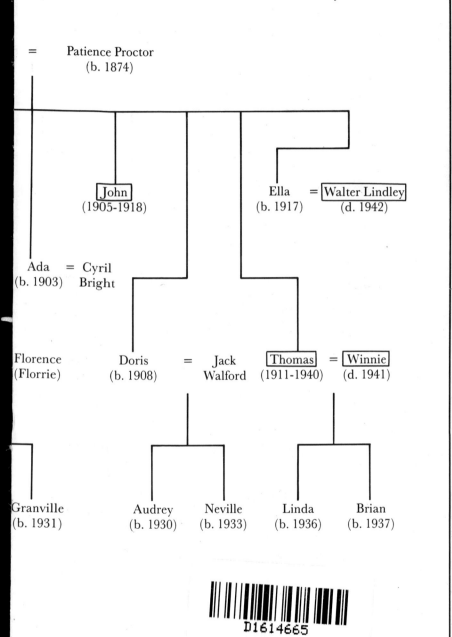

= Patience Proctor
    (b. 1874)

☐ John ☐
(1905-1918)

Ella   = ☐ Walter Lindley ☐
(b. 1917)   (d. 1942)

Ada   = Cyril
(b. 1903)   Bright

Florence   Doris   =   Jack   ☐ Thomas ☐ = ☐ Winnie ☐
(Florrie)   (b. 1908)   Walford   (1911-1940)   (d. 1941)

Granville   Audrey   Neville   Linda   Brian
(b. 1931)   (b. 1930)   (b. 1933)   (b. 1936)   (b. 1937)

NEXT OF KIN

NEXT OF KIN

Stan Barstow

Michael Joseph
London

MICHAEL JOSEPH LTD

Published by the Penguin Group
27 Wrights Lane, London W8 5TZ, England
Viking Penguin Inc., 375 Hudson Street, New York, New York 10014, USA
Penguin Books Australia Ltd, Ringwood, Victoria, Australia
Penguin Books Canada Ltd, 2801 John Street, Markham, Ontario, Canada L3R 1B4
Penguin Books (NZ) Ltd, 182–190 Wairau Road, Auckland 10, New Zealand

Penguin Books Ltd, Registered Offices: Harmondsworth, Middlesex, England

First published 1991

Printed in England by Clays Ltd, St Ives plc
Set in Baskerville 12/14 pt

A CIP catalogue record for this book is available from the British Library

ISBN 0 7181 3532 6

To my mother,
Elsie Gosnay
1900–90

PART ONE

ONE

I

A woman two tables away, in a hat with a feather, ate with her knife held like a pen. Ella changed the grip on her own knife before glancing furtively across at Howard. The handle of his knife was hidden in his palm, as hers had been. When she looked up she saw that he had been watching her. She blushed as he said, 'You were right before.'

'Oh.'

'Sorry. I shouldn't have . . .'

'I'd rather know,' Ella said. 'Have things right.'

It was the first either of them had said for some time. They were in the restaurant of the Gifford Arms Hotel in the middle of Calderford. Ella had never eaten in a place like it. Two men in tailcoats and a woman in black, with a white apron and head-dress, moved quietly about, attending to their customers. It was Ella herself who had stifled their conversation with her curt responses to Howard's remarks. Because the room was nearly full she thought everybody around them could hear every word they uttered and she was acutely aware that she might any second do something which would show her up and embarrass him. Now she had managed to embarrass herself by trying to be too genteel. But she wondered if he *was* right about

3

the correct way to hold your knife, and was surprised that she could doubt him in such a matter.

'Is that all right?' He nodded at her plate.

'Lovely.' She was eating lamb cutlets. She also had boiled potatoes, spring cabbage and carrots, which one of the tailcoated waiters had served separately from an oval partitioned dish. 'I could do to come here two or three times a week.'

'There'll be those who do. If you've got the money you can avoid the worst of rationing.'

'Well, it's very nice, I must say.'

He was smiling. 'Could you get used to it?'

'I wouldn't marry for it.'

'That's worth knowing.'

What a silly thing for her to have said. As if it meant something. His smile was gone. He was searching her face again in that way that so disconcerted her, as if he was going to have to draw it from memory. Coming into town on the bus she had tried very hard to bring to mind a sharp and detailed picture of his features, but all she could manage had been a generalised impression. He'd have changed, she told herself. He had changed every time she had seen him. Each time was like starting afresh; like waiting for the young man she had first seen and been so taken with to reoccupy the body and person of the man before her. But too much had happened for that now. To both of them.

'They've got jelly and ice cream,' Howard said, when the waiter brought the menu back, 'or jam roly-poly.'

'I wonder if the jam roly-poly's like me mother makes.'

4

'How does she make it?'

'With suet, and steamed in a cloth. Didn't she ever make it for you and Mr Keighley?'

'I can't remember that she did. Not for me, at any rate.'

'Oh, I think you'd remember if she had.' She smiled. 'Sticks your ribs together, me mam's roly-poly.'

'I'll ask him how they do it here.'

'No, don't bother. They've got college pudding an' all. I'll have that.'

'Perhaps I'd better join you, if we can't vouch for the jam roly-poly.'

When they had finished the waitress told them that there was no coffee but they could be served with a pot of tea in the lounge. Since Ella didn't drink coffee – had never, in fact, had a cup of real ground coffee in her life – this was what she would have chosen anyway. In the corridor outside the dining-room Howard took her elbow and steered her to a room with a glass door partly screened by a lace curtain stretched between wires. It was full of small tables and easy chairs. He seemed to know his way about. She would have to ask for the ladies before long.

'You didn't stay here last night, did you?'

'Oh, no.' He smiled. 'Lunch is about all it runs to. I hope you enjoyed it.'

'Oh, I have. Apart from anything else, it's interesting to see how t'better sort live.'

'How who? What d'you call them?'

'Sorry, it's my Yorkshire. The better sort.'

'I've never heard them called that before.'

'Haven't you?'

'I've heard them called the better off, but never

the better sort. You shouldn't think of them in that way, Ella.'

She wasn't sure what he was getting at, but she said, 'We're all in this war together, but I expect they'll still have the upper hand when it's over.'

'They certainly will if you insist in thinking of them as superior in quality instead of just wealthy.'

'Well, don't you think they will?'

'I don't know. There's a feeling among service-men, you know, that things mustn't go back to what they were.'

They had never mentioned politics before. Ella had not known where his sympathies lay, his background being so different from hers. What he had just said brought pleasure as well as mild surprise. It was what her father thought, though he was more pessimistic.

The tea came in a silver-plated pot that burned Ella's fingers when she reached to pour.

'You'd think somebody would have invented a teapot with a cool handle before now.'

'And silver's worse than anything,' Howard said. 'Shall I do it?'

Ella smiled at the suggestion that his hands might be less sensitive than hers and got out her hankie. 'No, I can manage. It's one sugar, isn't it?' She knew he was watching her intently as she poured, put in milk and sugar and added hot water to the depleted pot.

'What else do you remember?' he asked, and then, as she lifted her face, did something that took her completely by surprise: he put out his hand and touched the bridge of her nose. Ella had pulled away before she could stop herself. She gave a quick glance round to see who had noticed.

6

'What are you doing?'

'I've never asked you how you got that. It wasn't like that when we first met, was it?'

'No.' It had happened the year after Howard's only visit with Mr Keighley, in the last summer before the war. 'I got in somebody's way. They didn't mean it.' Now she felt for the small bump which had never gone down, and to whose detrimental effect on her looks she had resigned herself.

'Does it worry you?'

'No, not now.'

'As a matter of fact,' Howard said, staring at the point between her eyes, 'it becomes you, if anything.'

'A broken nose?'

'It gives you a sort of . . . of distinction.'

'You mean not everybody's got one like it? How many want one?'

'It's a lovely nose.'

'Oh, well then . . .' she said lightly.

'Have you still not got a photograph I could have?'

'Didn't you ask me once before?'

'Yes. Before they moved the battalion out of Daker. I regretted it later, not having a picture to remind me.' He sipped his tea. 'But it won't matter so much from now on, will it?'

Ella said after a moment, 'Howard . . . I still can't really understand why you want to keep coming and looking me up.'

'Can't you? Well, I've got a job here now.'

'Why here, though, out of all the places you could have picked from?'

'I took a liking to it when I was in military hospital here.'

'But you wangled the move here yourself, from that other place – Wilmington Park – and you'd no idea what it was like then.'

'You forget I had five days going round the district with Mr Keighley.'

'You're not answering my question.'

'If Mr Keighley hadn't been a bit of a penny-pincher I'd never have met you in the first place. What about that?'

'How was he a penny-pincher?'

'It was his tightness with money that made him lodge with your parents when he was up this way.'

'He was passed on to us by somebody else.'

'He could have put up at a commercial hotel. There's one near the railway station.'

'He was always highly satisfied with what we gave him,' Ella said.

'Of course he was. It was excellent value for money.'

'Though I must say,' Ella said, 'I always wondered myself why he came to us, when we hadn't a bathroom or indoor lavatory. Nor running hot water, come to that. I suppose he had all them things at home, a man in his position?'

'Of course he had. But he liked to make a bit on his expenses when he was away.'

Nineteen thirty-eight, Ella thought. Five years ago. It seemed now like half a lifetime. Now she had been married and widowed; then she had hardly put her mind seriously to the kind of husband she wanted, except that local lads were pushed into the back seats once Howard had brought charm and consideration from an altogether more desirable world elsewhere.

'If you want to know the truth,' Howard said, 'I took a liking to you the minute I walked into the house. You let us in. You answered Mr Keighley's knock and you were the first person I saw. Your father came up from the garden and into the house after us. Your sister was there with her little boy . . .'

'Our Doris,' Ella said.

'We were all standing about moving our feet, trying not to bump into each other, and I was afraid I'd crack my head on the ceiling.'

'I thought you well might. But you'd such a good thick head of hair I thought you'd cushion it. Fancy you remembering all that.'

'I've rerun it in my mind scores of times, like a film. I remember that you hardly took your eyes off me from the minute we walked in till your mother showed us upstairs.'

'That's your conceit!'

'No it isn't, and it wasn't then.'

'How did you know so much?'

'Because though *I* didn't stare, I glanced at you every ten seconds to make sure I was right – that you were interested in me – and my first impression of you hadn't been mistaken.'

'So what did you make of me with your shifty little looks, eh?'

'Do you want me to tell you?'

'You might as well now you've gone so far!'

'Well, I liked what I saw, your soft dark hair and your eyes, and your nose – though I like that even better now.'

'A good job you said so or I'd have thought you were having me on before.'

'I liked the way you held yourself. You're not

9

tall but you stand straight and you're not afraid of showing a certain fullness in your figure here and there—'

'Steady on!' Ella said. 'You're not sizing me up at market.' She glanced round the room again to see if anybody had heard.

'Are you going to let me finish?'

'Not if there's any more details like that.' She was amused under it, and flattered. She kept her face straight as she poured more tea.

'Before the few days were up I'd learned to like your direct way and I'd come to the conclusion that you were a girl a man could rely on completely. And I've never had reason to doubt it since.'

'Even though I went and married somebody else?'

'You must have thought you'd never see me again.' When she said nothing, he asked, 'Was that the only reason you did marry him?'

'Oh, nothing's as simple as that, Howard. I've never denied that things might have been different if you had come again. But that takes no account of all there was between Walter and me.'

Because their talk had taken too serious a turn too early in their renewed acquaintance, she asked before he could speak again, 'Do you happen to know where the ladies is?'

He began to get up. 'No, but I'll find out.'

She let him go, watching him as he left the room. The leg injury that had given him such a terrible time, entailing one operation after another, and finally bringing his discharge from the army, still showed in a slight stiffness as he walked; but it was nothing like as obvious as the permanent limp which had seemed the best outcome to be hoped for once the danger that he would lose the leg had passed. He needed to put on some weight. The blue double-breasted suit, made-to-measure, he'd told her, before the war, seemed to hang straight down from his shoulders, and you could see how thin his legs were from the way they now and then pressed against the full fall of his trousers as he walked. With his height, she was reminded of a circus performer on stilts. But he had grown his hair and while it had not quite regained the richness and lustre she recalled from her very first sight of it – its thick springy waves lit by near-platinum glints – it was a world of refound well-being away from the dull cropped stubble of their last meeting, over a year ago.

A watchmaker and jeweller by trade, Howard had been interviewed yesterday for employment with Kemp and Crowther, a Calderford firm which, among other things, made electric and clockwork mechanisms for weaponry and military installations. Confident of being taken on, he had arranged to stay over to look for lodgings and to see Ella, who had taken the Saturday morning off work to come and meet him. Wasn't there work to be had in Birmingham she had asked him? Plenty, but it wasn't where he wanted to be. What about family ties? There were none that were binding. Of that she knew little more than she had been told by his friend who had written to tell her that he was in hospital, wounded and black in spirit. He had a sister, married to a naval officer and living in Devon. His father was dead, his mother permanently in some kind of home or institution. Ella suspected it was an asylum.

Returning from the ladies she found Howard giving money to one of the tailcoated waiters. He slipped the folded bill into his top pocket as the man put the tea things on to a tray and Ella sat down.

'I'm thinking of changing *my* job,' she told him.

'Oh? In the same line?'

'No. I'm fed-up with weaving. They're setting women on at Daker Forge. It's a big engineering place.'

'You can't take your skills with you, can you?'

'No, but I can learn what they want me to learn. And it's more money.'

He nodded seriously. 'Perhaps one of these days you won't need to do any of that.'

'Walter—' she began, then stopped.

'Go on.'

'Walter wouldn't have wanted me to, once the war was over.'

'Neither would I.'

She was silent, unable to look at him.

'Well,' she said finally, 'thanks for a good – lunch.' Her hesitation before the word was so imperceptible she was sure he hadn't noticed. In her family the meal you ate at midday was your dinner. 'I enjoyed it.'

'We'll do it again sometime.'

'When you've saved up, perhaps.' She smiled at him now. 'What time did you say your train was?'

'Ten past four.'

'Do you think you'll be comfortable in the digs you've found?'

'Oh, yes. For the time being, anyway. Do you know where Cambridge Street is? It's near the cattle market. We could have a stroll that way, if you liked, then you'd know where it was.'

'Oh, I expect I could find it if I had to.'

'I couldn't take you inside in any case,' Howard said. 'Mrs Peel made it quite clear that she doesn't allow lady friends to be entertained on the premises. "I can't be having that kind of carry-on, Mr Strickland," was how she put it. "I keep a respectable house."'

'Quite right,' Ella said.

'But it'll do till I find a proper bedsitter, or a furnished flat.'

'Could you be bothered cooking for yourself and all that?'

'When you've had a canteen meal at midday you can manage without much cooking. I certainly prefer to be private, because I should like to invite you into what passes for my home.'

As to that, Ella thought, we shall have to wait and see. She turned her head to the window.

'Can you hear a band?'

II

It was a military band which wheeled in to cross the square, in RAF blue, with white belts and straps, led by a drum major in white gauntlets who flourished and spun his decorated baton, even launching it up to half roof-height, where it twisted and turned before falling back into his waiting, practised hand. And Ella thought, no doubt like scores of others in the orderly crowd observing from all sides now, 'What does he do if he drops it?' But she didn't know anyone who had seen one dropped and told about it.

13

She remembered what it was all in aid of the instant before Howard, beside her on the steps of the hotel, said, 'It's *Wings for Victory* week here. I saw the posters as I came in on the train yesterday.'

'It's brought some folk out,' Ella said. Every one on the street before lunch seemed to have multiplied by ten. 'They're coming up through the cracks in the pavement.'

With a jaunty swing to their step the band crossed the square and turned into Sovereign Street. Behind them marched a detachment of the RAF Regiment, shouldering arms. A squad of Girl Guides, then one of Boy Scouts followed. A contingent of the Church Lads' Brigade in pill-box hats, came before a more-strolling-than-marching group of nurses. There were some WVS women in green, among them her parents' neighbour, Mildred Sadler-Browne, and a motley collection of civilians with a variety of armbands. Last of all, marching with finicky precision and the utmost seriousness of demeanour, the local Home Guard, at their head an officer with a stick under his arm and a revolver holster on his belt. His moustache twitched as he passed. Ella thought mischievously that he was probably dying to scratch his nose and didn't know how to do it without damaging his dignity.

'Do you want to see where they're going?' Howard asked.

'We might as well.'

Once the procession had passed the crowd streamed on to the square itself and followed up the broad thoroughfare of Sovereign Street, from which all motor vehicles had been banned. Ella and Howard strolled up the middle of the road. She rarely came to this end of Sovereign Street; there were no shops, only administrative buildings, big, impressive: the law courts, police headquarters, the city museum and art gallery, the town hall. Outside the town hall a temporary platform of raw-looking timber had been erected and draped with bunting. There were Union Jacks hung on the fronts of several buildings and behind the platform, fastened to the stonework of the town hall, was a huge board painted with the words, 'Their wings are glorious. *Wings for Victory*. Beat the £1,000,000 target.' A big painted thermometer was marked off for recording the weekly progress of the appeal.

The crowd thickened in the area immediately outside the town hall. In a roped-off enclosure the RAF band set up to play while everyone waited for something to happen on the platform. The mood of patriotic high spirits was new in the progress of the war. The victories of the previous winter had infused everybody with new hope. An attempt to organise this kind of occasion before would have resulted in something more like a grim vigil. Not that anybody was singing or dancing now, but you could sense in the people that crucial transformation of the national mood. They knew now that they were going to win. How long it would take, they didn't know; but they were carried along on the certainty that all would be well in the end. There would still be a price to pay, and the cost to date could be measured in the loss of all those who could never know the outcome.

As that thought formed Ella was alarmed to feel

her lips tremble. She pulled herself up straight and took a deep breath.

'Can you see?' Howard asked.

She nodded as he glanced at her. He had taken her hand to draw her through the crowd to a good vantage point. Now she gently extricated it.

Small children were being hoisted on to men's shoulders.

'They ought to have Punch an' Judy for t'bairns,' somebody said nearby.

'There's enough clowns on t'city council.'

'Are *they* all comin' out?'

'What do you think t'platform's outside t'town hall for?'

'Well, they couldn't put it outside t'prison, could they?'

'Some of 'em ought to be locked up, all t'same.'

'I heard 'at Winston Churchill were comin'.'

'I heard Lord Beaverbrook.'

'*I* heard Uncle Joe Stalin. There were a chap with a fur hat and a big pipe wandering about down Moorgate end early on this mornin'.'

'Gerraway!'

'Aye. He'd snow on his boots.'

A door opened in the town hall and a man in a dark uniform peered out.

'That's t'mace bearer, si' tha.'

'How does tha know?'

'I know *him*. He goes wherever t'mayor goes.'

'I shouldn't fancy that.'

'Tha's no need to worry, as far as I can see.'

'Look, they're comin' out.'

The platform party filed out of the building and mounted the steps. Besides the Mayor and Mayoress, both in their chains of office, there was

16

a handsome RAF officer with wings on his tunic and a number of men in dark suits.

'Who are they all?'

The mace bearer stepped to the microphone. His voice boomed over the public-address system. 'Ladies and gentlemen, pray silence for His Worship the Mayor of Calderford, Councillor Raymond Lofthouse.'

'Citizens of Calderford,' the Mayor said, glancing at a paper in his hand, 'I'm proud to preside over this important occasion and to welcome to our city a hero of our fighting forces, Squadron Leader Nigel Norrington. Squadron Leader Norrington is going to speak to us in a few minutes, but before then it gives me great pleasure to hand you over to somebody you all know, the Member of Parliament for Calderford, the Right Honourable Horace Greenleaf.'

A well-built man in a black jacket and silver-grey tie took his place at the microphone. He spoke without notes, twisting the upper part of his body this way and that, his gaze ranging over the full spread of the gathering.

'My friends, you all know me. I've had the honour and privilege of serving this constituency at Westminister for the past eleven years and I hope to represent you for many more years to come. For the present, however, party politics have been put aside in the interests of winning this war and seeing off for good that evil man across the water and all his foul gang. As Chairman of the War Production Council it's appropriate that I should be here today to ask you – to beg you, my friends – to put all you can behind the great cause of *Wings for Victory*.

'His Worship has just referred to our guest of honour as one of the heroes of our fighting forces. Rightly so. That's just what he is. But men like Squadron Leader Norrington don't blow their own trumpet. Oh, no, they get on with their job and let other people do that. People like His Worship and me, who are only too proud to do it on their behalf. So at the risk of embarrassing the Squadron Leader – and I sometimes think it's a law of human nature that the braver the man (and the woman, ladies and gentlemen, and the woman) the easier they are to embarrass with talk of courage and heroism – so risking that I'll tell you a little about our guest that he wouldn't dream of telling you himself. First of all, he's the holder of the DFC and bar, which means he's not only won the Distinguished Flying Cross, he's won it twice! . . .'

Greenleaf went on to mention the Squadron Leader's participation in the 1,000 bomber raid on Cologne, 'Carrying the war back into the very heartland of the enemy,' while Ella watched the thin dark face of the flyer and thought of an advertisement she had seen in the local paper recently, asking for men between seventeen and a half and thirty-two years of age who were interested in being trained for flying duties to report at their local Air Training Cadet Headquarters. Some people had scoffed when Walter, the butcher's lad, had volunteered and been accepted for aircrew training, and he had always been thin-skinned about his failure to complete the course. But he had said from the start that they couldn't all be public-school boys and the advertisement proved he'd been right. He might now have even been offered another chance. And why this apparently sudden need for more men? Because the RAF's operations were expanding? Only partly that.

'We're asking for nothing you won't get back later – with interest,' Greenleaf was saying. 'You invest your money in National Savings and we can make the tools and put them into the hands of this gallant young man and his comrades – we can give them the tools to finish the job.'

And what we asked from *them*, Ella thought, was something that once given could never be returned, a forfeit more and more often being called in. The people were told of the successes in reaching targets, not of the losses incurred. That was a side of the story that wouldn't come out until it was all over. Walter had seen enough while still stationed in England. He had 'counted them out and counted them back in' and knew the difference in the totals. 'There are them that get back,' he had said, 'and them that you wonder how the hell they ever made it. I've seen men pulled out of kites like that.' What had brought that on? Some infuriating remark made in his hearing. If he hadn't walked away he would have hit somebody. 'I'd never have told you that otherwise,' he said. 'And neither would I if I were flying meself.'

No, hardly anybody talked about that, even the comparatively few in the know; and least of all on occasions like this. But as the Squadron Leader stepped to the microphone and spoke quietly and simply, with not one ounce of Horace Greenleaf's skill in holding a crowd, but holding this one all the same by the sheer magnetism of what he was, what he had done and all the colossal effort he represented, Ella wondered if inside that neat head, with its sleek black hair, the knowledge of more than any man's fair share of luck already used and the question of how much charm a charmed life ran to, wasn't in constant agitation, the ever-present counterpoint to all choices, decisions, conclusions; the last thought before sleep, the first on awakening, the colourer of every dream between.

The tears that were already drenching her cheeks might have gone unnoticed, but her helpless sobbing turned some heads. A middle-aged woman who made as if to come to her held back when Howard signalled his charge of her by putting a large clean folded handkerchief into her hand and drawing her arm firmly through his.

TWO

I

In an upstairs room of the house next door to the draper's shop, just along the street from the Masons Arms, somebody was practising the cornet, switching as Ella approached from scales to runs and repeated figures, sometimes a tongued note ringing like a bell in the still space between the buildings. The girl she had been following at a distance unexpectedly ducked sideways into the yard as she drew level with the house, and by the time Ella got there a door had closed on her.

'How long have you had t'musical renditions?' she asked when she had stepped into her parents' cottage and they had exchanged their customary brief greetings.

'Now then, lass.' Ella's father spoke from his wooden armchair by a fire burning with pale yellow flame. The evenings still turned cool.

'You mean t'cornet player next to Fowlers'?' Her mother glanced at Sugden as if for confirmation as she added, 'It must be four or five weeks now, isn't it, Dad?'

'All o' that.'

'I wonder I haven't heard him before.'

'He works shifts. You can sometimes hear him in a morning.'

'Hmm. I followed our Catherine along t'street. I thought she must be coming here, but she bobbed into their yard.'

'She's taking lessons,' Patience said.

'On t'cornet?'

'Aye. She were apparently going to him where he lived afore.'

'Well . . . I wonder what put that idea into her head.'

'Florrie says she's loved a brass band ever since she were kicking her legs up in her pram.'

'She were learning t'piano, though, weren't she?'

'Our Mary gave her a few lessons to start her off. I don't think it amounted to much more than that.'

'Hmm. She were carrying summat in a case, now I come to think of it.'

'Daker Band've lent her an instrument. They're all for encouraging young 'uns, wi' so many of their players called-up.'

'All this is news to me,' Ella said.

'You should take a bit more notice, then,' her mother said.

But it was because she no longer lived in the clearing-house for family information. It had all bobbed up in the small change of daily conversation. Now she had to be told, and much of it people assumed she already knew.

They were talking about Ella's niece, Catherine Palmer, one of her brother Wilson's three children.

'How old will she be now?' she asked.

'Well, how old is she?' her mother countered. 'She's fourteen.' In a moment she said, 'She'll ten

22

to one come on here when she's finished her lesson. She usually does.'

'If you want,' Ella's father said, 'you can walk out into t'street an' listen how she's gettin' on. One thing about learnin' a brass instrument – all t'world knows your progress.'

Which marked for the time being the end of their discussion of Catherine. What would be next? Ella had a piece of news. But Patience lifted from her knee a copy of the local paper and put it on the table. One small photograph, the head and shoulders of a man in uniform and forage cap, broke the narrow columns of grey print. Patience put her glasses beside the paper. She would have used them only to peruse the face, since she could barely read. Ella already felt the despondent sinking of her heart. Another one. She refused to pick up the paper, but her mother didn't miss the side-long way her eyes took it in.

'Well over twelve months, that one,' she said. 'Isn't that what it says, Dad?'

Ella's father nodded without looking round. It seemed he could no more play that game than Ella could. There was hardly a week without one; most of them missing since the fall of Singapore, in February, 1942. Now known to be alive and 'in Japanese hands'. Ella didn't want to hear about any more of them. She was glad for their kin, but she was also acutely aware of the false hope every one raised for the hundreds of parents and wives who were destined never to receive such joyous news. Walter was dead. She had lived through successive stages of grief. She couldn't live through them again. Thousands of men had been caught at Singapore; no wonder they were still being accounted for. But Walter's case had been different. He had gone on a reconnaissance flight he had no business to be on. His padre had written to tell her after she had heard from his CO that he was missing. They were all missing, the plane and everyone in it. They had known he was part-trained as air-crew and had offered him a treat. 'Fancy a trip upstairs, Aircraftsman? Room for a little 'un'. Had it been a treat or more like a challenge he couldn't resist? He'd dreamed about flying as he lay beside her, coming awake with the kind of start she knew sometimes when, on the edge of sleep, she was suddenly falling. 'You an' me,' he had said; 'we might just have a cushy little war.' She had found more happiness with him than she had ever expected. When she had fallen in love with the man she had only half-reluctantly married, he had been taken away from her. She had wondered for a while if she was big enough for God to spite.

She got the low stool and placed it opposite her father, on the other side of the fireplace. The range gleamed with the deep shine of blacklead, spit and elbow grease. Ella pressed her skirt down between her knees with her clasped hands, then told them what she had come to say.

'I've given me notice at Lidgetts.'

'What are you going to do?'

'I've got a job at Daker Forge. They've been advertising for women.'

'What to do?' Her mother again.

'They'll train me to use a machine.'

'But you're a skilled weaver.'

'It's more money, all the same.'

Sugden asked, 'Will they let you go?'

24

'They will now 'cos there's women waiting to come back. But I might not find it as easy later on.'

'What's your reason, though?' her mother asked.

'I want a change.'

But that wasn't good enough. Patience had lived her life in the firm belief that you should leave well enough alone.

'Herbert Godfrey gets more miserable every day,' Ella added.

'You can run into foremen like him anywhere you go,' her mother said.

'I'll have to risk that.'

'Are they makin' munitions down there?'

'Not as such. But it's essential work.'

'Have you heard 'at King George has a part-time job in a munitions factory?' Patience asked.

'Some o' t'women were havin' a laugh over it.'

'How does he get there?' Sugden asked. 'Bus, bike or Rolls-Royce?'

'Well, they'd never let him go on a bus on his own, Sugden.'

'What's t'point in him goin' at all?' Ella's father asked.

'Well, to set an example.'

'Like he does when he goes back home to Buckingham Palace?'

'Nay, they have had bombs on it.'

'But I'll bet there's a bigger air-raid shelter under there than we've ever seen.'

'You wouldn't go down an air-raid shelter if it had fitted carpets and . . . and a cocktail bar.'

'With a real live piano player,' Ella had added before she could brace herself for the onslaught of

25

melancholy remembrance her words unleashed. For she and Walter had spent the first evening of their honeymoon at Blackpool in a cocktail bar, and there had been a piano player. 'It's not officers only, is it?' Walter had asked the pageboy in the hotel lobby. Just over three years ago . . .

'I wouldn't go next door to a cocktail bar,' Sugden said. 'What do you know about cocktail bars?'

'Nowt. But I expect t'King an' Queen have one in their air-raid shelter.'

'They might have a private picture-house, for all I know. What I do know is he's got no job in no munitions factory, part-time or otherwise.'

'You can't deny they're doing their best, though, Sugden. They could ha' gone off to Canada, out o' t'way of it all.'

'I'm sayin' nowt against 'em. They've a job I shouldn't want, wi' all its benefits.'

'Daker Forge,' Patience said in a moment, as her thoughts shifted again. 'I'd an uncle worked there when I were a little lass. Me an' Cissie Cartwright used to take 'em their tea down in cans. They gave us summat like a penny a week for doing it.'

'They've a canteen now,' Ella said. 'You can get a hot dinner for ninepence.'

'Oh, it's grown so's you'd hardly know it,' Patience said. 'It weren't much more than a blacksmith's shop time I'm talkin' about.'

It was a lot more than that now. You could spend a long time never really looking at something that had been in sight all your life, and the sheer size of Daker Forge and Engineering, as it was called now, had, once she had concentrated

26

on it, so intimidated Ella she had nearly turned away at the gate without going for her interview, and might well have done had a uniformed commissionaire not come out to her.

'Talkin' about cocktail bars,' Sugden said.

'Who is?' Patience said.

'We were.'

'Ella and me's on to Daker Forge, aren't we, Ella? There'll be no cocktail bars there, is there?'

'In t'Managing Director's office, happen.'

Her mother was in one of her gently teasing moods, but Ella knew what her father was leading to. He fancied a drink and was going to ask her to take a jug to the Masons Arms. No one suggested he take himself off, for a change of scene and company. Unlike his surviving sons, Ronald and Wilson, and Thomas who had been killed in the pit, Sugden had little taste for pubs and not much sufferance for the talk of men at a bar. Like Ella's mother, he had seen the misery that excessive drinking could cause and had been abstemious all his life. But it seemed that tastes and appetites (and weaknesses) could skip a generation like physical features could, and he had had three boozers for sons, one of whom had beaten his wife.

As Ella stood at the jug-and-bottle window in the pub passage a thin woman wearing a scarlet slash of lipstick and dangler ear-rings came in from the street and passed her on a wave of scent. She heard the loose rattle of her cough before the best-room door closed behind her. The hatch opened and the landlord bent his head to look through.

'Now then, Ella. A quart for your dad?' He took the jug. 'How you keepin' these days?'

'Oh, you know . . .'

'Aye.' He nodded as though a sudden recollection of her loss had turned his enquiry into more than a routine pleasantry. 'Still in your own house, are you?'

'Oh, yes.'

'There's a lot to be said for keepin' your independence.'

'That's what I always think.'

From where she stood Ella could see little of the pub's rooms but almost everything of the clutter behind the bar: the pipes to the beer pumps, the driptrays, crates of bottles, a sink half-full of grey water, a cigarette burning in an ashtray, linoleum that looked nearly worn through in places. She shifted her stance to give room to a man in a cap and white scarf, with a small ginger moustache and no teeth, who came to the hatch to speak to the landlord.

'Has Clarry Hawksworth been in yet, Jim?'

'It's early for him yet, Wilf.'

'Aye. I'd come in an' wait for him, only I thought I saw our Jessie comin' this way.'

'She's in t'best room now.'

'Aye, well, it'll be as well if I don't bump into her tonight.'

'Have you got a message for Clarry?'

'I've got five quid for him. His bet came up.'

'Did it, by gum! That should be worth a back-hander.'

'Oh, Clarry'll see me right.'

'You won't want to leave it behind the bar for him, I expect?'

'No, no. I'll tell you what, pass us a half through here an' I'll hang on for him ten minutes.'

28

'What you been doin' to your Jessie, then?'

'Oh, that's a long story. A bloody long 'un. It started the day she were born . . .'

Ella, leaving with the jug, heard no more. The man was a bookie's runner. Off-course betting was illegal; but bets were made all the same and winnings delivered, tips gratefully received. She supposed there was a certain attraction to the life she had just glimpsed, that revolving round the pubs and clubs of the village. There would be some people who only ever went into one pub on one particular night of the week; others who, out early, went from place to place, having a drink here, another there, greeting acquaintances, but essentially solitary men. There would be darts and dominoes for the more convivial in men-only tap-rooms; ladies nights with sing-songs round the piano; hired singers and comedians in the clubs. It was a world women entered under sufferance, in which they were often objects of suspicion. But it was changing. More married women were going out to work. Their wages were improving. Having money at all outside what their husbands gave them granted a degree of independence. With a pound of their own in their pocket they could answer back.

II

When Ella got back to the house her niece Catherine had arrived. She was a stockily-built girl and the question was whether the weight she carried was the last of her puppy fat or an indication of the shape she would always be. Her Grandma Palmer was square and sturdy and, by way of her father, Catherine had Patience's auburn

29

hair too, though Patience now was entirely grey. Over her jumper and skirt Catherine was wearing the maroon- and black-striped blazer of Cressley Girls High School. She had been the first of the grandchildren – and so of the family – to progress to secondary education, though she had now been followed by her younger brother, Granville. Some had praised Wilson and Florrie for allowing her the chance, others believed the education of a girl past the compulsory age of fourteen a waste of time and a loss of her earnings. A boy, yes; but a girl would be married before you knew it and what use was her education to her then?

Catherine's mouth looked swollen. Ella said, 'I hope you won't spoil your looks by blowing that instrument.'

'Which looks are they?' her niece asked.

'You'll know in a year or two when t'lads start sniffin' round.'

Catherine pulled down the corners of her mouth. 'Mebbe.'

She sat on the stool that Ella had vacated, perfectly at ease with all three of them, at ease and affectionate without demonstration. She had never been the most eager to throw herself into her grandparents' arms, but she was now the most regular of them all at calling.

'Your Auntie Ella's got a job at Daker Forge,' Patience told her.

'Oh? Our George works there, y'know.'

'I know,' Ella said. 'I don't expect I'll bump into him, though, in that great place.'

'He were nearly in a bit of bother the other day,' Catherine said. They were talking about her elder brother, who was turned sixteen. They waited.

'He were walkin' across t'yard whistlin' the *Internationale* when the Works Manager jumped out of his office an' asked him what he thought he was doing. So George told him where he was off to but this chap said no, that tune he was whistling. So George tells him what it is and t'Works Manager's gettin' a right paddy up. "I know what it is," he sez, "and if I hear you whistling it again outside my door you'll find yourself walking up the road with your cards in your hand." Anyway, you know our George. Instead of leavin' it an' taking notice, he has to stand there an' argue. "That tune happens to be the national anthem of one of our allies," he tells this chap (what's his name? Mr Bascombe). "I know," George sez, "that the BBC stopped playin' the national anthems of the allied nations before the Sunday night news because they wouldn't play the *Internationale*, but that doesn't mean I can't whistle it if I want to."

'"It does if I hear you," Mr Bascombe tells him. "And if there's any more argument you can fetch your cards now."'

'Good heavens,' Patience murmured. Sugden was looking at Catherine with a steady attentive gaze.

'And just guess what George told him then,' Catherine said. 'You'll never guess in a hundred years.'

'Go on,' Ella said.

'He said to Bascombe. "That'll look good in t'*Yorkshire Evening Post*, won't it?"'

Sugden began to chuckle. He put his head back as it swelled into laughter. He slapped his knee. 'By gow, if that in't best I've heard in years.'

'So what did this Mr Bascombe do then?' Ella asked.

'George said he turned round and walked back into his office, saying over his shoulder, "Don't say you weren't warned."'

'He's a marked man now, though,' Sugden said, when he could speak. 'It's t'best thing I've heard in years,' he said again, 'but they'll get back at him some road or other.'

Patience said, 'Well, it's wartime. There's full employment. They can't really victimise t'lad, can they?'

Ella said, 'Y'know it strikes me as funny that your George, with all them ideas, is the only one of the three of you not to get to grammar school.'

'That's because he has no brains,' Catherine said at once. 'He's full of ideas but he's got no brains.'

III

On the day Ella left the mill the weather was mild enough for her and her closest workmates to take their midday break outside on the river bank. Daisy Marriott, Alice Cadman, Sylvia Hartley, Eva Watkinson, young Clarice Mellor and a few more were there with their sandwiches. They had a couple of bottles of black beer and two or three of lemonade, for making Sheffield stout. It was non-alcoholic so the lift it gave was purely imaginary, but it all the same lent the occasion something of the flavour of a party. The sun came out and glinted on the black surface of the water as they stood around suddenly lost for a subject they could all talk about. The only person missing at the moment was Olive Sims, whom Ella had last seen in the lavatory, washing her hands.

Olive Jessop she now was. Surprisingly was. A relationship with Olive outside work was something Ella had been reluctantly drawn into. She had never cared much for the thin inquisitive girl with the prominent eyes and the skin through which you sometimes thought you could see every vein as excitement or embarrassment sucked blood to the surface. Sexual excitement, usually. For gossip about sex, or revelations of others' sexual experience, was what had always fascinated her, despite her intermittent claims to be shocked by what she was so avid to hear. Ella had, though, found herself pitying Olive as she yearned – with all the desperation of one who knows in her heart of hearts that she has been forsaken – for loving words from the overseas soldier who was, Ella suspected, the one – the only one till then – whom Olive had given herself to. His clear signals that he wanted her had seemingly been enough for Olive. And he had been a friend of Ella's friend Howard. So involvement with Tony was also participation in the forbidden love of married Ella for the stranger who had come into her life, then disappeared, only to turn up again when it was too late. Olive had revelled in all that, as she had in finding herself present at more than one critical moment in Ella's life. She had been there when Howard, in uniform, suddenly came through a door towards her; there too when Ella had opened the nearly overlooked letter telling her of Walter's disappearance. Such was the intimacy she could claim, play on, enjoy.

'She's too busy living other folks' lives to live one of her own,' someone had once remarked, and perhaps the most surprising thing about her taking up with Harry Jessop had been the speed with which it led to the altar. Jessop was twenty years older than Olive, a widower in his forties, organist at the chapel Ella went to when she went at all; too old to need to beat the call-up and too respectable for the inevitable suspicion to be put into talk. They were married within six months of Olive's having been seen alone on the street with him. 'She were happen so eager to see what he had to offer her, he thought he'd better make it legal as fast as he could.' 'Nay,' another woman had said, 'I incline to t'opposite view.' 'What's that, then?' 'Like that upper-crust couple what got wed. He sent her upstairs on their wedding night while he finished his cigar. When he went to their room he found her stark naked on the bed except for one white glove. "You look beautiful, darlin'," he sez, "but why the white glove?" "Well," she sez, "I suppose I shall have to handle the 'orrible thing."'

The sun was drawing gold from two or three of the thirty grimy windows on this side of the mill. On the other side a train of empty wagons trundled along the main railway line. The black water slid by.

Ella had come here from school, at fourteen, starting by making parcels, then moving to manufacture. It was all she had known and she felt recurring twinges of panic at the thought of leaving its reassuring familiarity and the little group of friends whose ways she knew and could at worst put up with when she couldn't value or cherish them. Alice Cadman had even discarded her hair-curlers in honour of the occasion: squat Alice with the sexy legs, bringing up a growing girl born out of wedlock, in a husbandless home. Alice, it had to be admitted, seemed to like men in general too much to tie herself to one in particular. Pretty young Clarice Mellor, affectionate, open-natured, was surely born to make some chap deliriously happy, so long as she didn't choose a wrong 'un who would keep her in misery. Most of all Ella would miss Daisy Marriott. When you wanted good sense it was to shrewd, tolerant, even-tempered Daisy you went. For eighteen months or so now – ever since Ella had confided in her about Howard, and through the time of losing Walter – Daisy had been like an older sister. The main thing you learned from Daisy was that life could renew itself. Her first husband, and the father of her two children, had been burned to death in a foundry accident, but she had made a happy second marriage. There had been times when Ella felt strength from Daisy as tangibly as a field of strength.

Daisy came to her now. 'Alice is wondering if we should bother waiting for Olive.'

'Wait why? What's spoiling?'

'Alice wants to say a word, and she's got something for you, in that bag.'

Ella didn't overdo the pretence of surprise. A collection was usually made for anyone leaving who had been there for some time. Alice came up and took her arm.

'Let's get on with it. Trust Olive to be the awkward one.' She led Ella to an open space, placing her with her back to the river. As Alice began to speak Ella saw Olive come through the gap in the wall and stand watching. She had a funny little smile on her face.

'We're losing a pal today,' Alice said, 'and we want her to know we shall miss her. They say there's nowt wrong wi' right folk. T'only trouble is there's not enough of 'em about.' Alice lifted the bag and took out a stout cardboard box. 'We hope you'll like this little present an' think about your old mates here when you look at it.'

The box was heavy. Ella turned it in her hands as she looked for a way in.

'Get it open, Ella,' Sylvia Hartley called.

'I don't want to drop it.'

'You're standin' on grass.'

'All the same . . .'

Alice took the box back and held it so that Ella could lift out the handsome cut-glass bowl.

'Oh, I say, that's lovely.'

'It were that or a diamond tiara,' Eva Watkinson said, 'but we didn't want to embarrass you wi' owt flashy.'

Olive had come round the edge of the half-circle. 'Can I look, Ella? It's lovely. Alice an' Daisy went shopping for it . . .'

'Don't tell her everythin', Olive.'

'. . . and I haven't seen it properly.'

'You've had t'same chance as everybody else.'

'It'll look well on your sideboard, won't it?' Olive said.

'That's just what I was thinkin'.'

'Where did you get to, then, Olive?' Alice asked. 'We were waitin' for you.'

'I'm sorry. I had to go an' see Mr Kenworthy and it took longer than I expected.'

'Kenworthy? You're not in bother, are you?'

'Oh, no.' Olive took a deep breath. 'I was givin' in me notice. I'm leavin' as well.'

'You goin' an' all?'

'Well, copy-cat!'

'Is there summat goin' round that rest of us don't know about?'

'I hope you know we can't afford another whip-round so soon.'

'It's as catchin' as measles.'

'Are you goin' to Daker Forge an' all?'

'Oh, no.'

'What are you leavin' for, then, Olive?'

'Oh, Harry made it clear before we were married, 'at he didn't agree with a wife workin'.'

'There's a war on, though. He'll have to do like a lot more an' put up with it.'

'Y'mean to say Kenworthy's let you go?'

Beside Ella, Daisy said quietly, 'Is it too late to change your mind?'

'Oh, things could never be the same without Olive.'

Daisy chuckled as Alice said, 'Come on, Olive, let's be knowing why you're really leavin'.'

Olive's colour had risen. That odd little smile had come back. Ella suddenly recognised it as one of a deep and quiet satisfaction and realised in the split second before she spoke what Olive was going to tell them.

'I'm having a baby, if you must know.'

'You're never!'

'I am.'

'It doesn't show.'

'Nobody could tell.'

'I'm not quite three months, that's why. But it's definite.'

Ella found herself turning away from that smile and the glory of the moment shining from the bulging eyes. Sweeping over her, threatening to engulf her, was a feeling that both astonished and appalled her. She swayed on her feet. Daisy took her arm. 'What's up, Ella?' Ella thought she might faint.

IV

She let herself into the house in the short dead-end street behind the Temperance Hall. She had thought of getting a cat so that there would be some living creature waiting for her when she came in. The youngest of her family and the last at home, she had taken to heart her now-dead sister-in-law's advice in striking out for independence. Suppose anything were to happen to Sugden or, worse still, to Patience, Winnie had said – a chronic illness or a disabling one – who would everybody expect to shoulder the burden of caring for them? Why, the one living on the premises, who, childless, her husband away, had all the time the others couldn't spare from their own homes and families. Walter had slept with her here only once, the night before he left for his posting abroad, and she couldn't count the times since his death when she had longed to give it all up and retreat into the warmth and companionship of her parents' house. If ever her mother needed nursing or got past looking after things, Ella would still be the most likely person to be called upon. But by keeping her own home she had established herself as a woman entitled to a life of her own.

When she had put the box with the glass bowl in it on the sideboard she sat down in her coat and thought about the pure naked jealousy she had felt at Olive's news. Ella was twenty-five now. In a little over three months the war would be four years old and she twenty-six. Already ... Where were *her* children, being weaned, cutting their teeth, coming out of nappies, taking first steps, trying their first words? She had thought to wait till after the war, or at least till she had a home of her own. Then she had got a house. Then Walter had been sent overseas and the choice taken from her. Make plans with the world in turmoil? She had been foolish not to let events simply take their course.

'You'll keep in touch, won't you?' Daisy had said as they walked up from the mill together for the last time.

''Course I will.'

'You never know these days when you might need somebody to talk to.'

'Nobody does,' Ella said. 'I don't believe there's anybody free of it.'

'Have you seen your friend again?'

'Not yet. I expect he's not settled in yet.'

'You haven't frozen him off, have you?'

'I don't know what you mean, Daisy.'

'I mean you're a stickler sometimes for doing what you think's the right thing.'

'It's the way I was brought up.' They walked on. 'Howard'll be in touch when he's ready. I can't go chasin' after him.'

'Do you still want to?'

'I do want to see him,' Ella said. 'I'm waiting to hear from him.' She sighed. 'But folk change, Daisy. Things happen to 'em. You can't go back.'

'Just as long as you go on.'

Ella got down and put a match to the fire, which was ready laid. It felt a little wasteful to burn coal

39

when the evening was not yet cool enough to need it. But she needed the well-being the sight of it might give her. She filled the kettle and put it on the gas-ring before going to hang her coat at the foot of the stairs.

There was a letter on the floor behind the door. She picked it up. She didn't get many letters, and none of them now could fill her with the apprehension she had once felt at every one. That was over for her. It was a flutter of excitement she felt now, because she recognised at once who this letter was from. Howard, as he had promised, was getting in touch.

THREE

I

The vicar who had officiated at Mary Palmer's
wedding had just baptised her baby. To Ella's
surprise he stopped to have a word with her about
Walter. 'You have suffered a great loss since we
last met.' It raised him in her estimation.

Mary had her twenty-first birthday that
summer of 1943 as well. No one would have made
much of the coming of age of a woman who had
been married two years; but the birth of her child
called for a celebration because he was a first
great-grandchild for Sugden and Patience and con-
sequently the first in Mary's family of a new generation. It was getting complicated again, Ella
mused. That was because a big family spread over
a long time. Mary's eldest brother, James, while
Ella's nephew, was Ella's own age; for Patience
had had a child in the same year – 1917 – as her
daughter-in-law. And if ever, and whenever, Ella
had a child it would be younger than her niece's
first. Mary's boy would have a great-aunt with a
child younger than he was.

All this Ella solemnly read off to a young friend
of hers, whom she had once done a favour, then
become related to by Mary's marriage: a girl now
aged eleven, also called Mary and a cousin of Mary

41

Palmer's husband, Trevor Butterworth. Miss Mary Butterworth, as opposed to the Mrs whom Ella's niece had become.

'But I've forgotten who *they* are,' Mary said, indicating Linda, now aged seven, and Brian, aged six, who, in a gathering this size, at first stuck close to Ella's sister-in-law, Martha. 'They're not Mary's young brother and sister, are they?'

'No, Mary's the youngest herself. They're my brother Thomas's children. He got killed in the pit. Don't you remember seeing them at Mary's wedding?'

'Yes, but they had their mo—' Miss Mary Butterworth put her hand to her mouth. 'It was their mother who killed herself, wasn't it?'

'Yes, Winnie. Mary's mother and father took them in.'

'*I* heard *she* was havin' a kid an' all.'

'Oh, did you? Big ears don't allus hear what's good for 'em. Have you got your County Minor Scholarship results?'

'Yes.'

'Did you pass?'

'Yes.' Mary's mouth had set as she didn't enlarge.

'Is your dad still in t'same frame o' mind?'

'Yes,' Mary said again, only now her lips trembled and she turned so that she was facing away from the main body of people, who were engaged in the aimless standing about usual to these occasions, before being shown to refreshment.

Mary's father, according to her, did not believe in educating girls beyond the statutory minimum and wouldn't hear of Mary taking up the grammar school education her scholarship had won her.

'I'm sorry,' Ella said. 'I didn't mean to upset you. Isn't there anybody who could talk to him?'

'My teacher, Miss Parkinson, talked to him. What do you think he said to her? He said "Suppose she's clever enough to become a schoolteacher, like you? She's either got to stop a spinster all her life or give up her profession when she marries. What good's that?"'

'He told her that, did he?'

'Aye. I were so ashamed I didn't know where to put me face. She's a lovely woman, Miss Parkinson.'

'I can't say I know her.'

'You could imagine any man falling for her. It's not fair, is it? Why can't she get married *and* teach? Surely married women know more than single ones.'

'It's because t'jobs have to go to t'men first, love. And there's never enough to go round.'

Ella's niece had told a lot of people about the christening and a surprising number had turned up. All of them at first tried to pack into the cottage where Trevor and Mary lived, along an unmade cul-de-sac behind Daker Well Church. Once they had had a glimpse of the sleeping child, baptised Robert Ernest, and picked up a sandwich and a cup of tea or glass of beer, enough of them to ease congestion inside passed through into the small back garden where a gap in the hawthorn hedge gave access to still more space in the public recreation ground where there were seats and amusements for children in the form of swings, seesaws, roundabouts and slides. For children's use on other days but not today, the Sabbath. The baptism had taken place after Sunday morning

43

service; the pubs opened at noon, and some of the men slipped away to the Coach and Horses, nearby.

There was talk about the young couple's good fortune. The cottage belonged to Trevor's boss, a jobbing builder. The old woman tenant died when they had been married six months and living with Trevor's parents. That was just after Trevor's medical for the forces. Mary had married at nineteen to become Trevor's wife before he was called-up. But his medical discovered a heart murmur which the doctors assured him would very likely mend itself over the next few years, but which was enough to bar him from military service. 'He allus was a jammy sod,' a cousin in khaki was heard to remark. 'He's in for a right cushy little war.' Yes, Ella thought, just what Walter had predicted for her and himself.

Ella kept well out of the way of her sister Doris, who wasn't speaking to her. It had started with Doris's resentment at what she thought was the unfair influence Ella had with their parents after all the others had left home. A couple of spats, when Ella refused to give way, had been enough for Doris to embark on an extended feud. There had been occasions when Ella would have made up, but when Doris got her teeth into a grudge she worried it to the bone. Not even Walter's death had softened her. Ella had wondered at times whether Doris might even be vindictive enough to do her harm. Yes, she had one sister who was a bitch and another who had lived for years with the conviction that her job as housekeeper to a wealthy couple in Harrogate endowed her with something approaching their standing

44

and position; from echoing their opinions about the conduct of the war and their assessment of public figures, to dressing like a society lady come to bestow her bounty on those less fortunate. There was no doubt that her employers had treated Ada exceptionally well; she had none of those stories of abuse and exploitation common among people in domestic service, and her loyalty was understandable. Unfortunately, they were among those who would have treated with Hitler rather than oppose him and Sugden Palmer couldn't stomach the views she brought with her and tried to put forward as the only ones with reason.

Ada was here today, but alone, without Cyril, her husband. She was seen only rarely nowadays, since she was forced to make the lengthy journey by public transport. At one time Cyril had brought her quite often, finding some errand for his employer's car; but petrol rationing had finished that. It had finished Cyril's job as chauffeur in tandem with Ada's housekeeping. Now he drove a lorry for one of his boss's concerns and Ada – she couldn't stop talking about the injustice of it – had been directed into part-time war-work. It would have been full-time but her employer had found her a light job in one of his own factories engaged in essential work, and how she divided her time between the work she had been doing and that she was supposed to be doing now was largely at her discretion and that of her employer's wife. She had got off pretty lucky, everybody thought, and wondered how long they could stand hearing her complain that the war was ruining her life.

Mary's brother, James, was here with a

girlfriend. It was thought to be serious this time, but you never knew with James. Mary's second brother, Arthur, was away in the army. Like James, Arthur had worked down the pit and could have avoided military service, but he had volunteered after Winnie's death, when his mother had taken in her orphaned children. 'I wish he'd at least write and give us some news,' Martha said. 'We don't even know where he is.'

'I thought he was in Iceland,' Ella said.

'No, no, the Americans took over there. No, if it were James I could understand, perhaps. James is stubborn and wilful. But this isn't like Arthur. Or not,' she added, 'like Arthur as he was.' Before . . .

There was an unanswered question over Arthur's past. Ella knew more than his mother, but she had always been aware that she didn't know all.

The young soldier who had called Trevor Butterworth jammy came up to Martha as she stood with Ella by the back door of the cottage. He looked older close to.

'Did anybody tell you I'd seen your Arthur?'

'We've just been talking about him. When was this?'

'And where?' Ella added.

'It was in Alexandria. Oh, six months ago.'

'Alexandria!'

'Doesn't he write?'

'He wrote to say he was going overseas again and he couldn't get leave before.'

The young soldier's eyes narrowed as he looked from one face to the other and thought his thoughts.

'I shouldn't worry, y'know,' he said. 'No news is good news. You'd hear soon enough if owt was wrong.'

'You're not in Arthur's mob, are you?' Ella said.

'No, I'm in the West Yorkshires. He's the Koylis. We got knocked about in Crete, y'know. Whatever they've got lined up for Arthur's lot, they've something different in mind for us.'

What that would turn out to be would be bitter fighting in Burma when the advantage changed there. But none of them knew that then. Neither did they learn till later that at the moment he was being talked about in his sister's back garden Arthur Palmer was a member of an infantry brigade composed of battalions of Yorks & Lancs, The Green Howards and his own King's Own Yorkshire Light Infantry, which was fighting its way into the interior of Sicily after an unopposed landing in atrocious weather the day before.

Martha's eye had shifted to James's young woman, whose name was Avril. James had introduced her outside the church, with his usual heavy-handed grating humour. '. . . and this is me Auntie Ella.' She had probably been platinum blonde as a child. Her full lips turned down slightly at the corners. Her figure was the kind which might run to early fat, but drew men's eyes now because it suggested generosity and ease. She hadn't much to say for herself and commented on James's remarks with a succession of little digs, nudges and tugs. Ella thought – and was at once ashamed of the premature judgement it made of the girl – that James had always gone in for obvious and immediate pleasures.

47

'Has he left that lass on her own?' Martha said.

Ella had observed the dumb show between them in the rec., trying to read the twists and turns of the two bodies, the angles they took to each other, the language of heads and arms, before James left her, to walk away across the grass, turned and came part-way back, then walked off again, this time striding purposefully in the direction of the pub, while Avril put her back to him, looked at her feet, glanced over at the cottage, and strolled along a parallel line, neither coming nearer nor going farther away, her gaze down again as though searching for some small lost object in the cropped grass.

'He went to the Coach and Horses,' Ella said. 'He set off that road, anyway.'

'When has our James been known to stand outside a pub while somebody else was inside suppin' ale?' Martha asked, and expected no answer.

'Is she a shy lass?'

'Gawky, more than shy,' Martha said. 'I've learned how to get through to her, but the sight of Mary's family and Trevor's all at once is a bit too much for her. I'll go and get her.'

Ella wondered how Howard would have fitted in, if she could have defined her relationship with him clearly enough for her to have brought him, and if there hadn't been that episode in his past which stopped her from even telling her parents that she was seeing him. His good manners would have carried him through, without a doubt, and impressed most of the women.

Tidying herself as best she could in those awful works lavatories, she was catching a train into Calderford at the end of the Saturday morning half-shift. Howard met her in the station booking-hall when she arrived. He had looked the first time as though he would kiss her but he never had. He usually just took her arm above the elbow and led her into the street. He carried a folded newspaper in his other hand. Though he hadn't enough time to go to his digs before meeting her he was left with nearly an hour to kill. One day Ella thought a faint smell of beer clung to him and she wondered if he'd been waiting in a pub. But he never suggested they call in a pub when they met. As neither of them had eaten since breakfast the first task was to find food. The first time he had offered her the Gifford Arms again but she had balked at the expense and they found a tea-shop where they could get baked beans on toast and spam fritters and suchlike. The waitress re-membered them when they went back and told them about little treats that weren't on the menu. It was Howard she liked the look of, obviously. *She* found him different too, and deserving of special attention. He didn't flirt with the woman or crack jokes, and he certainly didn't suck up to her. He just quietly got on with finding out what was available, thanked her for what she brought them and always left a copper or two on the table when they went.

There was still something different about him for Ella, in spite of her growing familiarity with him. Most of the men she knew had similar back-grounds to hers; they shared certain assumptions. If their personalities differed and changed with time it was only within a limited range of possi-bilities. Howard, on the other hand, had a history that could surprise her. She couldn't jump to conclusions about him. It wasn't only his being a man that stopped her from knowing what went on in his mind: he was from a different tribe. He wore dark shirts a lot, in heavy wool and cotton, and with his bony height and the intelligence (and occasional haunted look) in his thin face, he reminded Ella of some lesser-known actors in the British films the war was throwing up, who played scientists engaged in secret war-work – 'back-room boys' and 'boffins' – or more mysterious men who might seem to have deserted from the armed forces and were hunted by everybody until it turned out that they were really intelligence agents on the trail of Nazi spies.

They usually went to the pictures after they had eaten. There were nearly always long queues at night but on Saturday afternoon it was usually possible to walk straight in, though there would be a few people waiting to join the continuous programme at the beginning of the main feature, or some other convenient point. One of the biggest cinemas, the Regent, had been a theatre. Ella could just recall pantomime there. One of the others had some double seats on the back rows where courting couples could sit without an armrest between them. They had been shown into such a seat once by a helpful usherette when they came in while the lights were down. 'We must look eighteen in the dark,' Ella said as they settled themselves. They sat shoulder to shoulder, thigh to thigh, while Ella wondered whether Howard might try to take advantage of their closeness. But he didn't. He had let her know his feelings at a time when he had no right to. Now that there was nothing in his way he hung back.

II

Ella kept checking on her parents. It was a habit that came from her having been the last left at home. Her mother was ensconced in the rocking chair to which she had laid early claim. It was in the living-room. The baby's cradle stood nearby, though it was empty now. With the viewing over, Robert Ernest had been put to sleep in a quieter place, upstairs. Patience seemed quite happy to have her tea-cup constantly refilled and to talk to Trevor Butterworth's grandmother and anybody else who came up to have a word.

Ella's father was sitting on a bench in the sun behind the house. With his hands resting on his walking-stick he listened to his grandson George while contemplating the square of garden about which he had been advising Trevor Butterworth, who listened with genuine interest because Sugden merely stated his own preferences and what his experience had taught him, without laying down the law. Trevor's uncle, Miss Mary Butterworth's father, had been sitting next to Sugden for a while but Ella hadn't needed to be near enough to hear what was said to know from Sugden's manner and small gestures that her father didn't like the man and found his company irksome. Meeting few people nowadays, Sugden was pleased if he found somebody congenial to talk to on occasions which brought numbers together, though he was cautious until he could distinguish the well-informed from the prejudiced. Not enough people, to his mind, were prepared to listen and discuss. He had learned a lot from Mr Keighley about the pleasure of quiet discussion.

51

Ella knew that those times – few in actual number – had become golden in his memory. It was as though most men acquired a set of views in early manhood which, like a good set of tools, were expected to last them a lifetime and which they dared not change no matter what the argument or evidence against them. He recognised a lot of this in himself. He was, after all, a product of his birth and upbringing; a working man, at the mercy of circumstances he couldn't control. He had spent a lifetime keeping out of the pub, going to work when he was well enough – and many a time when he wasn't – bringing up and providing for what were left of the nine children he had sired. He could *do* the work, but he couldn't *make* it. 'The rich man in his castle, the poor man at his gate ...' Why wasn't there a system – outside religion – which would satisfy the needs and aspirations of them both? George Palmer had something to say about that.

Almost everything he heard about his grandson these days seemed to delight Sugden. Although George's brother Granville and his sister Catherine were the exam-passers and George had gone to work at fourteen, he was the one who looked at everything a second time, questioned it all, took nothing for granted.

He was talking rapidly and intently to Sugden as Ella approached. He sat back as his grandfather tapped his stick on the ground and grinned.

'Tell your Aunt Ella,' Sugden said. 'I'd like to hear it again meself. Listen to this, Ella.'

It was about a sermon preached by the new minister at the Primitive Methodist Chapel. He had taken as his text the hymn *All Things Bright and Beautiful*.

'You know it, don't you?' George said.

''Course I do. Everybody does.'

'Can you remember all the words?'

'Not every verse, no.'

'What's peculiar about it?'

'I don't know.'

'Go on, George,' Sugden bade him. 'She's not sittin' an examination.'

George took a miniature hymnal out of his pocket and opened it at a marked place. '"*All things bright and beautiful,/All creatures great and small,/All things wise and wonderful,/The Lord God made them all*. Each little flower that opens, the cold wind in the winter, the tall trees in the greenwood . . ." It's all about nature – natural things – except for one verse: "*The rich man in his castle,/ The poor man at his gate,/God made them, high or lowly,/And ordered their estate.*"'

How far nowadays, the parson had asked, could we agree with what the writer of the hymn had meant to convey in that verse? Yes, the God who made all things made both the high and the lowly. Note the comma, he said, between 'God made them' and 'high or lowly'. Yes, God made all men, both those who were high and those who were lowly; he made the rich man just as surely as he made the poor man. But who made one man rich and another man poor? Surely that wasn't God's work, was it? The writer of the hymn believed so, though, didn't she? You could have thought she didn't, because of that comma. But she obviously did because the next line read, 'And ordered their estate.' Accept your lot, God said, according to this Victorian hymn-writer. 'I made you poor and him rich,' God was saying. 'Accept your lot and make the best of it.' Indeed, it was flying in the face of God to question one's place in society. But, the parson asked, is this really a state of affairs we can believe in here in the middle of the twentieth century? When we had won this war would we expect and accept that the high would still be high and the rest as lowly as they had always been? Was that what we were fighting for, that once the dust had settled things would go on in the same old way? Then he had, according to George, related what he was saying to the Beveridge Report, which had been debated in the House of Commons earlier in the year and filleted.

'Filleted,' George said. 'That's what he called it. A great welfare plan, a wonderful new order of social justice for all, and the guts cut out of it because of what it would cost.'

While George was talking Ella had heard the vicar taking his leave. Looking round for those he should not miss speaking to before he went, his eye had fallen on Sugden Palmer and he had come quietly up behind them while George was still in full flow.

'It's all very interesting,' he said now. 'I've heard that the Rev. Barraclough is a bit of a firebrand. But what amazes me is how anybody can base an argument on the premise that all men are equal when they're obviously not and never will be.'

'Nobody's saying they are,' George said. 'It's opportunity that should be equal. And if anybody thinks that being born into a rich family makes him better than me, I want to argue with him.'

'There are those who lead and those who are led,' the vicar said.

'Oh aye,' George said, 'but are you sure we've got 'em all t'right road round?' He added, 'I'm only askin'.'

The vicar's face was fixed now in that supercilious smile that Ella remembered from Mary's wedding and he was still wearing it after he had given his best wishes to Sugden and left them.

'If that's t'kind o' sermon they're preachin' at chapel nowadays,' Sugden said, 'it's happen time I started goin' again.'

'Nay,' George said, 'it's only Mr Barraclough, and I wouldn't like to say 'at all the congregation care for it.'

Men were drifting back from the pub. They came through a gate at the far corner of the rec. Ella saw Ronald, her eldest brother, Mary's father, now a grandfather at forty-nine. He strolled across the grass with Ella's other brother, George Palmer's father, Wilson. They were both wearing their Sunday go-to-meeting clothes: black jacket, striped trousers, bowler hat. It was a custom the next generation had not taken up; James, walking behind them, had on an ordinary grey suit.

Avril came out of the cottage and walked to the gap in the hedge. As James made to come through she took his arm and turned him round, but on a diagonal, which took them clear of the stragglers from the Coach and Horses. Standing alone again, Ella saw her give James a push and break away to walk apart. Martha came and stood beside Ella. She spoke quietly:

'She's in the family way.'

'Who? James's young woman?'

'Aye. She just told me, upstairs.'

'Does James know?'

'He does now.'

Martha nodded towards the young couple. Avril had turned to face James and was pummelling his chest with both fists.

'Will there be a wedding?'

'I reckon so. She's a nice lass. I wheedled it out of her. I knew there was summat wrong. She didn't know where to look, so I told her a bit of family history to console her.' Martha glanced at Ella. 'Who am I to cry shame on her, eh?'

'It's to be hoped she can handle him,' Ella said.

'Oh, they'll be all right. I'm not broadcasting it, but I thought you could p'raps tell your mam an' dad on your way home.'

'If you say so.'

'I don't want it to come from anywhere else.'

'No.'

Martha looked all round to make sure they were alone. Then she said, 'Summat for my ears only . . .'

'What?'

'Was Winnie taking our Arthur to bed?'

Ella sighed.

'C'mon, Ella,' Martha went on. 'I once told you 'at bairns came out with things.'

'I thought she was,' Ella said.

'Only thought?'

'Winnie never said anything straight out.'

'That bairn she was having was Arthur's, wasn't it?'

'I couldn't see otherwise, meself.'

'He thinks he made her kill herself, doesn't he?'

'But he didn't, Martha.' Ella's voice was insistent. 'Winnie was made that way.'

'It's why he doesn't write. He thinks everybody knows and wants nothing to do with him.'

'Oh, yes, I think that's true.'

'If I knew where he was I could write and tell him different.'

'You haven't cut him off with a shilling, then?'

'Of course I haven't. How can you think it?'

'I just wanted to be sure.' She said in a moment, 'Poor Arthur. Winnie didn't give him a chance to do anything. She took it all out of his hands.'

'She should never have done it. There was no need for it.'

'But she did it, Martha. Whatever went on in her mind, that's how it ended.'

Martha suddenly shivered, though the day was warm.

'I can do me best for her bairns, anyway.'

Ella said, 'I think that's the first time I've heard anybody call them hers, and not Thomas's. But you don't owe Winnie that, Martha. We all owe Thomas. You're just the one who shouldered the burden. And it does you great credit.'

'Look . . .' Martha said.

Ella followed the nod of her head. Across the recreation ground, in violation of all the regulations, James and Avril were sitting on adjacent swings and James had both legs round the seat of Avril's, pulling it in close so that she could keep her arms round him while they kissed.

III

Ella's father said, 'I suppose it's nobbut history repeatin' itself.' For James himself had been conceived out of wedlock, bringing a swift application

57

for compassionate leave and a wedding at which Patience had been pregnant with Ella. It was why Martha had no room, as well as no inclination, to criticise the girl.

'Martha only told me so's I could tell you,' Ella said. 'She's not telling anybody else yet.'

'We s'll have to save up for another weddin', Patience lass,' Sugden said. 'Eh?'

Patience appeared not to be listening. She sat looking into space. 'It's funny, in't it?' she said after a time.

'What is?'

'Life . . . How it . . . carries on.'

Sugden said, 'It's when it breaks into a gallop 'at it worries me.'

If, Patience said then, they had all been spared, what a clan they would have made by now. She was thinking not so much of Thomas, whose children Martha had the care of, but of the three lost sons who had never grown to marriage and fatherhood: Edward, killed on the Somme in the summer of 1916; David, dead before his first birthday, and John, too young for the war, who fell before the scourge of the influenza that swept across Europe as hostilities ended. Men who would now have been in their prime, with growing families. Six lads, Ella thought, standing shoulder to shoulder. They would have made an impressive sight.

Yet, as her mother said, life went on. The gaps were filled in time. The birthrate had fallen between the wars, apparently. Now they said it was on the increase again. Babies, babies, babies: Mary, Olive, Avril. It was nothing but babies. Ella sat and let her parents reflect and reminisce.

She supposed she seemed to them relaxed and at ease, after an enjoyable family occasion. But she wasn't. The restlessness she was hiding told her that she could only too easily surrender to another surge of the physical longing which had come over her as she watched James and Avril on the chilren's swings; a longing that drenched her skin with heat and struck deep enough to feel like a spasm in her womb. They had kissed, her nephew and the mother-to-be of his child. They had more than kissed; nibbling, licking, tasting skin with slack, wanton lips; and she had watched, fascinated, overcome.

Howard held her hand. He had held it all through *Fire Over England, Love on the Dole* and *The First of the Few*. It was like being back in a first courtship with a shy lad, scared to death of going too far too fast, each tentative move like a toe in the water, and there had been a time early in her knowledge of him when that, with a kiss or two, might have satisfied her indefinitely. But she had been married since then. She had known Walter. She had known the thrust of a man inside her and exulted in it. Then she had been sexually numb for so long after Walter's death she had doubted whether she would need a man in that way ever again. But Howard's fingertip approach had aroused her. Now it was winding her up like a spring.

FOUR

I

There was another Leslie Howard film showing in the town: *Pimpernel Smith*. She had heard good reports but it saddened her to think of it, for the actor had been killed earlier that summer in a civilian airliner shot down by German aircraft. Howard – her Howard, he of the first name – pointed to the posters as they passed the cinema. 'Did you know he wasn't English at all? He was Hungarian.'

Ella was disbelieving. 'Go on with you.'

'It's true.'

'Where did you hear that?'

'I can't remember. But quite a few Hungarian filmmakers came to England in the late 1920s. Alexander Korda, his brother Zoltan—'

'But they don't sound English.'

'Easy enough to change your name.'

'But Leslie Howard *looked* English. He looked more English than Winston Churchill and half the Royal Family.'

They got into some talk then about the antecedents of the Royal Family who, of course, were German not so far back, while Ella pondered upon that romantic English gentleman who had turned out not to be English at all. According to Howard.

She really would have to stop taking everything Howard told her as gospel truth. Of course, he knew a lot more than she did, about a lot of things; but, like others, he could be mistaken.

Today they had to wait a few minutes for a table in the café. There was a different waitress, a young girl, slouching, inexperienced. They could have a cheese omelette, something called Viennese fish cakes, or hot-pot.

'Would it be careless talk to tell us where the hot-pot comes from?' Howard asked the girl.

'I don't know.'

'Is it Lancashire?'

'They make it in the back,' the girl said. Howard was smiling.

'Is there any meat in it?' Ella asked. 'I'll settle for knowing that.'

'Yes, there is. Don't ask me how much, but there is some.'

Ella ordered it. She didn't like to ask what was Viennese about the fish cakes. Howard joined her and asked the girl to bring them a pot of tea while they were waiting.

'What would you like to see?'

There wasn't anything apart from the Leslie Howard that she could get excited about. *Life Begins for Andy Hardy* was at one place and something called *Tortilla Flat*, with a Laurel and Hardy in support, at another. Ella didn't want the war rammed down her throat at every verse-end, but watching a lot of these American films you'd never know there was a war on. Life just seemed to carry on as it always had done, with no rationing, no bombed cities, not even a blackout to damp things down.

'You don't have to be back 'specially early, do you?'

'No; why?'

'There's something I'd like you to see before we go to the pictures.'

No, there was nothing spoiling. Soon she would be taking care not to have to walk up home from the station after dark; but at present the reason she left him in the early evening was because once they came out of the cinema they found themselves trailing aimlessly round a town of closed shops, and even closed pubs.

'I've got the key to a flat,' he told her.

'You mean you've borrowed it from somebody?'

She wondered if at last he had found a bed to invite her into; or at least a sofa. Not for the first time she wondered what her response would be if he did, in fact, try to go all the way with her. She thought she was ready, but wasn't sure she was willing. But he was talking about a place to let, that he could have if he wanted it.

'Will you look at it with me?'

''Course I will.'

His paper lay beside his plate. Ella saw that he had been doing the crossword puzzle. As they ate his eyes strayed to it. He took out a length of pencil and filled in some more squares. He looked at Ella and smiled. 'Excuse me.'

'Carry on. Don't mind me.'

'Oh, no. I just spotted that one.'

'You would do. You've got it folded at the place.'

'Yes, it's thoroughly bad manners.'

'I don't know what's so fascinating about them.'

'They exercise the mind without engaging the emotions.'

'Is that good?'

'It's restful. You should have a go sometime.'

'I can't make head or tail of them.'

'Oh, surely. You read, don't you?'

'I don't read newspapers.'

'You read books, though. Don't you still go to the public library?'

'Yes.'

'What have you got out now?'

'Daphne du Maurier.'

'She's good, isn't she?'

'I like her.'

'What have I read of hers? Let me think . . . *Jamaica Inn*.'

'This is called *Frenchman's Creek*.'

'Well, you should have enough vocabulary. The main thing is to get used to the different styles. Some have a lot of anagrams; others hardly use them at all.'

'What's an anagram?'

'It's a word whose letters can be rearranged to make a different word. Like, er, "Draw" can become "ward". That's only a simple one. Others are more complicated.'

'Too complicated for me.'

'Oh, you'd get better with practice. This one's fairly easy. They'd sold out of my usual paper. Have a go at this one . . . The clue is "Waiting for no man".'

'Factory buzzer,' Ella said at once.

'Yes, but if you'll let me finish, it's three words: four, three, four.'

'Look,' Ella said, 'they only make me feel stupid and then I lose me temper.'

'Oh, really . . .'

'I'm warning you.'

'You'll kick yourself if you don't get this one.'

'No, I won't. It's other people I kick.'

'Have you really got no idea?'

'I'm not thinking about it.'

'"Waiting for no man",' Howard said. 'Four, three and four. Is the middle word "and" or "the", do you think?'

'It might be "cat" or "dog" or "fat", for all I know.'

'I don't think it's likely.'

'Stop trying to make me into something I'm not, Howard.'

'You stop making yourself out to be a duffer.'

'I don't know why you're so keen to draw me in.'

'It would be another thing for us to do on long winter evenings.'

'What long winter evenings, and where?'

'When I get a flat and we don't have to walk the streets.'

'Oh, I see. What a cosy picture.'

He smiled. 'Here's one ... "Loving couple." Five, three, four.'

'Romeo and June.'

'Clever! Think again. It's "Darby and Joan".'

Darby and Joan! She hoped he wasn't applying that to them.

'I'm not ready for a bonnet yet, Howard.'

'A bonnet?'

She explained. 'Women used to wear a bonnet when they got to a certain age. My mother's mother wore one. P'raps it was sixty.'

'I believe in some places widows wore them.'

'Did they? Well I'm not ready.'

'I'm glad to hear it,' Howard said. 'It shows you're looking forward again.'

Once more – and it happened so often now she had lost count – she wondered why he was so interested in her. If he wasn't desperate to get her on her back, what about her had brought him here, where he could see her regularly? She hadn't his brains: there were any number of things he could talk about that were a closed book to her. Why wasn't he bored?

'Is it far to this flat?'

'It's up by St Luke's. About ten minutes' walk.'

Ella nodded at the window. 'It's come on to rain.'

He turned to look. 'It won't last long. Why don't we have a cake while we're waiting?'

He meant a bun. A cake to Ella was bigger, something you cut into pieces. The others were buns.

'What I'd love', she said, 'is a jam and cream puff like they used to make at Daker Co-op Confectionery. Pastry light as a feather with real cream and strawberry jam inside.'

'*I*'d love a coconut macaroon,' Howard said.

There were no buns of any kind. They were given a couple of biscuits each. At least they had currants in them.

II

He had become more familiar with the back streets of the town than she who had lived in its vicinity all her life. He took her along thoroughfares and through ginnels she had never seen before. What she came to Calderford for had kept her to the shopping streets in the centre. Now she saw how close to the middle of town, hidden by the façades of shops and cinemas and pubs, were the red-brick terraces where the ordinary people lived. The better-off lived that bit farther out in stone-fronted houses on tree-lined streets, but still within easy walking distance of everything they needed. It was a compact town; you could see the tall spire of the parish church – All Saints – from almost any quarter. St Luke's had a kind of domed tower. It stood quite close to a main road. Behind it was an unfenced graveyard with well-tended grass between the markers. There was nothing recent: all the stones were old and weather-stained.

On two sides of the churchyard ran long terraces of tall houses in brick, with elegant high windows. There were three floors above ground level, the bottom one raised up to allow basement quarters. Iron railings ran on between flights of front steps. Some of the houses were beautifully kept and had huge brass knockers on their doors. Others looked a touch run-down. Quite a few of them, Howard told her, were already converted into flats and it was hard to see the others surviving long as private houses. Where were the professional people with the means? Where, if they had the means, could they find the servants? Ella could imagine carriages standing at the kerb, with grooms gentling waiting horses. 'It's like *Becky Sharp*,' she said. That was a picture she had seen, with Miriam Hopkins. But Howard didn't seem to take it in. 'Here we are,' he said. He had two Yale keys on a ring; one of them unlocked the front door.

Perhaps behind the doors they passed as they

went up and up lay drawing-rooms with chandeliers, big enough for couples to take a turn round the furniture. Perhaps as your fortunes improved you could work your way down the house to the very best accommodation, on the ground floor. Because there was no doubt that where Howard was leading her to was where the servants had slept. He opened one of two doors on the landing, which had a sky-light.

'How will all them stairs be for your leg?'

He had come up with no undue sign of strain, but not rushing, either.

'Oh, I shall manage. Come in and tell me what you think.'

'Is this the first time you've seen it as well?'

'Oh, yes.'

It was two rooms, the smaller one a kitchenette, the other containing a divan bed and a table with folding leaves as well as a couple of easy chairs.

She had never been in a furnished flat before. It smacked of the foreign life of cities, with people coming and going, all strangers, knowing nobody except those closest at their work. It faintly frightened her. The web of the family and familiar streets – a life at ground level – was a reassurance as well as an entanglement. She had learned to live alone but only within that context. The life represented by this flat was a step nearer the outer darkness.

Howard was poking around. There was a gas fire and a floor-standing gas cooker in the kitchen, with a coin meter.

'Who does it belong to?'

'An old lady I was introduced to by one of the managers at Kemps.'

'Have you looked at any more?'

'Yes, a couple.'

'Is this the best?'

'Oh, yes.'

'D'you think you'd be all right here?'

'Yes.' He nodded. 'I think I would.'

He joined her at the window. It looked out the other way from the square. The ground sloped. There was a pattern of allotment gardens beyond a lane and a small field. You could see for miles beyond them. Ella thought a distant spire could be Daker Church, the main one, on the hill.

'It should do for me until I have to look for something else.'

'When might that be?'

'If we were to get married, for instance.'

'Oh.' He was beside her at the window. She couldn't step away without touching him.

'It might be a bit cramped for two.'

'Don't you think you're rushing on a bit?'

'I don't know.' His arm across the window frame held her in. When she did turn they were very close. All he had to do to kiss her was move his face a few inches. He had been a lot bolder that time in Olive Sims's house, the night before the soldiers left Daker. She thought about meeting him halfway by standing on her toes, but a reluctance to offer herself till she saw what move he might make held her back. 'It's not such a disagreeable thought, is it?'

It never had been. And now there was nothing in the way. Except that she wouldn't walk with her eyes closed into anything so binding. The oddest thing was that she seemed to know him less the more she saw of him. Oh, she could anticipate his gestures, the way he performed certain actions, some figures of speech. But she felt no nearer the real heart and soul of him.

'Can you be patient a while?'

'Yes. I just wanted you to know how I felt.'

Yes, she knew. So far, she knew. He was always at pains to express himself clearly, but his words were from another mode of life. They weren't, to her, the language of love. They were too cool; they lacked the naked need that Walter had always let her see, even when she held him at arms' length.

Howard let her leave his side. She gave him an encouraging little peck on the cheek. That was how she left him at the station, with a swift touch of the lips to the side of his face. Like a sister. Or a wife of long standing. She looked into cupboards and talked about the things he would need – crockery, cutlery, pots and pans, bed linen – and where he might get hold of them in wartime.

'Does the window open?'

It was a sash. He tried it. 'Yes.'

'Good. It's warm up here. You'd think it was still the middle of summer.'

'Save on fuel bills.'

It was quiet too. They were lost. Out of sight above the bustle of the streets. Nobody knew they were there. It was the first time they had been alone together in private since that evening at Olive's. Then Olive had been upstairs with Howard's friend, and there was always the danger of Olive's mother coming home early. So that even the chaste hour she had spent in Howard's arms, in a dream of what might have been, had been spoilt by fear of interruption, not to mention guilt that she had allowed herself to stay in such a compromising situation; a married woman, messing about with soldiers while her husband was away.

Now they were really alone. But any minute they would leave and lock the door behind them. They would choose a film and spend three hours in a cinema. He would take her to the station afterwards, making arrangements for next week on the way. She would give him that friendly little peck on the cheek and leave him. And she would be no wiser than when she came; no further forward except in habit. She had not known when they came up the stairs, but she knew now. What she must do. She must find out what her feelings amounted to. And his. His feelings and his need. If she didn't take charge it would be habit that would bind them. But habit was for later.

'Well . . . If you're ready . . .'

Ella said, 'Couldn't we stop here a bit longer?'

He looked at her with a little frown. 'As long as you like. There's nothing much we can do, though, until . . .'

She was close to him again. She had put herself there. Her arms round his waist were inside his arms.

'Until,' she said, 'you kiss me as if you mean it.'

III

She turned her head abruptly from the glass above the chest of drawers as she became aware of the great healed wound running almost the full length of Howard's thigh. Through the dark hairs it ran, deeply cut into the curiously grey skin, deep and open and red, yet healed. He had put on a little

70

weight in his return from skin and bone, but not enough to fill and close what German shell fragments had torn open and surgeons' knives had extended then reopened, wound upon wound, to mend and save.

'Not a pretty sight, is it?'

He had seen her flinch from its violence. The urge that followed, to explore it with her fingertips, was hidden from him.

'Who's to see it?'

'You.'

'I don't mind.'

'Don't you? Doesn't it put you off?'

'Don't be silly.'

She had been unbuttoning her blouse. She took it off and held it in front of her before hanging it on the back of a chair, and thought, Why isn't he looking at *me*? As she laid her skirt across the seat of the chair she could see herself reflected in the glass, shoulder to waist, her own unblemished skin exposed to Howard's gaze any time he cared to look. She had on the cami-knickers she had made herself from some parachute silk that Walter had once brought her. Wearing the gift of one man to entice another. Offering the flesh one man had enjoyed to another, if she wanted to think that way. But Walter was dead. She had to live. So had this wounded man in front of her.

Why wouldn't he look at her? Walter had never been able to stop looking. All men wanted to look. If not at her at someone else. They wanted to look even when they daren't touch. And what was she doing here, half-naked with this man in this room heavy with the last of summer's heat, if she intended to stop him touching?

71

He was sitting in one of the easy chairs, very still, looking at something inside his head, his long bare legs stuck out in front of him. 'Spindle-shanks,' she might have said at another time. He still had his socks on, and his sock suspenders to keep them taut and tidy round his spare shins. The elastic was coloured in stripes, red, green, yellow. She wondered if they were his regimental colours.

She said, 'Howard, it doesn't matter, y'know,' before going to crouch beside him and reach for his hand.

'I know,' he said. 'I do know, really. You're not that kind of girl.'

'It's all right, then,' she said.

She twisted over his near leg and knelt between his thighs. A shoulder strap slipped. She left it. She herself had lost a little weight over the past fifteen months, but she was still well-covered. If Howard looked now he could see almost the whole of her breasts. Walter had loved her breasts. He had reached round her as she stood at the washbasin at Mrs Cheetham's, on their honeymoon, and soaped them for her. Soaped them for himself, more like, his hands, and his eyes in the mirror, renewing the awe he felt at the luck that had given her to him. That wasn't conceit: she knew that.

She closed her eyes. She wanted a man's flesh and it had better be this man's before it became someone else's. That thought frightened her. She had always understood bodily desire as a response to one man, in a deep and permanent relationship; something you could hold in easy abeyance when that man wasn't present; something which would

72

be to awaken all over again when that man was gone for good. But now she was disturbingly aware that what she craved might be seen apart from her feeling for Howard and she could comprehend how a woman might come to a moment of casual temptation, and almost understand how she might fall.

She put a hand on each of his thighs, her fingers spread. His legs twitched as she touched the scar and jerked convulsively as she made to probe its length.

'It doesn't still hurt, does it?'

'No, but it's as though there's a skin missing.'

The long lap of his dark green shirt was pulled down between his legs. Her little fingers touched its edge as, her hands reversed, she lightly rubbed the insides of his thighs.

'If I'd known I'd have brought some oil,' he said.

'Oil?'

'Some rubbing oil I have. It's supposed to keep the skin supple.'

'I'll do it another time.'

'It's especially soothing when somebody else does it.'

'Did the nurse do it?'

'Until she thought I was enjoying it too much.'

'I'll do it if you enjoy it.'

He glanced into her face and smiled. Yet she couldn't catch him looking at what she was offering him. He had claimed all along to love her yet she couldn't arouse him. He wasn't Walter and his needs would be expressed less directly. But there were clear responses he might make to show her.

'Shall we lie down on the bed?'

He let himself be drawn up. She held him round his waist and pressed her face to his chest as soon as he was upright. She felt his hand on her hair.

'Which side do you want to be?'

'Whichever suits you.'

'I have no preference in these things.' She was glad to hear the lightness in his voice. He said, '"His left hand is under my head and his right hand doth embrace me."'

'What's that?'

'*The Song of Solomon.*'

'From the Bible?'

'Yes. "Stay me with flagons, comfort me with apples: for I am sick of love."'

Walter had liked his left hand free.

'Perhaps I'll just go nearest the wall.'

'All right.'

'Remember that time at Olive's?' Ella said. 'Tony said he'd knock on the stair before they came down again. To warn us. And I said, "What do they think we'll be doing?"'

'And just look at us now.'

Ella lay down and turned on her side, facing him, as he stretched out beside her. It was the only way the two of them could fit on to the narrow divan. Suddenly, from wanting him to see her, she wished there were something to cover them and a light to put out.

'What was that bit again?'

'Which bit?'

'"Comfort me with apples . . ."'

'"Stay me with flagons, comfort me with apples: for I am sick of love."'

'Are you fed-up of love?'

'It doesn't mean fed-up, it means ill with it, poorly with it.'

Yes, Howard, she suspected, was capable of that, in the way of a lass who couldn't eat for thinking about a lad. She had, in fact, wondered before if he wasn't happiest when pining for something he couldn't have. Then he could build it up, make it into what he wanted it to be, safe from the reality that might spoil the dream. The reality being a woman he wasn't married to who stripped herself half-naked and persuaded him into bed.

Oh God, she hadn't meant to seem so brazen, but off the street and in the privacy of four walls he behaved as if he had no experience at all, leaving every move to her. Well, she was glad he hadn't been with a lot of women – especially the kind to be found behind bead curtains in the Middle East – but surely a natural longing should tell a man what to do. She felt tongue-tied, lacking all but the bluntest words to ask him why he didn't want her after all; why he wasn't caressing her in his need and bringing her to the point where she couldn't help but satisfy it for him. Wasn't that how it usually was: he persuaded, she gave in?

But she already wanted him. The spare flesh of his long body inflamed her. Her hands moved, searching, feeling for and exploring hard shapes. Everywhere she touched she felt an angle, a bone only lightly covered. The jut of his hip was like an outcrop.

She took his hand and, beyond all pretence of modesty now, guided it to the loose loop of silk at her crotch, slipping free the two small pearl buttons before reaching for him. She could have

75

cried out then. He wasn't anywhere near ready for her. She let her hand contain slack flesh for a few more moments, then withdrew it and lay still.

'I'm sorry,' he said.

'Don't worry about it. It's ... you must be ...' But what she didn't know.

'Has it never happened with you before?'

'No.'

'Did *he* never ... let you down like that?'

It wasn't the way she would have put the question herself, but she answered, 'No.'

'I thought not.'

So what did he want her to say?

'Was it always mutual?'

She let just an edge of impatience show in her direct answer, 'Yes!'

'Did he ever want you more often than you wanted—?'

'Howard – he's not here.'

'He is to me.'

So that was it! He had wanted to be the first. Or was it just an excuse, to cover up some deeper failure? Was he too fastidious to risk soiling his hands with living? Could nothing and no one ever match his standards? Well, she was flesh and blood. Being put on a pedestal, dusted down, given new clothes wasn't enough for her. Walter had changed that for her. It had been a copybook example of the way marriage was supposed to work: the modest girl coming unspoiled to be aroused by a loving and considerate husband. But she couldn't switch off now that he was dead. She still wanted warmth, touch, that intimate contact that went beyond the closeness of flesh, but which the closeness of flesh was the only passport to.

Only a man she cared for could offer that. She thought of all the women she knew who claimed they 'put up with it' and wondered why Howard couldn't think himself lucky that she was as she was.

'You'd never have come to me while he was around,' Howard said quietly. She was surprised by his clumsiness of expression. What could he mean? How could he reproach her for that, unless he was jealous of a dead man?

'He was my husband. He had the prior claim.'

'You wanted me before you wanted him, though. Didn't you?'

'I knew you for a week. Then you went away. How could I tell what I wanted?'

'You wouldn't be here now if you hadn't wanted me then.'

'People can change, Howard. What's here is now. What's past is gone.'

She pulled free as he sighed, and sat up in a burst of impatient energy.

'There's nowt I can do about it, then. I'm showing meself up to no purpose.' She waited for some response. 'I'll tell you straight, though, it'll be a long time afore you see me like this again.'

Her speech was broadening the more upset she became. She knew that she could easily work herself up now to the pitch of shouting at him as she accused him of shaming her, and wondered if that was the only alternative to tears as, clamping her teeth, she got up and dressed in silence.

She waited for him when she was ready to leave, thinking that for two pins she would go without him. But there would be no turning back from

77

that. And in spite of her shame, she wasn't finished yet. She couldn't guess how they might carry on, but throwing a tantrum would solve nothing. She could muster enough sense to realise that.

All the same, when he asked her, well-mannered to the last, if she still wanted to go to the pictures, she said, 'I think p'raps we've had enough for one day.'

It was too early for her usual train, so he walked her to a bus. That was painful in itself. All their growing physical ease with each other had gone. She didn't know how to match her step to his; how to stop and turn to cross a street without bumping into him.

There was a queue at the bus-stop. They stood apart from it.

'Won't you lose your place?'

'There'll be room.'

She could walk if it came to it. She felt, in fact, that it might be the best thing for her to do, using up some of her restless energy. But she thought he would feel compelled to walk at least part of the way with her.

As it was, though they kept at a distance for privacy, they had nothing to say. Only when the bus had trundled into sight did Howard ask, 'Shall I get in touch?' telling her that next Saturday could not be automatic for either of them. But whose feelings were uppermost in his mind – his or hers?

'If you still want to.'

She was last on and the bus was already moving as she looked for a seat. She could see Howard only by bending to the window and, occupied in

78

keeping her feet as the driver braked suddenly then accelerated again, she didn't manage to look out until he had turned and was walking away.

FIVE

I

'What do they call your friend, then? Is he a local chap?'

Darby Woodcock's voice was aimed into Ella's ear from a foot away, to counter without shouting the noise of the machine shop. She neither answered nor paused in what she was doing. She had just lifted an undrilled part on to the machine bed. When she went on, taking no notice of him, Woodcock picked up the part she had just dropped into the tub and checked it with a case-hardened steel template. It was essential, Ella had been told, that they did not vary by more than a few thousandths of an inch. If they did her machine would have to be reset. Not that she could do anything about it: the machine was in charge. The worst she could do was damage a drill-bit.

'You can talk and work at the same time by now, can't you?' Darby Woodcock said.

'Depends what there is worth talking about,' Ella said without looking at him. She had taken his measure early on. Excited by the number of women the wartime shortage of manpower had drawn into his world, he tried his luck constantly. If you cast your bread upon the waters often enough some of it was bound to come back buttered. At least he wasn't shifty about it; he made no bones about being interested. The main thing to remember was that you were unlikely to be the only one he was making up to. Or so she had been warned.

'I said is he a local chap?' Darby said.

'Who are you talking about?' Ella said, simply to be awkward.

'Chap I saw you down Calderford with, Saturday afternoon.'

'Oh, were you there, then?'

'I must ha' been to see you.'

'If it was me.'

'It was you all right. With a tall feller.'

'I never saw you.'

'Too wrapped up in your boyfriend.'

'I see nothing and nobody when he's around,' Ella said.

'*Is* he local?'

'What difference does it make?'

'It'll happen give me an idea how often he's likely to be around.'

'I see.'

'I've been thinkin' about askin' you to go down with me,' Woodcock said.

'You've been a bit slow, then, haven't you?'

'Does that mean your dance card's full up now?'

'Looks like it, wouldn't you say?'

'I'll wait for a "change your partner", then.'

'You never know your luck.'

Ella was aware that the need for him to stand close enough to make himself heard without shouting would be giving the appearance of an intimate conversation with Woodcock, but she had no time to glance round to see who might be watching.

81

'Is he in the forces?' Woodcock persisted.

'No.'

'Why not?'

'Why aren't you?'

'Oh, they've not got round to me yet.'

'You must ha' been hiddied when they went past.'

'Happen I'm a bit older than you think.'

Now Ella did turn her head to look into his face. He seemed unruffled by her insinuation. 'Are you asking me to guess?'

'You can if you want. I'm not an old man, mind. I've still plenty of lead in me pencil.'

'I'll bet,' Ella said. 'Is there a prize for droppin' straight on t'right year?'

'You can have a prize from me any time, pet.'

'Ooh, I'd better not tell the others or they'll all want one.' She smiled at him 'Or have some of 'em had theirs already?'

Fred Bickers, the foreman, came up, his stained trilby pushed back off his forehead. 'Is there owt amiss, Darby?'

Woodcock dropped the piece he was holding into the bin. 'Not that I can see, Fred.'

'Aye, well, don't overwhelm t'lass. We don't want her fainting into her machine.' He chuckled softly on a smoker's cough as Darby went on his way.

Grace Ellerington, on the next machine, a tall slim woman in her thirties, her thick fair hair held in a net snood, caught Ella's eye and pulled a face. Ella looked after the charge hand as he walked the length of the shop. She didn't dislike him. His shoulders were broad, his back flat. His features were strong, his nose prominent. Above a high

82

forehead his neat wavy hair had a silver thread here and there in the dark. They said he was legally separated from his wife. They said, surprisingly, that she was the one who had strayed.

Ella picked up another undrilled part. To her touch on a button a pneumatic clamp locked it into the jig. At the same time the guard came down. Then she manually guided the drillhead in its three consecutive operations, while coolant, like watered milk, fed on to the revolving bit. She dropped the finished piece into a metal tub on casters on her right and took the next one from the tub on her left. The parts weighed three pounds apiece and for some time, at the end of the shift, her forearms and the small of her back had ached with the bending and lifting. Apart from that, which was only troublesome now at a certain time in the month, the job suited her very well in her present state of mind. It was in its way as soothing and restful as a piece of plain knitting. She had no idea where the parts went from her or what they were for, and at the moment had no interest in finding out. Clinging without curiosity to the ritual of her current task was her shield against intimidation by the vast, complex spread of Daker Forge and Engineering, with processes of seemingly impenetrable mystery going on at every turn. Ella still felt that if she moved more than a few yards from her workplace except along the most direct route to the canteen and back to the main gate at finishing time, she would become hopelessly lost.

Woodcock appeared at her side as she walked to the canteen at lunchtime with a group of women.

'I don't want to stick me nose in where it'll get chopped off . . .'

'Oh, don't you?'

'But if circumstances should change, I hope you'll remember my invitation.'

'Did you make one?'

'If I didn't I will do as soon as you give me the word.'

'Don't hold your breath,' Ella said.

'I hope you're not offended.'

'Oh, no. How does a lass know what a chap wants 'less he tells her?'

He had deftly cut her away from the other women and now she quickened her pace and rejoined them as they entered the building. She didn't want labelling as Woodcock's latest try-on. But men – even 'fond' men – would rarely join a woman's table, and foremen and charge hands had their own corner. Woodcock left her once they were inside the canteen.

II

Few men would willingly have joined the table where Ella found a place, custom or not. Edie Crabtree was sitting there. Edie had a caustic tongue that she mostly used on men. She lacerated men; she scorned and reviled them. Very, very occasionally she would laugh at them; but humour was not one of Edie's strong points and men were too serious a subject for laughter.

Edie was thin to the point of being gaunt. She sometimes complained that she couldn't put on weight no matter what she did. Ella thought she might have a chance if she ate more and smoked less. She pushed aside her main course now, half-finished – 'Shepherd's pie. I don't know about t'shepherd but his boot soles are minced up in there' – and lit a fag, unmindful of where the smoke went until Ella, wafting an exhaled stream away from her plate, said, 'Keep it to yourself, till we've all finished, Edie.' Edie eyed her as if wondering whether to make an argument out of it, then docked the cigarette and looked round the faces at the table.

'Have you had t'AEU shop steward round your way yet?'

She addressed the question to Grace Ellerington, who shook her head. 'I wouldn't know him if I saw him.'

'Jack Broadhurst. You don't need to know him. He's makin' himself known.'

'What's it in aid of?'

'He's recruitin'.'

'What, women for the AEU?'

'Aye. Bloody marvellous, in't it, the way they can change their minds when it suits 'em?'

Ella supposed Edie to be in her late thirties. She was married and had a thirteen-year-old daughter. Her husband was in the army, somewhere overseas. Ella hadn't understood how he could have been called up, then somebody had told her that he had volunteered, and a couple of things Edie said revealed how savagely bitter she was about it. He had chosen to leave her when his age could have kept him at home. It wasn't the sole cause of her hatred of men but it helped to fuel it.

'What's in it for us?' another woman asked.

'Ask him yourself,' Edie said, lifting her gaze beyond the circle; 'he's comin' now.'

A harassed looking man with a lined face paused

at their table. He carried a school exercise book with a grubby cover. A row of fountain pens and propelling pencils showed across the breast pocket of his overall. He nodded warily at Edie.

'I want to ask you ladies if you'll stop behind for ten minutes after your dinner so's I can talk to you about the union's membership drive among women workers.'

'He wants to tell us that we're all gettin' equal pay with the men from next week,' Edie Crabtree said.

'I shall tell you nowt o' t'sort.'

Edie's eyes glittered as she took the point. 'Too bloody true, Jack. That's the last bloody thing you'll tell us, and don't we bloody know it. So happen you'll tell us what else you'll say 'at's worth our while listening to.'

'We have the negotiatin' machinery and if you'll give us time and your solid backing we might start gettin' somewhere on your behalf.'

'I earn two pound fourteen a week,' Edie said. 'Correction – I get *paid* two pound fourteen, which is a different thing. That simple bugger what brings me empty bins and takes me full 'uns gets over four pound. That's a rare old gap for you to negotiate away, in't it?'

'He's stronger than you,' Broadhurst said.

'Not in t'bloody head, he isn't.'

'I'm puttin' t'management argument.'

'Oh, are you? I suppose he constitutes part of this extra supervision we're supposed to need, an' all.'

'Aye,' Broadhead said. 'It's like the way they change a job slightly so's they can say there's no precedent for it and get out of paying you what

86

they previously paid a man for doing it. We know all their tricks.'

'And you reckon you can change all that?'

'I can promise you 'at you've more chance wi' t'weight o' t'union behind you than you have on your own.'

'But you see, Jack,' Edie said, 'that's just where I don't believe you. I believe you and t'management's in cahoots as far as we're concerned. We're a bloody nuisance 'at neither of you wanted, but t'government made you take us. Now you're finding out 'at we're better at some jobs than t'men and you're wonderin' what's goin' to happen when t'men start comin' home and asking for their jobs back.'

'You don't know what you're talkin' about.'

'Don't I? You mean you don't give a monkey's chuff for t'chaps 'at's away fightin'—'

''Course we do. What kind of union do you think we'd be if we hadn't their future prospects in mind? But you can't see beyond the nose on your face, Mrs Crabtree—'

'You notice how polite an' respectful he keeps it?' Edie said to the table.

'And you might be polite enough to let me finish.'

'Carry on, Comrade Broadhurst.'

'If you all get made up to full pay, what advantage have you got over t'men when they come back? What management is going to favour you then?'

'He means we're on a hidin' to nowt,' Edie said. 'We're cheap labour or nothing.'

And despite Edie's appetite for an argument and her eagerness to bait every man she came across, Ella felt that in this she was right.

'By, but there's some things goin' to have to change when this lot's over,' Edie said when Broadhurst had left them. 'An' there's some men in for a surprise when they come back an' find out what their women have been up to.'

'What d'you mean "up to"?' a girl asked plaintively. 'We're not all tarred with that brush, Edie. Some of us know how to behave ourselves.'

'I know you do,' Edie said impatiently. 'God, it's like talkin' to that bloody wall. You don't have to open your legs for every chap you meet to learn 'at women have never had a fair deal, that they've allus been handed t'shitten end o' stick and they allus will be unless they learn to stand firm and say no.'

'I don't know what you're talkin' about,' the same girl said. 'Bernard thinks the sun, moon and stars shine out of me. He'd give me anything he's got. He *does* give me everything he's got.'

'Keep him well wrapped up, love,' an older woman said. 'For God's sake don't let him catch owt. You could be a long time afore you find another as good.'

The girl was now in tears. 'He's not where I can look after him, that's the trouble.'

Ella wanted to ask how long the girl had been married, and offer her a little sympathy. But if that brought out the fact of Walter's death the lass would only feel worse.

As the meal ended and the men left, women began to gather at the end of the room near the stage, ready to listen to the union man. Ella found herself alone with Edie for a minute.

'Has that Darby Woodcock been pestering?'

'Oh, he's no trouble.'

'I thought he were sniffin' round. You're a war widder, aren't you?'

'Yes.'

'Darby doesn't mind whether they're livin' or dead, as long as they're far enough away. How he looks at it, it's them that's had it reg'lar that miss it most.'

'Isn't it a fact, though?' Ella said. Something in her wanted to provoke the woman.

'You think so, do you? If I never had it again it'd be soon enough for me. Sunday afternoons . . . All that thrustin' an' gruntin' an' then he's snoring in a lump an' you're crucified with indigestion.' She shook her head. 'No, I tell you, there'll have to be some changes when this lot's over.'

SIX

I

And wasn't it like her mother also to choose just then to quiz her about what she did in Calderford on Saturday afternoons and who she did it with?

'I know you like to keep things to yourself,' Patience said, 'and I thought, she'll tell me in her own good time. Of course, another chap'll come along. You're young. Your life's far from over. You'll want a family while there's still time. You—'

'Have you thought of a good day for t'wedding?' Ella asked.

'You what?'

'You're up to your old tricks – jumpin' to conclusions; seein' it all mapped out when it might not hardly have begun.'

'Now, Ella—'

'You were like that afore I married Walter. As soon as I got old enough to think about lads. I'd only to mention a name and you'd have him at home, his feet under the table, and plannin' what colour t'bridesmaids were going to wear.'

'All I'm sayin' is there's nobody to cry shame if you are seein' somebody. It's only natural.'

'Who's seen me?'

'Our Doris for one.'

'Who else?'

'A woman I met up t'village. She said she was glad to see you pickin' up the threads again.'

'Good of her to think so.'

'I wish you'd get it into your head 'at there's nobody runnin' you down.'

'Not even our Doris?'

'She didn't say a word against you.'

'Wonders never cease.'

'Not even when she knew 'at I knew nothing about it.'

'She'd be pleased she were first with the news.'

'It weren't as if she were bearin' malice.'

'She does bear malice, though.'

'Oh, Ella, I do wish—'

'She's got a grudge against me and I don't know what for.'

'Take no notice an' she'll come round.'

'She can please herself. I want nowt she's got, and that includes her sympathy.'

'I must confess I thought she might have softened a bit when you lost Walter.'

'Well, she didn't, an' I shall be a long time before I forget it.'

'You mustn't let things like that poison your life, Ella.'

'Oh, it won't do that. But I know where I stand with our Doris.'

'Mildred Sadler were askin' after you an' all.'

'I haven't seen her for a long time.'

'She were in a right temper when I were talking to her. She says Bobby Bainbridge went to tell her to stop her mother throwin' bread out for t'birds.'

'Is old Mrs Sadler goin' a bit doo-lally?'

'I haven't laid eyes on her for over a twelve-month. But Bobby Bainbridge told Mildred 'at he knew about a woman who'd been prosecuted and fined for the self-same thing an' if he heard about it again he'd have no option but to report her.'

'Fancy Bobby Bainbridge.'

'That's what I thought. I thought he knew how to keep well in wi' them that matter.'

'Do you ever see owt of Mildred's husband?'

'Neither hide nor hair. I think he must be away on some sort o' war work, but I've never liked to ask. It's allus seemed a funny match to me.'

'To me as well. I'm surprised they hadn't had somebody billeted on 'em afore now.'

'Who, for instance?'

'A couple of evacuee bairns, or at least an army officer. It doesn't seem right, just Mildred and her father an' mother in that great ramblin' place.'

'Oh, Mildred does her bit with her WVS work. When it comes to lodgers I expect she knows which strings to pull.'

'I wonder who told on old Mrs Sadler?'

'Mildred said Bobby Bainbridge weren't pleasant about it at all.'

'He's a bad bugger, Mother. We all know that.'

Patience took a mat to the back step and banged it against the house wall. She liked to be given a job when she visited Ella. She asked when she came back: 'Did you know Martha and Ronald had heard from our Arthur?'

'I didn't, no. Is he all right?'

'He was when he wrote.'

'Where is he?'

'Italy. There's a lot o' fighting there, isn't there?'

'Yes. Did he just write, out of the blue?'

'No, I thought you knew. Martha wrote him a letter and took it to Pontefract Barracks and handed it in for sending on.'

'Who thought o' that idea?'

'Martha herself. She asked our James to go and deliver it for her but he wouldn't.'

'That's him all over.'

'He said he wasn't going near the place 'cos they might try to rope him in.'

'He's just idle when it comes to doin' owt for anybody else.'

'Anyway, it's taken a burden off Martha's mind.'

'It will have.'

'You'd allus a soft spot for Arthur yourself, hadn't you?'

'I've more room for him than I have for James.'

'Oh, a lot more tender-hearted, Arthur was. I don't think he'll ever get over finding Winnie like he did.'

'That would ha' been a shock for anybody.'

'But Arthur ... after all the time he'd spent round there.'

'He did jobs for Winnie. She liked his company.'

'She liked more than his company, if I know owt.'

'Mother, what put that into your—?'

'You're not goin' to reckon *you* didn't know.'

'I'd like to know what put it into *your* head.'

'Summat Martha remarked set me thinking.'

'I hope Martha doesn't think you got it from me.'

'I've said nothing about it to Martha, but you and her have had a discussion by the sound of it.'

'It's not a subject for family tittle-tattle, Mother.'

'Now you've told me I'm right I shan't mention it again.'

'I've told you? How have I told you?'

'You've told me what you haven't denied. I must confess, it took a bit o' swallowin' at first, 'cos I couldn't understand what a tidy young chap like Arthur could see in a ragbag like Winnie.'

'Mother . . .'

'Oh, I know you shouldn't speak ill of the dead, but she wasn't what you could rightly call a young man's dream of love, was she?'

'She made a big effort towards the back end. You must have noticed that.'

'That were when that gamekeeper chap came sniffin' round.'

'He wasn't a gamekeeper, he was a farm labourer.'

'Whatever he was, he must have put Arthur's nose out of joint.'

'If there was anything between Winnie and Arthur it could only have been a passing thing.'

'She didn't go off wi' that other chap, though, did she?'

'She'd known him before an' preferred our Thomas. P'raps she still didn't fancy him.'

'So that bairn she were carryin' when she took her life wasn't his? Is that what you think?'

'How do I know whose it was?'

'Because you were closer to Winnie over that last twelve month than anybody else.'

'If our Doris gets hold of all this. Or our Florrie.'

'They won't from me.'

'I don't want Martha to think I've been gabbin'.'

'She knows you're not that sort.'

'I hope so.'

'Was that bairn Arthur's, Ella? That's all I want to know.'

Ella sighed. 'It couldn't have been Mole Templeton's because he told me he'd gladly have wed her.'

'Then it must have been Arthur's.'

'I couldn't see owt else for it.'

'What a shame,' Patience said. 'What a pity and a shame.'

'I've thought so many a time. I think it's why Arthur joined up. He couldn't face it coming out.'

'He'll find a good lass one of these days and then he'll forget it. He's nowt to blame himself for, has he?'

'No, but he does all t'same.'

Ella enquired about her father, who had been feeling run-down. He had never been the same, to her mind, since the war started. She had seen him age then, as though five or six years were compressed into one. The blow to his faith and optimism had taken a physical toll and the growing likelihood that the Allies would win was too late to restore his vitality.

They would relapse into silence for minutes on end while they went on with their light cleaning. Patience, offered nothing to appease her curiosity, finally asked, 'Do I know this chap you're walking out with?' which surprised Ella, who had been wondering what was holding back her mother's rebuke.

'I thought you said our Doris had seen him.'

'I did. She thought she'd seen him somewhere before, but she couldn't place him.'

'It's Howard Strickland.'

'So he's turned up again.'

'He works at Kemp and Crowther's, in Calderford.'

'Would he be workin' in Calderford if he hadn't wanted to see you?'

'Happen not.'

'Certainly not, you mean. Chasing you seems to be one thing you can depend on him for.'

'Mother, he never stole that money, y'know.'

'I can only go on what Mr Keighley told us, and what they decided in a court o' law.'

'There's no use saying owt about Howard Strickland to you. Your mind's made up.'

'It's been made up a long time. He deceived us all. He wasn't what we thought he was. What are you blushin' for?'

'I'm not blushin'.'

'I'm not blind. Your face is on fire.'

'I don't know why.'

'You're a year or two early for hot flushes.'

'About twenty-five, I should think.'

'Which means there are other things you're still capable of; so take care. One Winnie's enough in any family.'

'I'm not Winnie.'

'A word to the wise . . .'

'Howard's not like *that*, either!'

'I don't know what he's like. It's what you're like 'at concerns me.'

'Implying what?'

'What d'ye mean, "implying"?'

'I know what you're hinting at.'

'Does he want to marry you?'

'Yes, he does.'

'Does that mean he's proposed?'

'I wouldn't let him; not straight out.'

'There's nowt standing in your way now. You did your best by Walter. There's only you knows whether you can do the same by him.'

'I'm not marrying a chap you can't be right with.'

'Nay, Ella, it's your life. You make your own decisions. Your father an' me won't be here for ever.'

'Anyway, I've only told you what *he* wants.'

'What is it you want? And why are you blushin' again?'

II

He had written to her. His letter was under some linen in the sideboard drawer while she was talking to her mother about him. It had come on the Tuesday after she had seen him. She guessed he'd written it on Sunday, when he'd got his thoughts sorted out, and wondered if it had taken a long time or been dashed straight off. She could blush to think of its going astray and someone else reading it. She herself kept getting it out and reading it again.

'Dear Ella, I felt I had better write to you as quickly as possible before any further misunderstanding came between us. The most I can do is try to explain myself. I have spent some years building my image of you from what evidence I had. Now I find I know only a part of it and am faced with a side of your character which took me by surprise. As it happened, my reaction to this was impossible to disguise – one disadvantage of the male animal and something as distressing to me as it obviously was to you. Your strong sense of loyalty and keen feeling for right and wrong behaviour have been the keystones of my assessment of you, and I could admire them even when they were not to my personal advantage . . .'

But what the devil was he talking about she found herself asking out loud at this point? She had turned him off wanting her by showing him how much she wanted him? Another time? Safe inside the institution of marriage? It was hard to believe it would be any different. Easier to believe she had found him out in time.

She had thought that if he suggested they meet again as usual she would reply at once and say she needed time to think. But there was no such offer; just a promise to send her his address at the flat when he had moved and a wish – which she could interpret as sincere or a polite brush-off – that they might meet again before too long. Annoyed that he had not left that option to her, she decided not to reply. She couldn't anyway have expressed in a letter the most important things there were to say. They lay deep in an instinct, an impulse, which echoed a time, long ago now, with Walter. Howard wanted to know what he was to make of a woman who put off his proposal of marriage and five minutes later took him into bed. But what she had been looking for with him was what she'd sought that first time Walter had made love to her, in the open air, by the stream. Bridling at the

98

liberty he took she had then let him over the final threshold where she could have held him back. In two minds about him, she had thought to let it out of her hands, to offer herself to providence and the possibility of pregnancy. It would, she had decided, be a sign. So with Howard. In short-circuiting the slow pulse of habit she had thought to find out what was *meant*. And once again she had been denied a clear answer.

SEVEN

I

The cornet was playing in the house along the street. Ella didn't know whether it was that that woke her or the light touch of her mother's hand on her shoulder. For a second she didn't know where she was; then as the components of her whereabouts registered she had a sense of something missing. There was the flicker of firelight – rare in itself in an upstairs room of this house – and the occasionally wavering flame of the candle on the chest of drawers; the chair where her mother had been sitting, opposite; the fog-shrouded silence of the house ... and ... What? No sound that her ear could catch from the bed in the corner. She started, as violently as out of a dream of falling, and gasped. 'Oh!' Her mother leaned over her. Ella's hand reached up to the hand on her shoulder, grasping as though in appeal. Had she slept while the worst happened? Had she after all left her mother alone?

'Is he? He isn't ... ?'

'He's sleepin',' her mother said. 'As quiet as a bairn.'

'Ah ...'

'It's a good sign.'

Yes. Her neck was stiff. She must have been away a good while.

She didn't think there had been a fire up here in three years; not since the winter of 1940, when *she* had had a couple of days in bed with 'flu. Now nearly every household had somebody down with it. Her father had been in bed for two weeks. His chest was his weak spot. Any infection there was a danger. They had feared pneumonia. Dr Flint had called every couple of days and muttered consolingly in his sometimes impenetrable Scottish brogue. There were no magic medicines, only nursing. 'Keep him warm; give him plenty of liquid; try to keep his breathing free. Keep him in his bed if you have to tie him to it, until I tell you otherwise. I know he can be a stubborn man, but he's not as young as he was.'

It was a Saturday afternoon in December, one of the shortest days of the year. The fog had not lifted all day. The fifth Christmas of the war was nearly on them. Many people couldn't bring themselves to make anything of it now. Others might go to midnight mass, exchange a few simple presents. Prayers would be said. The Allies were winning the war but it was costing lives. People with men away had their hearts in their mouths every time the letter-box clacked. What they feared most, though, was the boy who delivered telegrams. Who had ever seen a telegram that didn't bring bad news?

On Boxing Days before the war as many as a couple of dozen people had crammed into this cottage. Numbers had reached their peak with the birth of Thomas and Winnie's two and the first of the grandchildren – James it was – to bring the lass he was courting. Ella wondered what had happened to her; if she knew that James was married and soon to be a father. Only weddings, christenings and funerals brought any number of them together now. Gone were the times when they had gathered for the sake of it, in their old home. Sugden had been amiably complaining by then that numbers were getting out of hand; but that hadn't been what stopped it. There were too many losses, too many ghosts; too much cause to sit haunted among the laughter. That was the reason; wartime shortages were merely the excuse.

Ella stretched her neck. 'I'd gone right off for a minute.'

'You were asleep for half an hour,' Patience told her.

No wonder her neck was locked up. She kneaded it with the heel of her hand. There was no air in this room, and no way of introducing any without letting in the fog as well.

The cornet was now playing a long, solemn melody. Ella had heard it only in scales and difficult phrases. She liked what she could hear now but asked her mother if she should go and get the man to stop.

'He might not play long.' Patience had taken her seat again. She drew in a long breath and let it slowly out. 'I feel a lot easier now.'

'Yes. Shall I go and make some tea?'

'I could come down for it.'

'Stay where you are, if you're warm an' comfortable. I'll see what the fire's like downstairs.'

The smell of something cooking slowly in a pot in the coal-oven met her as she went down. The living-kitchen was in darkness except for the red glow from a fire that needed mending. But before attending to that she transferred the partly heated kettle of water which always stood on the range to the direct heat of the coals, then put a lighted twist of paper to the gas mantle, the soft glow seeming to repel the fog-laden darkness pressing against the window panes. She closed the curtains and opened the door to look out. Immediately she was embraced from head to foot by chilling air. The fog stood before her like a wall. She couldn't even make out the Sadlers' big house across the width of the yard. When she stepped up into the street and looked right and left she could see and hear nothing. The cornet had stopped. She could have been in the middle of a huge field.

Shivering, she went back in. She laid a tray, mashed the tea, then put coal on the fire before carrying the tray upstairs.

'Did you find them arrowroot biscuits?' her mother asked.

'I never thought to look.'

'Never mind. Try not to bang about,' she added as Ella put the tray on the drawers and began to pour. They spoke to each other in low clear voices.

'I just had a look out,' Ella said. 'It's an awful night.'

'It'll happen keep folk inside their own homes, where they belong.'

'I don't fancy the walk back to my house.'

'There's nowt spoilin', is there? I've been sleepin' in your old bed. You could come in with me.'

It was a tempting offer. Fogs like this one were worse mid-week when the factories and mills were working. But industrial smoke never properly cleared except during the mass shut-down of a general holiday. To walk out now with a handker-chief over your face would show in ten minutes how much sheer filth you were breathing in.

'I'll see what I feel like later on,' Ella said.

'There's some rabbit stew in t'oven.'

'I could smell it.'

'I thought I'd make a few dumplings to go with it.'

'Oh, I'll stop for a bite to eat,' Ella said.

'I'll see to that presently,' Patience said. She put aside her tea-cup and got up to bend over the sleeping man. She remained there for a couple of minutes, standing with her head on one side as she listened to his breathing.

'I don't mind admitting now,' she said as she sat down again, "at I were a mite worried about him last night. He were coming to and going off again. And talkin'.'

'What about?'

'Owt that came into his head.'

'Wasn't he making sense?'

'To his-self, happen. He were askin' at one point for your Uncle Mauritius.'

'Mauritius?' That was a name from the dim fringes of family lore and one she hadn't heard for years. It could almost have been something she had dreamed or imagined. 'Uncle Mauritius?'

'Aye. They've not laid eyes on one another in donkeys' years and if they had I don't think they'd have spoken.'

'What did they fall out about?'

'Oh, it's never just one thing, though it's often one thing that finishes it off. There were some quarrel over the inheritance of this cottage.'

'Is he still alive, then?'

104

'I've heard nowt to t'contrary. An' he's a year or two younger than your father.'

'Where on earth did he come by a name like Mauritius?'

'His real name's Austin. Austin Herbert Palmer. But he's had Mauritius since he were a lad.'

'How do you spell it?'

'Now you know there's no use asking me that, Ella. If I'd ever seen it written down I shouldn't have recognised it. As I recall, it came from a place he was allus on about goin' to. He had wanderlust afore he was out of short pants, Austin did, an' he was allus on about this tropical island he was goin' to visit an' see some day. Mauritius, it were called.'

'Did he ever get there?'

'That I don't know, but he must ha' been nearly everywhere else.' Patience let herself be given another cup of tea. 'The thing *I* remember, 'at scandalised everybody, was him marryin' his housekeeper a month after his wife died. It were done so quick your father said he must have asked t'parson to post t'banns while he were conductin' Cora's funeral. A nice woman, Cora. Put up with his ways without ever a grumble 'at I ever heard. 'Course he weren't at home three-quarters of their married life. Then she fell poorly an' spent the last two years of her life bed-fast. That's where t'housekeeper came in. She's dead an' all now, as far as I know. Aye, I met this woman on t'street. "You weren't at your Austin's weddin' were you? Are you still not speakin'?" One of them women you want to tell to mind their own business the second they utter. But she'd taken me by surprise, you understand, and I'd said "I didn't know Cora

105

had passed away" before I could collect meself. "They buried her six weeks ago", she said, "and your Austin had his housekeeper in church inside the month." An' what do you think your dad said when I come in and told him? He said "Where have they gone on their honeymoon, then – Mauritius?"'

'He sounds to be quite a lad.'

'Have you never run into him, Ella?'

'Not to know about.'

'Him and your father parted before you were born.'

'Me dad said he wanted to see him?'

'Aye. It made me very uneasy, I'll be candid. When folk who's poorly start wanting to mend their quarrels . . .'

'Well, he's round the corner now.'

'He'll very likely not remember most of what he said.'

'It seems a pity they won't have a chance to make it up.'

'Oh, some folk are just not worth botherin' your head about,' Patience said. 'Is that our door?'

'Somebody's come in,' Ella said. She heard a voice. 'It sounds like our Doris.'

Patience said quickly, 'Nip down and stop her afore she comes up. Go on, your limbs are nimbler than mine. She'll be sure to wake your dad if she gets up here.'

The stairs' door, which had stood ajar, opened fully as Ella went down. Doris changed her mind about calling up as she saw her sister.

'Oh, you're here, are you?'

'I'm surprised you've turned out on a night like this, Doris.'

106

'Oh, are you? We're not all fair-weather visitors.'

Doris turned her body to let Ella pass and would have gone straight up if Ella had not taken her arm.

'Me mam says not to go up just now.'

'She says or you say?'

'Me dad's asleep.'

'Why should I waken him any more than you? Are you in charge o' t'sick-visiting rota now?'

'I'm only tellin' you what me mam sent me down to tell you.'

'I'll believe it better when she tells me herself.'

'Doris, if you wake him out of his first peaceful sleep for—'

'You'll what?'

Ella wanted to say 'I'll claw your silly face for you,' and felt that she could without hesitation have put her nails to the mask of undisguised malice through which Doris challenged her. But they were saved by Patience's tread. Doris stood back as her mother reached the bottom step.

'You fratch on sight, you two, don't you?' Patience said. 'When you speak at all.'

'Am I to be told by madam here when I can and can't see me own father?'

'I sent her to tell you when I heard you come in. Your father's come through a crisis and I don't want him disturbed.'

'An' I've turned out on t'worst night in t'year an' I reckon I've as much right as she has—'

'You've just as much right, Doris.'

'Well, then. I've a family to look after. I'm not like some, who can pick up any time. If I were I could happen take better advantage of it.'

'Say what you mean, Doris,' Ella said. 'If you hadn't a family you could spend all your time here, poisonin' me mam an' dad against t'rest o' t'family, which is what you seem to think I do.'

'If t'cap fits—'

'As for your family, you want to think yourself lucky an' look after 'em, including your husband, who sleeps in his own bed every night.'

'My husband does his own bit in his own way.'

'Nobody's callin' him. You just want to learn to stop walkin' all over him an' thank God you've got him where you can see him.'

'Who says I walk all over him?'

'Just about everybody when they talk about it. Which isn't often, I'll admit.'

'Will you stop it!' Patience glanced at the ceiling and lowered her voice to warn them. 'If you don't give it up I'll rattle your earholes for both of you!'

Ella felt sullenly unsatisfied that the exchange had led to no decisive outcome. But what did she expect? This kind of quarrel could last a lifetime.

'Have you come through t'streets on your own?' Patience asked her middle daughter.

'Jack brought me.'

'Why didn't he come in?'

'Oh, you know Jack.' Doris shot a warning look at Ella as if daring her to make some sarcastic comment. 'He doesn't like sickness. He's coming back for me at seven. He'll very likely look in for a minute then.'

Ella stepped back to where she could see her father's watch hanging beside the fireplace. She was being driven out. She didn't think she could bear nearly two hours of Doris's company.

Doris had taken off her hat and coat now. She

patted her hair and secured the hat-pin in the hat. She didn't sit down.

'Well, am I to be allowed to go and see him or not?'

'I suppose you'll have to go,' Patience said, 'or we s'll never hear t'last of it.'

'I think you can rely on that.'

Her sister was beginning to look middle-aged, Ella thought. Doris had always carried herself rather stiffly; now she had a substantial bosom to balance, and thickening flesh round her hips. She had a way of standing with her feet apart, her feet turned out slightly, which gave her a look of being ready to take on anyone who came near her. The suspicion and aggression she had shown as a child had grown with her into womanhood.

'Well you listen to me,' Patience was telling her. 'Go up quietly and neither touch him nor speak to him. I want him to have this sleep out.'

As Doris went her mother protected her hand with a cloth and opened the oven to stir the contents of the earthenware pot inside.

'Do you think,' Ella asked, 'that in a strange place they'd know our Doris an' me for sisters?'

'You're more alike than you seem to realise,' Patience said, 'so don't you go putting on airs.'

'Mmm.' Ella put her head back and pointed at the ceiling. 'Listen.'

They had heard Doris's weight on the floorboards. Now there was another sound. Her voice. Patience sighed.

Ella said, 'It's no use going up to her. You don't want an argument in front of me dad.'

Ten minutes went by before they heard Doris cross the bedroom floor to the door.

109

'I think every board in this house creaks,' Ella said.

'You'll creak if you live to t'same age,' her mother said. She faced her other daughter as she emerged through the stairs' door.

'It's some good talkin' to you.'

'He woke up an' spoke to me afore I'd hardly crossed to his bedside.'

'Probably heard us playin' Happy Families down here,' Ella said.

'How does he seem to you, anyway?' Patience asked.

'His temperature's down.'

'Aye, that's a good sign.'

'He said he wanted to go to sleep again.'

'I'm pleased to hear it.'

'He, er, he seemed to be wanderin' a bit.'

'He weren't bad, were he? He did know who you were, didn't he?'

'Oh aye. But he wanted to know if anybody had been to fetch Uncle Mauritius.'

Ella turned her head to the window. Faintly, from the house along the street, she heard the cornet start again.

II

A goods train on the rails overhead filled the pedestrian tunnel of the viaduct with a threatening rumble. A man mounting the steps at the other end hoisted his bicycle on to the running-board provided for it and wheeled it along at shoulder-height, nodding to Ella as they met somewhere about the middle. His lips moved in some pleasantry that the wagon wheels wouldn't let her hear, and she smiled in acknowledgement and passed on.

It was Sunday morning. The worst of the fog had cleared, but mist still shrouded distances. Ella was dressed to face the still cold, in winter coat, scarf and gloves, and a close-fitting woollen hat that she had knitted herself. When her feet touched the ground again she was on Balk Island, the strip of land between river and cut. A simple hump-backed bridge straddled the canal. Between her and that were a row of cottages, an ale-house in an overgrown garden, and an open space among tussocky frost-rimed grass and the thick brittle stalks of riverside weeds where a goat was tethered among a group of tarred timber sheds beyond which Ella could make out one window and a corner of the house where she had been told she would find her father's brother.

As soon as her shoes scuffed on the packed lumpy earth of the yard a dog began to bark. She stopped, apprehensive, as it hurtled into sight, black, smooth-haired; a lot of the labrador in it, she thought. It came to a halt as though at the end of a chain and stood barking at her.

'Delilah,' a voice commanded, 'that's enough.'

It was a man's voice with a curiously blurred and throaty articulation. He came from behind a shed and half-bent to fondle the dog's head before giving any attention to her. Ella was mildly surprised. She knew him.

'Hullo, Josh,' she said. 'What are you doin' here?'

Saliva bubbled at one corner of his mouth and ran in a thread down the side of his chin. He was one of those simple-minded men who never seem

111

to age, remaining fixed in late adolescence, until you see their skin near-to and notice the threads of grey in their hair. The jacket he wore, tweed, a size or two small for him, could have been the one she had seen him in the time she particularly remembered. He had a woollen jumper under it, but the frayed shirt was open at his throat and, with neither gloves nor topcoat, he seemed uncaring of the cold. The dog had sat on its hindquarters by his leg. Josh stared at her, his black buttons of eyes unblinking.

'Don't you know me, Josh?' You ought to, she was thinking. You cost me a broken nose, my lad.

He spoke. 'I come down here,' he said. 'I come to help. I'm reight handy.' Someone had told him so.

'Mr Palmer lives here, doesn't he, Josh?'

'Mr Palmer, aye. He lets me come an' help him.'

'I bet you're handy to have about the place.'

'I am.'

'Will you show me where I can find him? Or tell him there's somebody come to see him?'

He stared at her. She reminded him. 'Mr Palmer, Josh.'

'Aye.' He turned and walked away. Somewhere out of sight somebody had begun to chop wood.

The dog remained. She walked slowly towards it and bent to stroke its silk-smooth cranium. 'Delilah, eh? That's what they call you, is it?'

She wondered if her uncle had been living here when she had played in and around the viaduct, as a child. But they had been rare, the treks after boys or the search for novelty which led down here. There were places nearer home to play and always boundaries, either taken for granted or cited as lines beyond which gangs of strange rough lads lurked in wait for the unwary.

The woodchopping stopped a few seconds before another man came out where Ella could see him. He was bareheaded too. There was a neckerchief inside his collarless shirt. He wore an open waistcoat over the shirt, and moleskin breeches and leggings. The long-handled axe hung loosely from his hand. Ella was looking for resemblances to her father as he sized her up before speaking.

'D'you want me, young lady?'

'Uncle Mauritius?' Ella asked and watched his eyes narrow. 'I'm Sugden Palmer's youngest daughter.'

His grey hair was cropped in the fashion her father favoured and he had the same spare build. It was round the mouth, as he spoke again, that she suddenly discerned an unmistakable family likeness, but there was more vanity in the way he shaped his moustache. Josh stood watching from a few paces behind him.

'I wouldn't ha' known thee.'

Ella noticed his immediate drop into the familiar before she said, 'I'm not surprised.'

'Is there owt amiss?'

'No, no, nowt like that. Well, no, not what you might be thinking.'

'What might I be thinking?'

'I'm not bringing that kind o' news. Me dad's been poorly, though. He's had 'flu right bad. We've been worried about him.'

'Comin' round, is he?'

'Yes. He were ramblin' a bit. He were asking for you.'

'While the balance of his mind was disturbed,' Mauritius said. 'In't that what they say? "Not responsible for his actions?"'

'I wouldn't have put it like that.'

'Happen not. But what might thy name be?'

'I'm Ella.'

'Ella. And t'youngest lass, tha says?'

'T'youngest of 'em all.'

'Not too young to be appointed *emissary*, by t'look of it. *Emissary*. In't that right? Come wi' terms for peace?'

'I don't know.'

He was surprising her by the second.

'*Negotiator-in-chief*, no less.'

His delivery in any case was a slow drawl, his voice light, so that what he said seemed to be released to float between them; but when he launched a long word he put his head back and gave it time to hang in the air like a coloured balloon while he observed it, chuckling.

'Aye, aye ... aye ... Well, tha'd better come thisen inside where it's warm. It's no mornin' for standin' about.'

A cottage of flaking sandstone with a sagging roof stood behind the sheds. There were some hens in a wire enclosure and a vegetable garden with a few rows of cabbage stumps. A huge fire was piled in the grate, though the house door stood open. Josh followed them in and stood just inside the doorway as Mauritius waved his hand at a sagging armchair. 'Sit thisen down. An' thee put t'wood in t'hoil, Josh lad.' Ella rather wished he wouldn't as the cold air from outside cut the thickness of the odd smell, something like animal feed, which caught at her throat and for a moment made her want to gag.

114

'Tha knows my assistant, does tha?'

'Oh, yes, everybody knows Josh.'

He had sat down on a stool behind the door, watching Mauritius fill a teapot with water from a blackened kettle off the hob. At the last summer feast before the war Walter had remonstrated with three lads who had shouldered Josh roughly aside, then found himself in a fight, first with one of them then with all three as the other two joined in to save their mate. Ella had tried to drag Walter clear of the impossible odds, and got an elbow in her face. Meanwhile, Josh had taken to his heels.

'He follers me like a shadder,' Mauritius said.

'Don't you mind?'

'No, no. He fetches an' carries a bit and saves my back. But best on it is, he listens.'

In a cupboard he found Ella a surprisingly delicate china cup. He poured tea into that then filled pint mugs for himself and Josh. He offered her sugar, then a flat half-bottle of whisky.

'Does tha fancy havin' it fortified with a drop o' Johnnie Walker? No? Never press strong drink on a reluctant imbiber. Allus been a rule o' mine. Comes in handy at a time o' shortage. Aye . . . aye . . . Just a touch for me, then . . . Oh, aye,' his tone changed, 'he listens. He sits wi' me an' listens by the hour.'

'What do you tell him?'

'Everything, lass. The bloody lot. He's had my life story in every jot an' tittle. Aye, wi' footnotes an' all. He'd know as much as I do by now if he could understand any more na one word in half a dozen. Well he does understand more words na that. It's when they're strung together into sentences 'at meaning escapes him. Aye.' He put his

115

head back and chuckled as he prepared to release another balloon. 'He's what tha might call *non-cognisant*, tha sees, Ella. Or should it be *incomprehensive*? Happen so. Aye. No bloody matter. It goes wi'out sayin' 'at poor bugger's *non compos* bloody *mentis*. Tha'll have known some folk what's elevenpence ha'penny in t'shilling, no doubt. Well I reckon Josh is about eightpence. Aye. But tha's no idea how peaceful it is to talk while he sits an' listens.'

'I hear you've travelled a lot, Uncle.'

'Oh aye. The wide world over, lass. Aye. I set off to Canada first. Found me way down into t'United States from there.'

'Did you see any cowboys?'

'I never dropped across Tom Mix, no. But I did eventually join up as one o' Teddy Roosevelt's Roughriders, in t'Spanish-American War.'

'Ridin',' Josh said.

'Hear yer,' Mauritius said. 'He remembers. Does t'name o' Teddy Roosevelt mean owt to thee, Ella?'

'No.'

'Theodore Roosevelt as he become. Twenty-sixth president of the United States.'

'I thought he wa' called Franklin D.'

'Nay, lass, tha's just jumped thirty-year an' dropped on another chap altogether.' He twinkled at her. 'Tha'll have to come an' sit an' listen wi' Josh.'

'It sounds like it.'

'I come home an' joined up for t'Boer War then. There were three on us from Daker: Clarry Normanby, Billy Melchett an' me. Does tha know, when we arrived back they'd Daker Silver Band

116

waitin' for us at railway station. Full complement. They played us in procession up t'village while folk cheered an' waved. Oh, aye. That's when I got wed t'first time. I had me pick an' I thought I'd better get job done afore t'enthusiasm ran out and t'choice dwindled. Heroes aren't heroes for long, tha knows, Ella. They start shrinkin' in stature as soon as they put their uniforms away. Aye. I went to Australia then. After I'd worked round here for a while.'

'What did your wife think of your roamin'?'

'Oh, she were a very patient woman. An' I painted her a rosy picture of the kind of life I'd have waitin' when I sent for her.'

'You came back, though.'

'Oh aye. My disease, tha understands, Ella, were in allus thinkin' there were somewhere else.'

'You're settled at home now, seemingly.'

'T'only place I make for nowadays is Euphoria. Tha gets there by walkin' across to t'pub wi' a couple o' bob in thi pocket. Oh aye. T'next destination for me lies inside t'pearly gates. Least, I hope it'll be there an' not t'other place, "May the devil find out you're dead half an hour after you've arrived in heaven." Has tha never heard that? Irish. Not that I'm takin' any insurance for it, tha understands. Whatever's in store 'ull come to pass wi'out me joinin' t'Sunday mornin' fox-fur an' mothballs brigade. Oh aye. I think we can be sure o' that.'

'How long have you been on your own?'

'Oh, some while now. I thought I might look round for number three to tend me in me declining years, but I had no luck. I see you're wearing a wedding ring.'

'I married Walter Lindley. Happen you'd come across him when he worked in t'Co-op butcher's.'

'Can't say he registered. Is he away in t'forces?'

'He got killed in the Far East eighteen months ago.'

'Ah . . .' Mauritius shook his head in a gesture of sympathy. 'I lost both mine through natural causes. If tha can call a lingerin' death wi' consumption o' t'lungs natural. That's what took t'first one. There's folk live up mountains in Switzerland an' in t'Arizona desert 'at never get that, tha knows. It all depends on t'luck o' t'draw.'

'Me mother says she were a nice woman, your first wife.'

'Aye. There's no argument about that. Cora were a queen. "Look after him, Nellie," she said to t'woman what came in to see to things. "There's nowt I can do while I'm laid here." Aye. There were talk when I took Nellie to t'altar afore Cora's funeral flowers had wilted. But she'd begrudged me nowt an' I thought it my place to make it official as soon as possible. She'd ha' waited a while hersen. Happen she knew 'at rushin' like that 'ud make folk certain o' what they'd only previously suspected. Eh well. I hope I'm not shockin' thee with all these snippets of family history 'at tha's nobbut heard as gossip afore.'

'No, no.'

'No, tha looks like a young woman wi' red blood in her veins, not rose-watter. Aye . . . You'll go out to work, I reckon?'

'Yes. I was a weaver at Lidgetts, but I work at Daker Forge now.'

'Not much weavin' there, is there?'

'No, I'm on a machine. I'm like that song o'

Gracie Fields's: I make whatnots for thingume-
bobs.'

'I see. Aye. So here we are, then. Sugden's
poorly an' he fancies he'd like to see me. Did he
send thee his-sen?'

'No, me mam sent me. I think t'first time he
began to ask for you it made her uneasy.'

'It would do. It comes under t'headin' o' tidyin'
up loose ends, tha sees. *Consanguination*, Ella lass;
meanin' blood's thicker than watter. An' it is. Oh
aye. Aye. No denyin' it. All t'same, an' never-the-
bloody-less, this is summat 'at requires a bit o'
thought. If tha'd come an' told me he were at
death's door I'd very likely ha' put me coat on an'
gone straight back wi' thee. But when tha says
he's on t'mend it gives me time to look at it from
all angles. Aye.'

'Can I ask what it was you fell out about?'

'It were over that cottage tha were brought up
in. It belonged to thy Uncle Hedley, thi father's
brother an' mine.'

'I never knew him.'

'No, he died before tha were born. He never wed
an' he had no issue. I suppose tha knows 'at one
doesn't allus foller from t'other, even in t'best o'
families, but it did in Hedley's case. He talked to me
about it. He said he didn't think he were t'marryin'
kind an' if it should come about 'at he passed away
wi'out offspring, his cottage should either be sold
and t'proceeds divided between thi father an' me,
or one of us could live in it an' t'other get his share in
t'form o' rent. Now I were on t'other side o' t'world
when Hedley cocked his clog and by t'time I got
back thi father had his family installed in Hedley's
house an' claimin' it were his by right o' seniority.'

119

'Oh, surely . . .' Ella couldn't help questioning her uncle's version of events.

'Oh aye. I know you don't like to hear that sort o' thing about your father, but there it is.'

'And you've never had anything out of it?'

'Not a meg.'

Ella wondered if she dare ask her father for his version of the story, and which one she would feel compelled to believe.

'And don't think that's the end of it,' Mauritius said. 'It'll cause bother among you lot – Sugden's bairns – when him an' your mam have gone. Oh aye. I can see ructions still to come.'

Mauritius leaned forward, picked a piece of wood out of the hearth and pressed it into the middle of the fire.

'Any road, I'm pleased to have made thi acquaintance, lass, an' I hope tha'll come again an' bring me news of thi father's progress. In t'meantime I think tha'll have some under-standin' why I'm not already half-way there on me bike.'

'Bike,' Josh said. 'Ting-a-ling! Ting-a-ling!'

'Harken to him,' Mauritius said. 'I sometimes think he's like Pablo's bloody dog: tha says t'right word an' he's off. Go an' get it out, then, if tha wants. I let him ride it round t'piece,' he said as Josh went out. He eyed Ella. 'I've given thee food for thought, haven't I?'

'You have.'

'Happen I should ha' kept it all where it belongs, between Sugden an' me.' Ella made a little gesture. 'But I sometimes think livin' on your own doesn't mean you talk less; it means you talk all the more when t'opportunity arises.' They both sat quiet for a time. Then Mauritius asked, 'Could tha do wi' a two-or-thri eggs?'

'Me dad's hens are laying, thanks.'

'Well then. I'd a pig an' all at one time, but I couldn't be doin' wi' all this *fandango* o' licensin'. Can't kill it when tha wants to an' gi' somebody a couple o' chops. No. Not for me, all that. Let some other bugger be bossed about an' spied on.'

EIGHT

Ella's father died in his sleep and was buried two days before Christmas, 1943. The family had had a baptism, a wedding and a funeral within the year. A single life ended; life itself was renewed: James's wife, Avril, was big with Sugden's second great-grandchild.

There were a lot of people in the chapel, though numbers dwindled once the coffin was taken out and the family was allowed its privacy at the graveside. The brothers, George and Granville, stood side by side. There were tears on Granville's cheeks, while George watched dry-eyed the putting in earth of the man he had drawn close to in Sugden's last eighteen months. Their sister Catherine, normally unseeking of demonstration, could not contain herself and buried her choking sobs in the rough tweed of her mother's coat, to the upper sleeve of which Florrie had stitched a small black diamond badge of mourning.

Ada had come with her husband, whom none of them had seen for some time. Ella was disturbed by the change in Cyril. He had been easiest brought to mind with his sleeked hair, his dentures flashing as he bantered and chaffed, the life and soul of any party. Now his eyes had a strange wandering and unfocused look, as if he wasn't a hundred per cent sure where he was and why. Ada had managed a black coat that was more suitable for the occasion than the weather. All she seemed capable of was murmuring time after time, 'Oh, this wicked, wicked war' – as though she thought it directly responsible for her father's death – while she wept with admirable control and touched a tiny handkerchief to her nose.

For noisy weeping of a kind most likely to upset Patience, no one could beat Doris, who, once she let go, shook with great honking cries and gasps for breath, even at one point gabbling aloud a run of words that Ella couldn't make sense of. One of Ella's thoughts was that her father wouldn't, after all, see the end of the war; would not know who did win and how it all turned out, finally. What she still hadn't learned then, and never would fully take in, was that nothing ever was, in fact, final. There was always something else. Nothing was ever settled except in the way it was now for Sugden Palmer. Unlike four of his children, he had lived his life to its full biblical span. She wondered if he had had the time, or the inclination, to ask himself what it had all been about. And whether there had been an answer.

An elderly man at the gate, looking lost, stepped forward as Ella went out. She knew him, though she had not seen him for a long time. He knew her. He asked, 'You're Sugden Palmer's youngest, aren't you?'

'Ella, Mr Dews.'

'Well, lass, I'm hopin' 'at what I've just stumbled across isn't what I think it is.' He craned his neck as he spoke and even lifted on his toes as he looked past Ella as though for the one person present he couldn't yet see.

'I'm afraid it is, Mr Dews.'

'Your dad.'

'Aye.'

'I've been stoppin' with me eldest daughter at Thurnscoe, or I might have heard.' He took a quick catch of breath then pulled a face, a grimace that was near to a totally humourless grin. 'Otherwise I'd ha' been here. That I would. We dug some tons o' coal between us, me an' your dad, in t'old days at Elder Bank.'

'I know. He'd talk about it many a time.'

He stood in silence, then shook his head. 'I can see your mother. I don't think it'll upset her too much if I just go an' have a word.'

'She'll be disappointed if she knows she's missed you.'

The little man had taken her nearer to the tears she had not yet shed. The public ones, that was, not those she had given way to on her own. She looked round distractedly. People were lingering. Somebody should marshal them. They were only a step from the Co-op Hall where the funeral tea was waiting.

Mauritius was behind her. She had spotted him at the back of the congregation as they had followed the coffin out.

'Thomas Henry Dews,' he said to the back of the man who had gone to speak to Patience.

'Yes.'

'Worked with your father for years.'

'He did. He's just had a shock. He hadn't heard.'

Nobody had thought about Mauritius, but he

had heard and turned up. He wore a shabby but well-fitting navy-blue Melton overcoat, elegantly shaped at the waist. Ella had not told her mother what Mauritius had said about his quarrel with his brother. When asked if he was coming she had answered, 'He will when he gets round to it.'

'Have you managed a word with me mother?'

'I have. She said Sugden had been askin' for me. I told her 'at t'gravity o' t'situation had escaped me, or I'd have come. Aye, aye.' He looked at the ground and murmured, 'It's what you might call a bugger, Ella lass. It leaves a feller feelin' he hasn't done what he should ha' done.'

'We all thought he was on the mend,' Ella said. 'Anyway, she'd ask you to come with us for a cup o' tea, didn't she?'

'She did, but I told her I'd summat else to do. T'bosom o' t'family's hardly t'right place for me. If I'd seen your father it might ha' been different. But I didn't.'

The Rev. Mr Barraclough came up as Mauritius left Ella's side. Ella wanted to tell him how delighted Sugden had been with George's story of his analysing the hymn. She herself had heard him preach two or three times since then.

'Are you comin' across for your tea, Mr Barraclough?'

'Oh, yes ... yes ... I've a feeling I'd have liked your father.'

'He knew about you.'

'Did he really? What did he know?'

'That you sometimes ... you sometimes upset people with your sermons. *All Things Bright and Beautiful* ...'

'Ah ...' The parson nodded. '*All Creatures Great and Small* ... Yes. Come, shall we walk across together?'

PART TWO

NINE

I

A bandy-legged old man was leaning on his stick as he morosely contemplated the blackboard propped against the open door of the Masons Arms with its chalked message: 'Sorry, no beer'. He looked round when Ella spoke to him. 'That doesn't look so promisin'.'

'No. I mun as well go in, all t'same. They'll happen have some o' t'smell left.'

'They won't charge you for that, either!'

She passed by and went into the cottage. It was Saturday dinnertime and she had just walked up from work. The smell of cooking met her. The heat of the fire drawn under the oven seemed to have left a pocket of cold air at the back of the room and Ella shivered suddenly as she took off her coat.

'Is it cold out?'

'I think that mild January's made us all soft.'

She took a place on the hearth beside her mother, who stood with an oven-cloth at the ready.

'Meat an' tatie pie.'

'Lovely.'

'I put a jam pastie an' an oven-bottom cake in while I were at it.'

129

'Grand.'

There were times now when Patience tempted her like a woman pleasing a favoured suitor, though she would have resented any suggestion of an ulterior motive. 'Come home,' was the unspoken message. 'Why condemn yourself to that cold, unwelcoming house when there could be a fire and a hot meal waiting every time you walk in the door?'

'Is there some bother brewin' in t'pits?' Patience asked as they waited.

'It looks like it.'

'What's it all about?'

'This minimum pay award they've brought in.'

'I thought t'miners had allus wanted a guaranteed weekly wage.'

'They have, but not one what does away with their differentials and piece-work.'

'It's a fine time to be stoppin' work.'

'Oh, aye.'

Patience brought the pie to the table. Steam rose through the incisions in the crust, which had taken hardly any colour at all. She put out hot plates with a warning to Ella to watch her hands. They sat down, Ella having drawn herself a glass of water. There was a little less beef and a little more potato in the pie than there would have been normally, but Ella was happy enough with what there was. She thought sometimes that she could have satisfied herself with crust and gravy. Her mother's crust. She had never quite acquired Patience's knack with pastry.

'They've run out o' beer at Masons.'

'Oh, have they! That'll spoil a few weekends.'

'I expect so.'

'It'll happen save a few women from black eyes, an' all.'

'You never have expected owt of men with a few pints inside 'em, have you?'

'I've preached enough sermons ow t'subject for you to know that.'

'Aye.'

Ella was still conscious of her father's empty chair. It was in her sight without her looking directly at it, though she was drawn into giving it repeated sideways glances. Her mother sat with her back to it. Perhaps she allowed herself to brood on it when she was alone. She seemed to manage, stoically, during the day, when she could find jobs to do; but she had refused from the day she was widowed to sleep in the cottage alone. Ella had stayed with her every night. It was a kind of dependence that Ella had not foreseen. Patience was well and needed no waiting on; but she was afraid to be by herself at night. Ella had begun to feel trapped in a ritual that would be hard to break.

She asked as she accepted a second helping of pie:

'Have you thought about it, then?'

'Thought about what?'

'Having a go at stoppin' on your own for a night.'

'Oh, that.'

'You'll never master it, y'know, till you set yourself.'

'It's the thought of locking that door an' knowing I'm on me own till mornin'.'

'I didn't like it when I first moved to Temperance Street, but I vowed I'd get the better of it and I did.'

'You're younger than I am.'

'Granted.'

But she had lost someone too. Not a man she had shared her life with for fifty years; but the nights had been when the ache of losing Walter had come to her undisguised, with nothing but the slow tally of further nights to render it endurable.

'Happen when t'days draw out a bit,' her mother said.

'By that time it'll be past changin'.'

'I can't see what it's interfering with. It's only like it was when you were at home. You came an' went as you liked then. It's no need to stop you doing what you want to do now. Has it stopped you courtin' Strickland?'

'No.'

'Summat has, though, hasn't it?'

'How do you know?'

'You're not hoppin' off to Calderford every Saturday afternoon, like you used to.'

'We decided to give it a rest for a while.'

'Both of you, or just one?'

'Oh, it was mutual.'

'You're happen well rid of him. Give yourself a chance to find somebody more your own kind.'

'There doesn't seem to be all that many about.'

'There will be when this lot's over and t'men start comin' home. There'll be a lot wantin' to settle down and start raisin' families.'

Oh, yes. If you had one who wouldn't come back you had only to wait for another. There'd be plenty to go round, surely. There had been nothing like the slaughter of the last war, when any number of women had been left to endure life on their own. And in any case, she, Ella, was comely, pleasing to the eye, warm-hearted, warm-blooded. She could, given the chance, make any man happy, if he wanted what most men wanted. So all she had to do was wait, try to keep cheerful, and life – the real life of marriage and children – would sooner or later seek her out.

She had been on the point two or three times of writing to Howard, saying just enough to tell him she was willing to see him again. It wasn't that she actively missed him, not painfully, not in every empty moment of the day. Often now her feeling was one of a lurking irritability, which could grow into exasperation at the suspicion that she might have been judged and found wanting; that she had shocked him so much he was avoiding any involvement. It was this that she couldn't leave alone. It wouldn't rest. It called for a resolution that Howard seemed in no hurry to seek; an outcome that she herself couldn't define, involving a man for whom she had feelings she couldn't analyse. Sometimes she put it all down to pride. He had dented her self-esteem. She couldn't bear to think of him going about thinking worse of her than before. He had wanted a lady and found himself with a woman who, surprisingly, had suddenly begun to behave like a whore. But Walter had thought her a lady. 'Our Ada's the only lady in the family,' she had once remarked, to be answered with his instant contradiction: 'That's where you're wrong. You're the real lady. She only thinks she is.' Nor had that opinion stopped him from enjoying what she gave him in bed, and thinking all the more of her for the willingness with which she had come to offer it. No, she was all of a piece. There was no contradiction between the woman the world saw and the one who had offered herself to Howard. It was his fault if he couldn't see that, and good riddance. She had nothing to be ashamed of, nothing to hide.

They sat by the fire when they had finished eating. On impulse Ella took her father's chair. Her mother observed but made no comment.

'I'll go and get me mucky self washed.'

'Are you goin' out?'

'Later on.' Ella waited, then said, 'Am I comin' back here, then, or not?' Her mother's lips tightened.

'Don't come if you don't want to.'

I've not wanted to any number of times, Ella thought. But she had done it. Because it was her duty.

'I'm goin' to have to learn to sleep in me own house again,' she said.

'You must think it's worthwhile.'

Patience's manner was turning sullen. Ella hated the idea of persuading her against her will. On the other hand, she had become aware that she would not be released from her obligation unless she made the first move. Her mother could talk about the change that longer days might bring, but by then the habit would be firmly rooted and there would be no way back. On the contrary, it would be seen as only sensible for Ella to move back in and abandon this inconvenient business of trying to run her own house.

'I've got me own life to live,' she heard herself blurting, and hated the injured tone of it.

'I'm sure I don't want to stop you.'

'I might be out late.'

'You've got your key. As long as I know you're

coming you can stop out as long as you like. What d'you call "late"? Midnight? I don't know where you could find to go after that. Nothing stops open late nowadays, because there are no buses running.'

'I think you should give it a try for a couple of nights.'

'A couple? You started with one.'

'You *ought* to try it for a *week*.'

'Go on, make it grow. I know what you're after. You're after leavin' me altogether.'

'I can't be trailin' down here every night for the rest of me life, Mother. The sooner you get used to being on your own the better for everybody.'

'For you, nobody but you.'

'Oh, yes, I can see that I'm goin' to come out of this as the most selfish bitch who ever walked shoe-leather. That's what you get for doing your bit while everybody else is twiddlin' their thumbs.'

'Who's better suited for it?'

'I wish I thought it were me good nature you were talking about, but I suspect it's only me circumstances.'

'I don't know what you're talkin' about.'

'I'm talkin' about me livin' on me own when there'd be more sense in me livin' here.'

'You admit it, then?'

'I admit nothing. I left this house when me father were alive and I'm not coming back now he's dead.'

'You can sit in his chair an' say it, an' all. You know full well what he thought about it.'

'He came round when he saw I hadn't done it just to spite him.'

'He never set foot over your threshold, you'll remember.'

'Oh, he was like that. There were some things he had no curiosity about. But the rug he made me is on my hearth, and that's good enough for me.'

'I don't know what's so attractive about livin' on your own, 'less you're up to summat you don't want other folk to know about.'

'It's simple, Mother. When I shut me door on a night and lock it I know that the outside world's on one side an' I'm on the other, in me own little kingdom. If I want to scrub it and polish it till I ache all over, or let it stand till it's deep in dust, I can do. An' if I want to paper it sky-blue-pink with yellow dots, I can do that an' all.'

'Do as you like.'

'I shall do. Within reason.' She got up. 'I'm going now, then.'

'All right.'

'I'll be round in the mornin' to see how you've gone on.'

'Just as you like.'

'Thanks for me dinner.'

'You're welcome.'

'Righto.'

'Aren't you goin' to take your nightclothes with you?'

'I'll leave 'em here for the time being.'

'You don't seem very confident.'

'What about?'

'That I'll learn to manage.'

'We'll see about that. But they're not in anybody's way.'

'Won't you need 'em?'

'I've more than one nightgown.'

'There's your dressing-gown an' slippers an' all.'

'I'll collect 'em another time.'

'Wrap 'em up while I'm not lookin', eh?'

'Why should I do that?'

'Because you're ashamed of yourself.'

'Oh, God!'

'Don't think I can't tell. There's things about you I've been able to read all your life. Strongest of all is when you can't fashion to hold your head up. Like now.'

II

She came away. She would have liked the last word, but let her mother have it. Words couldn't touch a sense of grievance. You could only do what you intended to do and hope that time would change things. She had never thought her mother an unreasonable woman. Stubborn, sometimes, and often illogical. But not selfish. Perhaps, then, she *was* afraid. Not just timid but genuinely afraid.

Ella was nearly home but she stopped and turned, then walked back a few steps. There had been rain that morning, but now pale sunlight lit the brick fronts of some houses across the street. The year they had been built was carved into a small stone over one of the doors: 1898. She had walked past them a hundred times yet she couldn't recall seeing that before. Her mother would have known the site when it was green fields. She had been married before the houses were built and mother to Ronald and Edward by the time they

137

were finished and that stone put into place. They had never – her mother and father – spent a night apart since their wedding day. Not one. Patience had had all her babies in her own home. Since the age of nineteen she had known no life but that shared with Sugden: making a home for him, bearing his children, grieving with him at the untimely loss of four of them; sympathising with, when she couldn't wholly share, his disappointment at their shortcomings. His life had been her life. So what was left to her now that his life had been taken away? Ella stood, trance-like, on the edge of the pavement, her resolution ebbing as she contemplated, as if for the first time, the extent of her mother's loss and the void it had left in her existence.

She started as somebody spoke to her. A middle-aged man:

'Has it gone for good, then?'

'What? Sorry. What?'

'Whatever it is you've lost.'

He smiled, lifted his hand and went on.

She couldn't go back. Hard as she now judged her decision to have been, to go back would be grudging, and grudgingly acknowledged, leaving nothing resolved and bad feeling stirred up for no reward. She must look at it in the long term.

She turned again and walked on, passing in a few minutes the picture house as the uniformed commissionaire came out through the door to the stalls and released the roar of children at their matinée. Another few minutes and she was shutting her own door behind her.

She seemed to have hardly been in the place for weeks; passing briefly through to pick things up, never stopping long enough to light a fire. The house was cold. Her bed would not be fit to sleep in. Before taking off her coat she carried the portable electric fire upstairs and plugged it in at her bedroom socket. She drew down the blankets and sheets to hang along the edge of the bed and turned the fire so that it would air them. Downstairs again she sorted old coals and arranged them in the grate to form a support for a cradle of sticks and firelighter, then carefully piled new coal on top before lighting it with a match. She put another match to the pilot light of the water-heater over the sink then went upstairs once more and opened her wardrobe to look at her clothes and decide what to wear. That jumper would be warmer than a blouse, but it was a bit on the tight side and emphasised the shape of her breasts. She preferred a skirt and either a jumper or a blouse to a frock, though, because she hadn't a winter-weight frock that she felt her best in. If she probably wouldn't have to take her coat off she might settle for the jumper. She wanted to feel attractive without seeming to be putting everything she'd got on offer.

An hour later she woke out of her nap on the sofa in front of the fire and sat up, pushing aside the blanket with which she'd covered herself. She had left her wireless set on. Now it was playing music from a tea-dance at a big London hotel. She could see them in her mind's eye, slow fox-trotting among the bamboo furniture, the women in hats, the men in double-breasted suits with gold cigarette cases to whip out the moment they sat down. 'Virginia on this side, Turkish on that.' Now where had she got that from? She made

139

herself some tea, building up the fire while she waited for it to mash.

Then she fetched her clothes for the evening and spread them out along the sofa. After her tea she switched on the light and closed the curtains. She ran hot water into the sink and, stripping completely, stood in a bowl on the floor and washed herself all over. Dressing, she felt the pleasure of clean underwear next to clean skin. She had a pair of nylons she'd paid a small fortune for to a man at work who seemed to be able to put his hands on anything you wanted, at a price. She'd had them since before Christmas but never worn them. She smoothed them along her legs and fastened her suspenders. Then she slipped on her shoes and stood up, managing by propping a mirror against the sofa to see herself at the back from her heels to the hem of her skirt. The sideboard glass let her examine herself in the jumper. Its being a pale colour – a sort of light stone – showed her shape all the more. But why should she hide a bust worth showing? They were all the thing now. Hollywood films were full of girls in clinging sweaters and those underslips that looked as if they couldn't come off without being taken to pieces. American bombers flew with such as Betty Grable and Lana Turner bulging out all over them. All right. She brushed her hair, securing it with a couple of enamelled clips, and applied rouge and lipstick to her face. A dab of scent under each ear and she was ready.

Her topcoat had been a dreary grey until she had dyed it navy blue. It had come out a touch lighter than she had intended – a kind of French navy, she supposed – but it looked surprisingly good. It had wide revers and a tie belt and a collar deep enough to cover her ears when necessary. She liked herself in it and people looked at her when she had it on. Some garments were like that; their effect had nothing to do with what they had cost.

She filled a hot-water bottle and took it upstairs. When she had remade her bed she put the bottle into it and unplugged the fire. Back in the living-room she pressed a briquette block of compressed coal-dust into the middle of the fire, piled it round with coal and shut off the draught before standing the fine-mesh guard in place.

Her heels clacked on the flagstones as she walked back along the street. One of the last things her father had done before taking to his bed had been to fit metal protectors to these shoes. He had always done little jobs like that, keeping the necessary bits and pieces, acquired over years, in a tall toffee-tin with a hinged lid.

His death had taken the last man with influence and authority out of her life. Her brothers, Ronald and Wilson, had enjoyed brief dominance in years gone by, but she had never had the kind of relationship with them in which she instinctively tested her actions against their esteem. Her father had always had that place. Walter had won it with his simple integrity and his dogged cherishing of her; Howard through his own persistence and his suggestion of routes into a different life. Now they were all gone. She was left with moments when she felt cast adrift. Then she knew that her only chance lay in an even more determined assertion of her independence, and survival on her own terms. 'I'm sorry, Mother,' she muttered as

141

conscience nudged. 'I'll try never to let you down; but you'll have to allow me to be the judge of what that amounts to.'

She quickened her step. The light was fading fast now and she wanted to reach the railway station before darkness fell. Her cheeks glowed in the keen air. There would probably be frost later on.

III

There were a middle-aged couple and a quite grown-up girl in the compartment Ella chose. At the last second, though, just before the guard blew his whistle, they decided they were on the wrong train and should be waiting on the other platform. They scrambled out and slammed the door, which was suddenly wrenched open again as the train began to move. A man jumped in and dropped into the seat opposite. He laughed as he recognised her. Darby Woodcock.

TEN

I

'What are you doin' here?' she asked before she could stop herself.

His smile became puzzled. 'I'm on me way to Calderford to meet you. I thought you'd things to do there before I saw you.'

'Oh, I got held up.' It was her first small lie.

'So did I. I thought I'd be late. But it doesn't matter now.'

His smile was soon back. He observed her in a series of little sidelong glances, as though constantly checking that she was still there, his eyes full of a silent glee. She had never seen him in any but working-clothes and she took him in in her turn. A yellow paisley-pattern scarf filled the neck of his double-breasted navy-blue overcoat – a real navy, not the hit-and-miss home-dyed colour of hers. The dandy she had suspected was confirmed by his yellow kid gloves and, even more, by his patent-leather shoes, which winked and glittered in even this feeble light as he crossed one leg over the other and sat back in his seat. He had no hat; his hair was brilliantined neatly close to his head as always, his cheeks smooth after a recent shave. He looked new-pin clean; in a different style, though, from Walter, who had been one of the cleanest-looking men she had ever known, in a well-scrubbed and shining way. 'A proper toff,' he might have said of Darby, his tone suggesting mild disparagement of the vanity involved in such care with appearance. She had already come to the conclusion that Darby was in his early forties as she observed him, keeping him in her watchful eye-corner over the weeks, while he regularly reminded her that his invitation was still open. As soon as she let into her mind even the possibility of going out with him she had realised how desperate she had become for new company. She never went anywhere these days, confined as she was to the three-cornered circuit of work, home, her mother's. And where was the harm in it? She could put up with the talk, though a desire not to shout it from the rooftops was what had led her to arrange to meet him in Calderford rather than openly travel with him from Daker.

She met one of his smiling glances.

'You look pleased with yourself.'

' "If at first you don't succeed . . .",' he said.

'Oh, you're better off trying something else.'

'But "Faint heart never won fair lady," did it?'

'They say not.' But don't you go counting your chickens before they're hatched, she thought.

'You don't smoke, do you?'

'No.'

The cigarette case he produced was not the battered one he used at work but an ultra-thin one in coloured enamel. He sat and inhaled, seemingly at a loss for words now.

'Well, here we are at last.'

'Yes, here we are.'

'I don't suppose you'll tell me what made you change your mind?'

'What does it matter?'

'If it's something I'm doing I can do it a bit more.'

Ella gave him a vague smile and looked away. The train clacked steadily on through the thickening darkness. Not a flicker or glimmer of anything out there.

'What happened to the tall chap?'

'Which tall chap?' she felt bound to ask, stalling.

'Him I saw you down Calderford with.'

'Oh, him. What should have happened to him?'

'Don't you still see him?'

'What difference does it make to you?'

'I don't know,' Darby said. 'That's what I'm trying to find out.'

'You'll have to wait and see, then.'

'I do like to know where I stand.'

Resentment at his prying and his implied claim on her gave her the temper to be blunt: 'You don't stand anywhere much at present.'

'Oh, thanks. As long as I know.'

'You might do better if you didn't push too hard.'

'You wouldn't be here now if I hadn't kept pushing.'

'Well, here I am, so you can hold your horses a bit.'

'Right, ma'am. If you say so, ma'am.'

'Is there any heat on at all in here?' Her voice sounded peevish.

Darby got up and strained at a lever. 'It won't budge.'

'A good job we're not going all the way to Hull.'

'Where do you feel it?'

'In my feet. They're like blocks of ice.'

'If I knew you better I'd ask you to dance.'

Ella smiled. She stood up and took a few steps between the bench seats, stamping her feet. There was no corridor to walk in.

'Any better?'

'No.'

'Sit down,' Darby said, 'and take your shoes off, one at a time.'

'You what?'

He sat forward as she took her place again, opposite him.

'Stretch your leg out. Come on. No need to be shy.'

She extended one leg. He took her foot into glove-warmed hands and gently kneaded and pressed.

'For God's sake be careful with me stockings,' Ella said. 'They're the only pair I've got.'

'Did you get 'em from Cadge Whitfield?'

'Yes.'

'Paid a price, I expect.'

'Everything's a price these days.'

'I'll get you some more.'

'I don't wear nylons every day. You be careful and they'll be all right.'

She knew she sounded churlish but it wasn't as if she had collapsed and needed attention, and there was something unbecomingly intimate about the feel of his hands round her foot. It ran in her mind that Darby had, in fact, some qualification in first aid. But here they were, their first time together socially, and already engaged in familiarity.

'No corns or bunions, eh?'

'You what?' Was he a chiropodist as well?

'Healthy feet are a boon.'

'I must be lucky.'

'You heard about the fashion-plate that went into a shoe shop, didn't you?'

'No.'

'She told the assistant, "I take a five, but if you can squeeze me into a four I'll have a three."'

'Oh, some women . . .' Ella said vaguely.

It was very pleasant – she couldn't deny – the feeling of Darby's hands and the warmth returning. If she had known him better – quite a lot better – she could have leaned back in her seat and given herself up to enjoyment. But as he took up the other foot she gave a little warning yelp.

'Ooh! Be careful.'

'What is it?'

'A chilblain. I'm not as free from blemish as you thought, y'see.'

'Does it itch sometimes?'

'I'll say it does.'

'That's poor circulation,' Darby said. 'And toasting your feet at the fire instead of wearing warm socks.' He paused. 'Do you want me to carry on?'

'What – rubbin' me feet or tellin' me off?'

'Advice is good for them that'll take it.'

'If it's good advice – and asked for.'

'I have some salve I can bring you for chilblains. It's wonderful.'

'I thought you were too clever to get things like that.'

'I lived with a woman who got 'em reg'lar every winter.'

'Lived with her?'

147

'In a state of unholy matrimony.'

'Oh.'

Ella couldn't help her curiosity about Darby's wife and whether she had, as all accounts made out, run off and left him; but she decided she would let him tell her about it in his own time.

'How do they feel now?'

'A lot better, thanks.' She expected them to be frozen again in ten minutes, but they should be getting off the train by then. She pulled up the foot he had just released on to the seat beside her and gently massaged the chilblain.

'Leave it alone,' Darby said.

'I can't.' It was one of those pleasures on the edge of pain. She half-closed her eyes.

'You'll only make it worse.'

'It was all right till you set it off.'

'That's the thanks you get.'

'I'm sorry.'

'They keep picture-houses warm, don't they?'

'Only just. Haven't you been lately?'

'Must be more than twelve months.'

'Don't you like the pictures?'

Darby shrugged. 'I have other interests. I like me wireless and a good play, and I read a lot.'

'What about when you go out?'

'I go for a drink and a game o' darts. Summer I play bowls. I quite like dancing, when I can get a partner.'

'Well . . . I'm sure I don't want to—'

'No, no. It'll be a pleasant change. I'm lookin' forward to it. You'll have to choose for both of us, though.'

Oh, God, Ella was all at once thinking, I hope this isn't going to be a miserable washout. For coming over her now in an unexpected but engulfing wave was something mounting close to panic, an overwhelming fear that she would never again find a man with whom she could fulfil herself, one who could lift her into joy. This was the way her awareness of loss could ambush her, paralysing her will and wearying her very soul.

Darby was watching her intently, sensitive to every change of mood. 'What's wrong?' he asked. He leaned forward. 'Joke over. What's upset you?'

Her sudden tears brought him across the aisle to sit beside her. She allowed him to put his arm round her shoulders and hold her hands with his free one. 'Why are you crying?' When he turned his face to her cheek it was as if to confirm her tears by tasting them. The dimly lighted compartment moved through the endless darkness while a man she had never touched before held her in his arms and comforted her with words made urgent by his own desire.

'Ella, Ella, don't cry, lass. There's no need for it. You're lovely. You can have anything you put your mind to. You've all your life before you.'

He turned her face and put his mouth to hers. Instead of resisting she relaxed her lips and let them open. His arm tightened. He drew her closer.

'Oh, Ella, I've wanted to do that ever since I first saw you.'

'That's enough for now, though,' Ella said, drawing away. Like telling him to come back for more later, she thought. Which wasn't what she'd intended, pleasant enough though the moment had been. 'We should be there any time now.'

'You're coming round,' Darby said. He

squeezed her hand before returning to his own seat. 'What brought it on?'

'Oh, memories. Just memories.'

'Oh, memories,' Darby echoed. 'You never know when they'll cut to the quick.'

'Sometimes you feel selfish,' Ella said. 'As if nobody else ever lost anybody.'

'They did, though,' Darby said.

For a moment he was inside himself. She opened her powder compact, which had a mirror.

'It's hopeless in this light.'

'And every other light,' Darby said, coming out of his private thoughts. 'Which means folk can't see *you*.'

'Women can tell when a woman's been crying, Darby, light or no light. So if you don't want 'em giving you funny looks I'd better get a bit of powder on in the right places.'

He held up a small battery torch.

'Would this help?'

'It might.'

'If I shine it on your face from behind the mirror.'

'Let's try, anyway.'

He leaned forward and shone the light. Ella turned her face from side to side, dabbing with the powder-puff. She supposed she looked good enough. She could check in the ladies at the pictures. But exasperation flared in her. 'What bloody dodges we have to get up to,' she exclaimed. 'What flamin' tricks. Won't you be glad when it's over – when it's finished an' done with? Aren't you just about sick and tired of it all?'

Darby was watching her with a smile on his face. Her irascibility seemed to amuse him. They

150

were trundling into the station where there was just about enough light to get you off the train and into the street – where there was no light at all.

'I mean,' she cried out, 'what is there – where's there a single thing – to cheer you up?'

II

To be taken out of yourself for a couple of hours helped; to be drawn into a Technicolor world of Arabian Nights fantasy, of wicked caliphs, and princes turned into mongrel dogs; of genies released from bottles, magic carpets, mechanical horses which flew when wound up, and princesses who languished until brought safely into the arms of their true love. *The Thief of Baghdad* had won over *Lady Hamilton*. Ella wished for no sad stories tonight, nothing which might reinforce her own lurking melancholy. Even Darby, one of those men, Ella suspected, to whom the cinema was a triviality fit only for the amusement of women and children, had been impressed, chuckling a couple of times at especially dazzling effects. He had left her alone, what was more, unpestered by roaming hands; so she was all the more disposed to try to please him when, as they stood putting coats back on in the foyer, he asked her, 'Will you let me take you for a drink now?'

'Where?' she asked. 'Here?'

All pubs to Ella were places of loose behaviour and potential iniquity; and city pubs were worst of all.

Darby said, 'No, I know a place somewhere else, cosy, with a good crowd. I think you'd like it.'

151

'Is it far?'

'We'd have to get a bus.'

'What about getting home after?'

'Oh, that'll be all right.' He looked at her. 'I wouldn't take you anywhere low.'

Not on purpose, she thought, but it could be a matter of opinion. She said, though, 'All right, lead the way.'

She watched the pleasure break in a smile across his face. Was it her destiny always to hold the gifts, to bestow or withhold them as she wished? Had Howard seen it so? Had he needed her permission to renew his claim? Could he really still want the girl she'd revealed to him? What was there for her in the man she'd found him out to be? Every time she set foot in Calderford she was aware that she might run into him. But she hadn't. The odd thing was that each time the question recurred in her thoughts the more distant and detached it seemed, as if it were becoming someone else's problem. All she was in love with now was a memory of a tall, fair-haired young man from somewhere else, whom she had known for a few days; and he was no more to be resurrected than was the impressionable young girl who had first watched him step into her parents' cottage.

'You've gone away again,' Darby said.

'Have I?'

'More memories?'

'Not that kind, no.'

They had crossed the street to wait at a bus-stop.

'I could take you straight home, if you'd rather.'

He really was a very considerate man.

'No, no, we'll go where you said. We both deserve a bit of fun.'

'You're right!'

The low shape of a single-deck bus was moving towards them. 'We're lucky, see,' Darby said. He stepped out and waved his arm.

For a time Ella felt no curiosity, assuming they were going somewhere strange to her. Even when they had left the bus she was a moment or two before she recognised her whereabouts. She was holding on to Darby's arm as they crossed the little hump-backed bridge. They were approaching the place where Uncle Mauritius lived, from the other side.

'I know where we are.'

'I thought you would. Have you ever been in this pub?'

'Oh, no.'

'How many Daker pubs have you seen inside?'

'Only the Masons. And only that to get me dad's jug filled. I once went into one of the Calderford pubs with me husband. Opposite the theatre. We'd been to a variety concert.'

'You don't come from a teetotal family,' Darby said.

'Me dad was always abstemious. For as long as I remember. But I'd three brothers who could drink their share.'

'I know,' Darby said. 'I was a member at Trades at one time. I knew your brother that got killed. Your Thomas.'

'Oh yes? Our Ronald and Wilson have quietened down a lot. Happen our Thomas would've done, if he'd lived.' And perhaps not, she thought, married to Winnie.

153

'Perhaps I ought to tell you', Darby said, ''at though I'm very partial to pubs, it's for the company as much as the drink. I'm no stranger to moderation.'

'So long as we know,' Ella said, amused by the solemnity of his declaration. Her mother would be pleased, though she had no intention of telling him so. Nor, for that matter, did she plan to talk to Patience about Darby unless challenged. There were things about him more open to question than a liking for drink, such as what had made his wife leave him and how many women he'd known since.

They had come to the neglected garden she had noticed. Darby said they must go single-file here but she should hang on to his coat-tails and step carefully over the broken flagstones. The moon had come up now, though, which made things easier. The frost she had expected was forming. She could make out the shape of the pub, but only the faint sound of voices inside gave any indication that it was open.

The full blast of noise met them as Darby carefully closed the outer door and opened the inner one to usher Ella through. The place seemed packed. Men stood in the passage, getting their drink at the serving-hatch by the door to the far room, in which, in soft gaslight, Ella could see people sitting and others moving about carrying glasses. On the left along the passage was the door to another room, like a small sitting-room. There were people in there as well, women among them. Darby spoke to a couple of men who greeted him in return.

'Darby . . .'

'Now then, Darby.'

They nodded at Ella. One spoke: 'Evenin'.'

Darby looked past them into the main room then turned to stick his head into the smaller one, the snug. 'We'll perhaps be best in here.' Ella followed him in. There were people whom she had not been able to see for the door. A fire burned in an open grate. 'Room for a little 'un here,' Darby said. People hutched up to make a space for her. Darby leaned over her. 'What would you like?'

'I don't honestly know.'

'Is there owt you can't stand?'

There could be a dozen things. 'Bring me a surprise.'

A woman sitting two or three seats away, across the corner, was listening, her gaze solemnly shifting from Ella to Darby and back again. 'If I'd said that,' she remarked when Darby had gone, 'it'd be a gill o' beer. T'cheapest drink in t'place.'

'You're not likely to say it,' the man next to her said. He sat in his flat cap. A tie was neatly knotted round the bare skin above the neckband of a clean white collarless shirt. 'Tha knows every drink in t'house.' The woman half-rolled her eyes.

'Is it cold out?' she asked Ella.

'Turning frosty.'

The woman nodded. Darby came back carrying a pint of beer and a small glass containing a brownish liquid. He managed to create more room to squeeze in beside her.

'Try that.'

Ella lifted the glass and sniffed. 'Is there peppermint in it?'

'It's rum an' pep,' Darby said.

155

'A lovely drink,' the woman said. 'A lovely drink.'

'Ask her if there's owt *she* can't stand, Darby,' the man with no collar said.

'That is a lovely drink, though,' the woman said.

'I thought it might warm you through,' Darby said.

'Oh, I'm plenty warm enough now,' Ella said. She was thinking about taking off her coat in the baking heat of the fire and that radiating from the press of bodies filling the place.

A piano accordion started up in the other room. People began to sing: *Bless 'em all, bless 'em all, the long and the short and the tall* ... The woman near Ella joined in in a queer little strangulated voice. The man without a collar picked up his empty pint glass and went out without a word to her. The woman watched him go then looked at her glass. She picked up the small stout-bottle standing on the table and held it over the glass and shook it. Nothing came out to add to the half-inch of nearly black liquid in the glass and the woman picked up the glass and gazed into it for a moment before emptying it down her throat. She took out her purse. All the time, except for the few seconds of actual drinking, she had kept on singing, only she'd lost the words now and made do with 'dah, dah, dah, dee, dee, doh.' ... *You'll get no promotion this side of the ocean, so cheer up me lads, Bless 'em all.*

A man stepped into the room, glanced round and went out. In a few minutes he came back with a pint of beer in his hand and looked carefully about, nodding as people spoke to him. Darby lifted his arm. The man came across.

'Darby lad. How you doin'?'

'Middlin', Mauritius. Aren't you goin' to sit an' have a word?' There was a spare stool. Mauritius sat down opposite them.

'There's some folk in here tonight, Mauritius, in't there?'

'There might well be, Darby lad. We've been suppin' baht ale all week, tha sees. Bert nobbut took delivery this mornin' an' a few of us have been trying to drink him dry ever since.'

'Do you know this chap, Ella?' Darby asked.

'Not as well as I ought to,' Ella said, 'seeing as he's me uncle.'

'Gerraway!' Darby said.

Mauritius was narrowing his eyes as he peered at her.

'Well by shots if it isn't thee, Ella lass. T'negotiator-in-chief herself. Tha'll have to pardon me not owning thee straight away, lass. Either tha's been doin' summat to thisen or my eyesight's more pitiful than I knew.'

'A bit o' warpaint,' Ella said. 'And you wouldn't be expecting to see me here.'

'No, you're right there.'

'I brought her,' Darby said. 'She didn't know where she was coming to. And I'd no idea you were related.'

'One o' my long lost kin, is Ella,' Mauritius said. 'Made herself known to me last back-end. How's your mother makin' out, Ella lass?'

'Oh, she's managin'. She doesn't care for sleepin' in the house on her own.'

'Some folk never do take to it. I've only just been thinking I might call an' see her.'

'Oh?'

157

'Aye. There were never owt wrong between Patience an' me. Be a pity not to offer me services in any way I can, now she's on her own.'

Ella said, 'You haven't got your shadow with you tonight, then?'

'Josh, tha means? Oh no. No, no. This is no place for him. There's some kinds o' deficiencies in t'old brain-box, y'see, Ella, that are aggravated by alcoholic beverages. An' Josh is that sort. Aye. A couple o' pints could be all 'at's needed to send him berserk. Oh, aye. Yes. Beware a good-natured simpleton inflamed by strong drink.'

'Are you talkin' about Josh Cutshall?' Darby asked.

'That's him. My loyal amanuensis.'

'Did you ever hear how he got the way he is?'

'He were born that way.'

'Yes. I heard it was through his mother tightening her stays because she refused to believe she were havin' him.'

'Oh aye, could be, could be. *I* heard one silly bitch say it was a punishment for her conceiving him out o' wedlock.'

'I heard that,' the woman across put in. 'Josh's father weren't the only man his mother had been with.'

'Aye, well,' Mauritius said, 'if every bairn got that way turned out same I might see some logic in it. As it is all I can see is some folk wi' no powers o' cogitation.'

Darby nudged Ella. 'That's a good 'un for this time o' night, Mauritius. Cogi-what did y'say?'

The woman across cackled. 'Full of 'em, is Mauritius. Leaves us baffled.'

158

Mauritius glanced up from his tobacco tin, where he was detaching a cigarette paper.

'Nah then, Darby lad, don't thee be playin' silly buggers an' all.' He got up with his nearly empty glass and swigged the last drop on his feet.

'Let me get that,' Darby said as he turned for the door.

'Tha're reight,' Mauritius said over his shoulder.

'Swallowed a dictionary, Mauritius,' Darby said. 'He makes me chuckle.'

'I think he knows without being reminded,' Ella said. She recognised what Mauritius had said to Darby as a rebuke. Perhaps his refusal to accept a drink was another. But he had left his makings on the table, so must be coming back.

The piano accordion was still going, leading in another song: *We'll build a sweet little nest, somewhere in the west, and watch the rest of the world go by* . . .

Darby had finished his pint. He stirred in his seat and nodded at Ella's glass. 'Is that to your liking?'

'It's very nice, yes.'

Darby got up and left the room. When he came back he was with Ella's uncle. He put another drink in front of her. Well, one more wouldn't harm her. Mauritius sat down and finished rolling his cigarette.

'I can't recall t'last time I were in a picture-house,' he said. Darby must have been telling him about *The Thief of Baghdad*, at the hatch. 'I think I've seen one since they started talkin'.'

'Oh, it must be all of a twelve-month since I were there,' Darby said. 'It were a Robert Donat picture. The Adventures of Tabu. Sabu. No, that's him that was in the picture tonight. Summat like "Tattoo."'

'Tartu,' Ella said. '*The Adventures of Tartu.*' As she said it she realised that what Darby was short of to complete the figure he cut was the kind of thin moustache that Robert Donat had worn in the film.

'"Tartu"!' Darby said. 'That's it. Robert Donat was living in England, though he was born in Romania. They roped him in to go back and sabotage a poison-gas factory over there.'

'Who did?' Mauritius asked.

'British Secret Service.'

'Which war are we in?'

'This one.'

'Quick off t'mark, aren't they?'

'Oh aye.'

'Did they say who won?' Mauritius asked dryly.

'Oh, we won that round.'

'We always do,' Ella said.

'I expect t'Germans allus win in their pictures.'

'Robert Donat's not Romanian,' the woman across the corner said. 'He was born in Oldham.'

'It were only t'part he played in this picture.'

'Leslie Howard was Romanian,' Ella said.

'Leslie Howard?'

'Never!'

'He wasn't English at all,' Ella said. 'He looked it and sounded it, but he wasn't. He came here about fifteen year ago with a lot of other film people from the same place.'

'Oh, I can't believe that.'

'Oh, no.'

'Sorry!' Ella cried. 'I'm wrong.'

''Course you are.'

'He wasn't Romanian, he was Hungarian. It was Hungaria he came from.'

160

'Just as bad.'

'Same difference.'

'You've been dreamin'.'

Two or three other people had joined in.

'A friend of mine told me,' Ella said. 'He knows all about such things.'

Darby said, 'I'd like to put a little bet on that. Anybody else here say he was Hungarian?'

But there were no takers.

'You don't believe me either,' Ella said.

'Oh, I believe you, Ella. I just don't believe whoever told you. I just wish he were here. I'd have ten bob on it with him.'

'How would you find out if it was true or not?'

'I'd write to t'*Daily Herald*.'

'If it's not general knowledge it might be confidential.'

'And it might be all me eye and Peggy Martin. I think somebody's been pullin' your leg, lass.'

She was being made fun of. She didn't like it.

'I'll have half a crown on it with you,' she said.

'Oh, come on . . .'

'That's a fair offer,' Mauritius said.

'I couldn't take her money.'

'Tha might end up losing some,' Mauritius said. 'I've seen and heard things on me travels 'at tha'd find harder than that to credit.'

'I've heard some of 'em,' Darby said and nudged Ella again.

'And I'll tell thee,' Mauritius said, 'if tha could subtract all t'knowledge there is in this pub this minute from t'sum total there is in t'world, tha'd not be able to see an iota o' difference.'

'Oh yes,' Darby said.

'Does tha foller me meanin'?'

'Oh aye. We're all ready to learn.'

'Thee speak for thiself, Darby lad. Tha might be in a minority o' one there.'

'There's more things in heaven an' earth . . . is what I'm sayin',' Darby said.

'Aye.'

'On the other hand, I weren't born yesterday.'

'There's no flies on thee, I can see that.'

'No,' Darby said. Ella sensed that he was beginning to flounder. He saved the moment by asking, 'Are you going to have that drink with me now?'

'If tha're insistin', Darby lad, I won't throw kindness in thi face.'

Ella took a note out of her purse. 'Get it out of this.'

Darby and Mauritius said 'Nay!' in unison. She pressed the note into Darby's hand.

'I go out to work an' all, so don't argue. Get one for yourself while you're there.'

'First outing, is it?' Mauritius asked when Darby had gone.

'Yes.' Ella glanced at the woman across the corner, but Mauritius had pitched his voice low. 'He's very persuasive,' she added.

'A good-hearted lad, though. Give him his due.'

'Oh, yes.'

Mauritius nodded, his fingers busy with tobacco and paper again. 'A fair question, Ella lass.'

'Go on.'

'Does tha think thi mother's likely to show me t'door if I do come callin'?'

'I don't know why she should.'

'Oh . . .'

'She's not a quarrelsome woman.'

'I've always understood so.'

'Do you want me to mention it to her?'

'No, no. I don't want her sittin' an' waitin' an' wonderin'.'

'Do you think she would?'

'You know her better na me.'

'She might,' Ella conceded.

'And I don't want thee comin' back wi' an invite 'at involves t'best cups an' saucers. No, I thought I'd just bob in as I were passin'. Just to enquire how she's keepin'. No fuss. Eh?'

'As you like,' Ella said.

'Aye. Well, we'll see.'

Darby was back. He carried two full pints and another drink for her.

'I've hardly started on me second one,' she said.

'Couldn't leave you out.' He put the change into her hand before lifting his glass. 'Your good health.'

'Aye, all the very best, Ella lass,' Mauritius said. 'What does tha think of our little tavern, then?'

III

She liked it, the amiable company, the hum of sound, the way, near the end of her second drink, she had felt the tension leave her calf muscles and her weight transfer itself fully on to her seat. No one had seemed the worse for drink; one or two showed signs of being better for it. She felt that way herself. As she followed Darby and his pocket torch through the dark tunnel of the viaduct her mood was marred by nothing more than a lingering irritation with him for trying to get her to join him in laughing at Mauritius. But that he wasn't taking the opportunity offered by the darkness

163

inside the viaduct for getting fresh went a long way to mending her opinion of him.

Once across the river they walked for some way along the boundary wall of Daker Forge and Engineering, where they would both be back at work on Monday. Steam billowed over the wall at one place, from a boiler blowing off. There was always somebody in there looking after things. Darby told her a story about an accident involving a number of men and their fight to prove the management's neglect. Coming into almost everything he'd told her about work all evening had been the figure of the managing director, Andrew Broadley, whom Ella had never seen, a stern master who didn't hesitate to sack people on the spot. 'There was this lorry in the yard one day,' Darby said; 'one feller loading on to it, the other leaning on his shovel while he had a drag. Round the corner comes Andrew with a couple of visitors. He takes one look at this second chap and tells him to go and get his cards. You're sacked, he tells him: I don't employ you to lean on your shovel and smoke. You don't employ me at all, this chap tells him.' Darby chuckled. 'He worked for a contractor they'd hired. "I'm sure the man who pays your wages will be interested to hear how much of his time you spend doing nothing," Andrew says. And this bloke says . . . he says . . .' Darby couldn't get it out now for laughing. 'He says, "Well, he's here. Tell him now," and calls over to his mate doing the shovelling. "Cliff," he says, "bloke here wants a word."' Darby laughed for some time. 'Make no mistake, though, he doesn't usually come off worst.'

'I'll watch out for him.'

'Oh, he'll have no need ever to notice you. And if he did he'd be charm itself. He is with all the women, even though if he had his way there wouldn't be a woman employed on the premises, apart from canteen washers-up. His own private secretary's a man.'

The frost was settling and they walked at a brisk pace. Ella's nose was so cold it felt to have a permanent dew-drop. She wished she had thought to bring her woolly hat. Once Darby glanced down at her feet as her heels rang on the pavement. 'You believe in lettin' folk know you're comin', don't you?' 'I've nowt to creep round for.' All the same, they were mostly early to bed along her street, with one or two poor sleepers among them, and she was aware that after a certain time every sound was heard and noted. She was glad, then, that though it would be known what time she had come home, only the keenest ears would detect that she had not been alone, especially since she warned Darby not to talk as they rounded the corner by the Temperance Hall. She had thought to say goodnight to him there, but he insisted on seeing her in.

'Be quiet, then, or you'll get me talked about.'

'I'd better ask you now, then, if you'll invite me in for a cup of tea.' She looked at him. 'Just to get me warmed through before I set off home.'

'Ten minutes.'

'Ten minutes.'

As she switched on the light and checked the curtains she said, 'I've just realised how famished I am.'

'We should have looked for some fish an' chips. Have I to go now?'

'No, they'll have shut by now. Do you fancy a slice of toast? It's all I can offer you.'

'That'd be welcome. On the other hand . . .' He took a packet from his pocket and opened the paper. 'What about this?' She was looking at two slices of gammon, each the size of her shoe-sole.

'Where on earth . . . ?'

'The pub. There's a chap I know.'

'It looks wonderful.'

'It will be. So what do you say?'

'You mean do I want one? Can you spare it?'

'I mean if you're willing to get the frying-pan out we can have it with that slice of bread.'

'Oh, but you'll want it tomorrow.'

'I'm hungry now, since you mentioned it.'

'So am I. All the same . . .'

Things were moving quickly into a familiarity she had never envisaged on their first time out. She had thought it quite possible there wouldn't be a second time and had seen herself keeping her distance, making it easier for her to refuse him. Now here he was, inside her house, asking her to cook for him.

'Am I putting it away again or are we going to enjoy it now?' Darby asked.

'Give it here, then. Take your coat off and give the fire a poke.'

'That's more like it,' Darby said.

Ella lit the gas-ring and bent to get the pan out of the cupboard. She put fat into the pan and cut bread while she waited for it to heat up. Flames were appearing where Darby had broken up the fire. He was looking round the room.

'Is upstairs as nice as down here?'

'Yes, but you'll have to take my word for that. I'm not going to show you.'

166

He frowned. 'I shall have to watch what I say. You can misconstrue anything.'

'You said you liked to know where you stand. I'm just telling you.'

'Hmm.' He appeared to change the subject. 'Will your mother be all right, d'you think?'

'Oh, yes. She wouldn't be if she was never made to try.'

They had made a small detour to pass the cottage. It had been in darkness, with the curtains closed. Ella intended to go down first thing in the morning.

'Do you like living on your own?' Darby asked now.

'I never planned it this way.'

'No . . .'

'Did you?'

'No.'

'The only alternative is to go back home.'

'The only alternative at present,' Darby said.

'Well, yes.'

'You don't want to do that, though, do you? You want to be able to come and go as you please. Invite a chap in for a bite of supper if you feel like it.'

'Yes.'

'I mean, what would you have done tonight if you'd been living with your mother?'

'If I'd taken you in – and it's a very big if – she'd have probably left us and gone to bed. Then she'd have laid awake listening for wedding bells.'

'Would she?'

'Oh yes. My mother sees no reason why a woman should spend time with a man unless there's to be a wedding at the end of it.'

'What do you think?'

'*I* see no reason why a woman shouldn't go out with a chap without strings, providing she enjoys his company.'

'Have you enjoyed yourself tonight?'

'Yes.'

'You're not altogether sure.'

'Did it sound like that?'

'What bit did you like best?'

'I liked the pub, surprisingly enough.'

'Good!'

'I've always been a bit wary of pubs.'

'They're a life-saver if you know how to use 'em.'

'Yes, I can see that now.'

'Will you let me take you again?'

'You can always try asking.'

'Good.'

With the ham sizzling in the pan and the room growing warmer, Ella went to take off her coat. There was a small glass in the lobby and she patted and pushed her hair in that. She felt Darby's gaze on her immediately as she returned to the room, pulling down the welt of her jumper and taking a deep breath of temporary well-being. She reached for her apron then and covered herself.

ELEVEN

I

It was only just light the next morning when Ella left her house to walk briskly through the empty streets to her mother's cottage. She chided herself for turning over when the alarm clock rang and losing twenty minutes. Patience had always been an early riser and Ella had planned to be there when she came downstairs. She had slept exceptionally well, though she had thought she might not, on a full stomach. The ham had been a delicious treat. By the time they had eaten it, drunk a cup of tea and Darby had enjoyed a smoke, midnight was behind them. She had let him kiss her then, in the lobby, just before he left. Of course, he had tried to prolong that, hoping for more response than she was willing to give; but she didn't blame him and the tone in which she curbed him was far from rough: 'Don't spoil it, Darby'. Not for the world, he'd said. Would he please not call goodnight once he was out of the house, she'd asked him. Perhaps next time, he said, she would come and look at his place, though he couldn't pretend that his neighbours were any different from hers. Which got him away on a shared laugh and a nice feeling that nobody's pride had been hurt.

169

This morning she wore shoes that didn't announce her coming and let herself into the cottage as quietly as she could, pleased to see that all the curtains were still closed. The door to the stairs was open. She listened there a moment then closed it, trying not to rattle the sneck. She left the curtains for the time being and lit the gas. The fire had burnt out. There was coal in the bucket, she was glad to see, and she always chopped firewood as soon as the supply in the box looked low, following her father's routine. Creosote or something similar in the wood made it spit and crackle as the flames took hold. She stood the draw-tin on the high hob, where the draught could flow underneath. She had put the kettle on the gas-ring before busying herself with the fire and she made tea and fitted the padded cosy round the pot. At any moment she expected to hear her mother's tread, but all remained quiet. She could still hear nothing from the foot of the stairs, either, when she opened the chamber door again so that she wouldn't have to do it while carrying the tray. A first tremor of unease tried to tell her that something was amiss. But no, her mother had heard her and was simply sulking; waiting for her to speak the first word. She took the tray and started up the stairs. The door of her mother's bedroom stood open. Dim light filtered through the curtains. Ella couldn't see all of the bed from here, only the black-lacquered rail at its foot; but she knew with complete certainty before she stepped in that there was no one there.

Downstairs the fire was roaring up the chimney. She took down the tin and muffled the flames with more coal. She poured herself tea and sipped it, looking into the fire from her father's chair. There was no use getting into a state about it. Her mother hadn't been kidnapped, nor would she have wandered off into the night. What Ella felt now was less concern than a rising anger at being constrained by another's foolish weakness. 'I've got no sympathy,' she said out loud. 'There's no need for any of it.' She felt helpless, inert, waiting for whatever would happen next. After a time she got up and opened the curtains and put out the gaslight. She cut a slice of bread and toasted it on the end of the long fork. There wasn't yet enough red coal in the fire for good toasting, but she could make do. Nor did the dark, mealy national bread make toast to compare with that pre-war. But while the fire would get better, the bread was the best they would get till the war was over. A spread of beef-dripping from a pot she found at the cellar-head improved it no end.

There was no sound outside. All the village slept, apart from some tradesmen and a few delivery boys with Sunday newspapers; and none of them had got into this quarter yet. Ella's eyelids drooped. Her head fell forward and she came to with a start. She shifted in the chair so that she could rest her head back, then let herself drift into sleep. She dreamed, whisked from one situation to another as a succession of scenes flashed by. Darby Woodcock was standing at one end of a table full of women in the works canteen and pointing at Ella. 'I don't make a fuss of her,' he said. 'That would never do.' Then Darby and her mother were coming along the street together in Mr Tyson's horse-drawn trap, Darby driving while her mother with fantastic dexterity flicked measures of milk from the big can directly and

171

accurately into the jugs customers held waiting at the roadside. 'We've gone into business,' Darby cried. 'You wouldn't think she daren't stop on her own at night, would you?' Ella said to a woman standing next to her. When the woman turned her head Ella saw that it was her sister Doris, her face contorted in venomous hatred. 'It was you 'at drove her to it,' she spat. 'Nobody but you.' Then the rap on the door that woke her also told her as she half-staggered across the room that all that last part could not have taken more than a couple of seconds of real time because it was Mr Tyson himself on the step with the milk, and the actual sound of his pony and trap that had intruded into her dream and shaped its climax. He smiled as he saw her blink in blurred incomprehension.

'Mornin'. Not been to bed with your clothes on, have you?'

'Dropped off again in the chair.'

She found the jug and took it to him. He lifted the gill measure and poured. There were coins to the required amount on the window ledge near the door. Ella passed them over. The pony chomped on its bit and shook its head, snorting steam into the frosty air. Mr Tyson touched the wavy brim of his old trilby and hopped on leather-gaitered legs back into the trap.

'If I don't make much of you at work,' Darby had said, 'don't get the wrong idea, will you?'

'Oh, no.'

'Let other folk mind their business and we'll mind ours.'

'Ours.' His and hers.

'Don't you fancy making another arrangement now, while we're on us own?'

172

'I'd rather leave it a day or two, Darby, if you don't mind.'

'It's entirely up to you.' A pause. 'There's nothing wrong, is there?'

'No, 'course not.'

'You'd tell me if there was, I hope.'

'Would you tell me?'

He shook his head. 'There's nothing to tell. Nor likely to be.'

Oh, some of these grown men, so seemingly level-headed, yet as doting and blinkered as young lasses.

Footsteps in the street now, running. The letter-flap was lifted and something substantial pushed part-way through. She went to look. When she'd lifted the draught curtain out of the way she found a folded newspaper jammed in the slot. They hadn't had a Sunday paper delivered in years and Ella had never even seen this one before with its huge pages of small print. Some new lad had got it wrong. Opening the paper carefully so as not to tear or soil it, Ella read at random. There was still bitter fighting in Central Italy, which made her think of her nephew, Arthur. A large force of British troops had been landed behind the Japanese lines in Burma, which made her think of Walter. A report that women teachers were to be allowed to marry without losing their jobs brought young Mary Butterworth to mind. She'd have lost her scholarship now, whether or not this made a difference to her father's attitude to educating girls. Too late. It would have seemed sadder if Ella hadn't suspected that such restrictions and injustices had not formed Mr Butterworth's opinions, but were merely useful in justifying them.

173

Butterworth wanted his girl in work at fourteen and that was the end of it. The trouble in the pits dragged on. As soon as agreement seemed to be reached in one area, men came out in another. There were now over 80,000 miners idle in South Wales. When would it affect the men in her family?

The paper probably belonged to the Sadlers, next door. Ella wondered if the lad had left another paper there and would have liked to see Mildred Sadler's face on finding herself with the *News of the World*. On the other hand, perhaps she had a taste for that kind of juicy scandal. She folded the paper neatly, as it had come, and put it on one side for taking round to the big house. Perhaps she should take it now, give herself something to do while she waited. She had no idea how long she would have to wait: her mother could stay out all day, wherever she was, if she felt like it. But she wouldn't. She wouldn't be able to relax for thinking what neighbours and passers-by might conclude from the closed curtains. As she reached for more coal Ella considered letting the fire burn out, washing the tea things and closing the curtains again, leaving the cottage as though no one had been. She could come back around dinnertime, say, as if she knew nothing. After all, she did know where Patience must be, didn't she? From a choice of three places, one was much more likely than the other two. It was a likelihood Ella dreaded having confirmed, but dwelling on the trouble it would bring rekindled her anger and prevented her from facing the only other possibility – that her mother had had a brainstorm and gone off alone.

She mended the fire and made fresh tea. Then she waited.

II

It had gone half-past nine before she heard voices she recognised in the street. She clearly heard her mother remark on the curtains being open before two pairs of calves and ankles passed the little window facing the road. When the door opened Ella could see Patience behind the woman whose bulk blocked out the daylight. 'She's here.' Doris.

Ella had got up to move alongside the table.

'What are you doin' here?' Doris again.

'Why shouldn't I be here?'

'I thought happen your conscience wouldn't let you sleep.'

'My conscience is all right, thank you.'

'There's summat wrong with it, then.'

'Now, Doris,' Patience said.

'I'll tell her if you won't.'

I will not be drawn, Ella told herself. I will not sink to her level.

'How long have you been here?' her mother asked.

'Since a quarter to seven. I came to light your fire and see how you'd gone on.'

'If you'd been where you should ha' been you'd ha' known how she'd gone on,' Doris said.

'I don't live here. What made you go to our Doris's?'

'She came to me because I'm her flesh an' blood, which is more than some seem able to remember.'

'I couldn't go to Martha or Florrie,' Patience said.

175

'No, because you'd have shamed her,' Doris said.

'I've nowt to be ashamed of, Doris.'

'Then I'm ashamed for you.'

'Enjoy it. Me mother's handed you a right treat.'

'I couldn't settle,' Patience muttered.

'You didn't try. From t'look of your bed you didn't even take your clothes off.'

'I knew I wouldn't. I told you I wouldn't. I asked you not to go.'

'No, you didn't.'

'You knew without me sayin' it straight out.'

'Mother, I've told you, all you need to do is stick it for a week and you'll be over it.'

'You're a callous bitch, Ella,' Doris said.

'There's nothing I can say, Doris, that'll make a ha'p'orth of difference to you. You've dreamed up a grievance and you're determined to spend the rest of your life feeding it. You've not had a bonus like this for some time. I can just see you lickin' your chops once you'd got over the inconvenience of me mother turning up on your doorstep.'

'My mother knows where she's welcome and who has her welfare at heart.'

'If you care all that much, sister, you can come and stop with her every night, because there's a vacancy.'

'I've a family to look after.'

'It looks as if I shall never have one while I'm tied to this place.'

'Is that all 'at's stoppin' you?'

'You know the main thing that stopped me, Doris.'

'You've not been short of followers since then, as far as I know.'

'What do you know about my followers, as you call 'em?'

'I know you're not short. So what makes it so important to sleep in your own house? Is it so's you can entertain?'

Ella felt the blood surge then subside as she looked to her mother for an intervention and saw only a dejected old woman with her head in one hand. But in a sudden flash of insight she realised what was driving Doris in her malice. She was near her wits' end with jealousy. She was jealous of Ella's freedom. Doris had her husband and family but she had married a colourless man who gave her no joy, and her life was without flavour. She was better-looking than Doris – always had been – and she had choice. In her twisted thinking Doris might even feel that Walter's death, after so brief a marriage, had restored that choice to her.

'I ought to feel sorry for you, Doris.'

'Why's that?'

'Havin' to live with such a mucky mind.'

'I'll give you mucky mind, madam.'

'But I'm not charitable enough to forgive you,' Ella said. 'You're poison. You poison everything you touch.'

'If I touch you you'll think it's more than poison.'

'You daren't touch me, Doris. I've warned you before. Don't you bloody dare.'

'Is there never going to be any peace between you two?' Patience said.

'Not as far as I can see,' Ella said. 'You've just given her enough to keep her going for another five year.'

'I weren't concerned with your quarrels.'

'You'd better be now, is all I can say.'

'There's no need for it.'

'Tell her that.'

'I'm tellin' you both.'

'You won't come straight out and tell her what an evil-minded bitch she really is, will you?'

'I'm warnin' you—'

'Just keep out of it for a minute, Doris. I'm talkin' to me mother. You won't, will you?' she asked Patience again.

'I won't be forced to pick an' choose between me own flesh an' blood.'

'All right.' Ella drew herself up. 'I'll do it for you.' She threw out her arm to point at Doris. 'That's the lump of your flesh an' blood you can rely on in future, 'cos I've finished.'

'Ella, I don't know how you can—'

'No, you can't, and that's what sticks in my craw. I'm just giving somebody else a turn. I wouldn't like to keep all the best things for meself. They can come out of it with a medal, or the kind of slaver I've had to put up with. It's no concern of mine.'

'You're washin' your hands of it, then,' Doris said. 'I'm not surprised. You've been waitin' for a good excuse.'

'Is it a good 'un, Doris, or are you just sayin' the first malicious thing that comes into your head, like you allus do when I'm around?'

'All I can say is I'm glad me father's not here to witness it.'

'If he'd been here there'd have been no reason for it.'

'You'd ha' found another one, sooner or later.'

'There's allus you, sister, when all else fails.'

Her father's empty chair faced her. Into her mind as she pulled on her coat and tried to gather words of leavetaking came the memory of him coming into the house from some saddening family errand, years ago. Trouble between Thomas and Winnie. 'A bloody fine sample we've raised between us, Patience lass ... Our Ella here's t'best o' t'litter, an' she's hardly been tried yet.' Yes, he had 'picked and chosen' that day. And she had been tried since. And tried him. She didn't like the picture of herself she could see today, but it was all she had to offer. Angry, disappointed, lost, drifting ... tired of it all, in fact. She knew she would show them tears if she stopped another minute.

'I don't know what any of it amounts to any longer,' she managed as she flung towards the door. 'You can sort it out between you.'

TWELVE

I

'Did you know', Martha asked Ella, 'that our George has been directed down the pit? He's going to be a Bevin boy.'

'I ran into Florrie,' Ella said. 'She told me. I've never known her to be so upset.'

'But do you know what she said to me?' Martha said. 'She said, "If your Arthur had stopped in t'pit where he belonged, 'stead o' slopin' off into the army, there'd have been one less job to fill."'

'She never did.'

'Oh, aye, she did. So I said, "Where would you prefer your George to be, then; sleepin' in his own bed an' workin' where his father works, or getting shot at in Italy?" She said she'd like him to be still in his job at Daker Forge, only they'd refused to apply for exemption for him.'

'He'd ha' done better in that respect if he hadn't gone round spoutin' Communism.'

'Is that what he did?'

Ella told Martha the tale young Catherine had told her and Sugden and Patience, about George and the Works Manager.

'That all seems pretty harmless to me,' Martha said.

'Aye, but you know how it is, Martha; if somebody starts accusing you of things you sometimes behave as if you're out to prove 'em right.'

'True enough,' Martha said. 'I sometimes wonder, though, whether Florrie hasn't got an old dish-cloth between her ears instead of a brain.' Ella laughed.

'Wilson and Florrie have sworn since George and Granville were bairns that neither of 'em would go down the pit.'

'Well, I only hope it's not going to be an excuse for a long-running family quarrel,' Martha said. 'We've all managed to get on reasonably well over the years.'

'Some of us have,' Ella said. 'Some of us haven't.'

Martha took her allusion.

'It's a pity Doris has to spoil things between you and your mother.'

'Nay, you could say I spoilt it when I refused to go on sleeping there every night.'

'What's your mother doing now?'

'She's going round to Doris's every night.'

'*Can't* she settle on her own?'

'She won't try. I've never known me mother to be so . . . so . . .'

'Exasperating?'

'Like a wilful bairn.'

'She's never had it to do.'

'I'll make a little bet with you, Martha. She'll have it to do once our Doris gets fed-up of 'em all hutchin' up to make room for her. Once Doris gets over preening herself for rescuing me mother when I'd let her down, she'll make her do. You mark my words.'

'And in the meantime . . . what about you and your mother?'

'Oh, I put me head in once a week and we both sit and sulk.'

'After you've always been so close.'

'Times change,' Ella said. 'And folk change with 'em.'

They had met on the street, she and Martha, and Ella had responded to her sister-in-law's pressing invitation to call and see her. It was such a long time since they had had a real natter, Martha said. Ella liked Martha, but she had been avoiding seeming to look for those among her relatives who might side with her in her quarrels.

Double summertime had once more brought long light evenings and Linda and Brian were playing in the street with other children, whose shouts could be heard. It was a safe street, with no though traffic, so Martha could get a bit of peace without constantly worrying about them. Eight and seven, Thomas's children were now, and Ella sometimes wondered whether Martha ever regretted giving them a home.

'Do they get more of a handful or less?' was her tactful way of asking.

'Oh, they keep me young,' Martha said. 'With Arthur in the army and both James and Mary wed now, what would I find to do without 'em except sit and brood?'

As she spoke she craned her neck to see something through the window.

'That looks like our James now. He's having a word with Linda and Brian.'

'Is he on his own?'

'Yes.'

'I keep going to bob round and see them,' Ella said.

'You want to. She's a friendly soul, Avril. Still a bit awkward in company, but she's a good mother and she's made our James a grand wife.'

'He's dropped lucky.'

'Aye. After playin' fast an' loose with a dozen you might say he did.'

The street door opened. James called hullo as he opened the door into the living-room.

'Now then, Ella, how're you keepin'?'

'Pretty fair. How's your family?'

'Mother an' daughter both doing well.'

'Good.'

'Call round an' see Avril sometimes. She'll be pleased.'

'Your mam's just been sayin' so.'

James said, 'Has me dad gone out?'

'He's at a union meeting.'

'He went, did he?'

'Shouldn't you be there?'

'It's not compulsory.'

'Your father seemed to think he ought to go.'

'I don't know what there is to talk about. T'decision's been taken.'

'What decision?'

'Hasn't he said owt about it?'

'About what?'

'About stoppin' work. T'men had a pithead meetin' this afternoon an' voted to come out.'

Martha's jaw dropped. She seemed lost for words.

'Me dad's gone to see if t'union'll make it official, but I don't think they will.'

'They've come out against t'union?'

'T'men *are* t'union, Mother. Without t'men there'd be no need for t'union.'

'What do you appoint union officials for if you can't agree with 'em?'

'We appoint 'em to protect us against t'coal-owners. When they start gettin' into bed wi' t'owners 'stead o' fighting for us, we have to do summat about it ourselves.'

'Colliers an' coal-owners!' Martha cried. 'You'd think they were the only folk involved.'

'Well aren't they?' James asked. 'What's it got to do wi' anybody else?'

'If you don't bloody know I can't tell you,' Martha said. 'But I'm ashamed you should have to ask.'

'Ey up,' James said, 'I didn't come here for a row. If all I'm gettin' is this kind o' slaver I'm off now.' He turned at the door. 'You can tell him I called.'

'I'll tell him you called,' Martha promised. 'I'll tell him some other things as well.'

James cocked an eye at Ella. He wasn't alto-gether put out. 'I'll be seein' you, Auntie. If t'vol-cano rumbles any more I'd make meself scarce before me dad comes home, if I were you.'

'Oh, get off with you!' Martha said. Her colour was up. She turned her face away from him.

'By bloody hell!' she said softly as the door closed.

'Will our Wilson be out an' all?' Ella asked.

'I expect so.'

'I thought there were negotiations going on at national level. I thought them that had been out had gone back.'

'So did I,' Martha said. 'But our lads must think they're being robbed of their turn.' Her voice was heavy with sarcasm. 'It's like measles: it'll have to go all round before it's done with.'

The colour of her anger gradually subsided, but the muscles of her face remained tight and she occasionally reclamped her mouth as her thoughts fuelled her rage. She was as upset as Ella had seen her; but when Ella got up to take her early leave, she said, 'No, don't go yet. You haven't had a minute with the bairns. If it's Ronald you're bothered about, he won't be back for a while. He'll have to have his pint before he comes home.'

The light outside was fading and she called the children in. They came without grumbling. Martha was firm with them, but fair. They knew that when she said something she meant it and would stand by it. Ella hoped there would come a day when they would realise the extent of the luck that had come to them when she, apparently out of the blue, had decided to take them in, and brooked no opposition from Ronald. Linda was the one Ella had her doubts about, the one who had seemed to know how to turn things to her advantage from the moment her brother came into the world; the one of whom, Ella hoped, the sly-ness in her character would never be employed in anything damagingly underhand.

They wanted to know why she never took them anywhere nowadays.

'Well, you can manage the tuppenny rush on your own now, can't you? You don't need me to look after you.'

'They have right big picture-houses in Calder-ford an' Cressley, don't they?' Brian said. 'Colossal places, wi' organs what come up out o' t'floor an' change colour as they play.'

' "Colossal",' Ella said. 'That's a grand word.'

185

'Gigantic's another,' Brian said.

'I want me Auntie Ella to take us to t'seaside again,' Linda said.

'Do you?' She had taken them with her to Southport the summer she had lost Walter, wanting to get away anywhere herself, but preferring not to be alone. 'Well, then, we'll have to see what the warmer weather brings.'

'Don't make any promises,' Martha said.

'Oh, they know it's not a promise. Don't you? I promise to think about it, but that's not a promise we're going.'

Martha fed them and got them off to bed. James's moving out had given them a room each before it was strictly necessary.

'If I moved them back in with each other, I suppose I could manage your mother for a while. I mean if the worst came to the worst.'

'Don't think about it, Martha. It's not your worry.'

'Well . . .'

Ella said, 'I wonder if I could get 'em away to the seaside again.'

'P'raps we could take 'em together,' Martha said. 'It's no use askin' Ronald. I can't get him off the spot these days.'

'It's summat to think about.'

'He might not take kindly to being left to fend for himself, o' course.'

'You've a daughter and a daughter-in-law, Martha. He ought to survive.'

Ella was thinking that Darby Woodcock would jump at the chance of accompanying her to the seaside; preferably without children, but probably accepting them if they provided the only excuse.

186

Did she wish to take her involvement with him quite so far, though?

'Do you know what Florrie said?' Martha asked all at once. 'About the bairns.'

'No.'

'She said, "It's to be hoped they never repay your kindness by bringing trouble to your door." As if you don't have that risk with your own.'

'Have you heard from Arthur lately?' Ella asked and immediately wondered if Martha would make the same connection.

'A fortnight ago.'

'Can you get any real idea of how he is?'

'On himself, well enough. How much danger he's in, no. I saw some newsreel pictures of that Monte Cassino place the other day. Over three months they've been trying to prise the Germans out of there. The Germans are makin' our lads fight for every yard. That's what makes this strike business so—'

She stopped in mid-sentence as they both heard the house door open. Ronald glanced into the room as he took off his cap and raincoat. He nodded.

'Ella . . .'

'Now then.'

He was avoiding looking directly at Martha, who said now, 'Our James was round looking for you.'

'I've seen him.'

'He knew where you'd be, then?'

'He found me, any road.'

'What had he to say?'

'He says you gave him a mouthful.'

'Only half a one. He didn't stop long enough for t'rest.'

'You'll have saved that for me, I reckon.'

'And some more to go with it.'

Ronald pulled out a straight chair from under the table. He sat down and rested one forearm. More and more Ella came to see his resemblance to their father. A moustache would have conjured up the man she remembered from her childhood. He ran his fingertips through the short stubble of his hair, then drummed the fingers of his other hand lightly on the table top. Ella could smell the beer on the edge of cool outside air that clung to his person. Look like her father he might, but there had been times when she had dismissed him as insensitive to anybody's feelings but his own. Unpredictable in temper too, especially after drink. She prepared herself to leave as soon as he showed a sign of retaliating to Martha's onslaught.

'Why didn't you tell me the men had had a meeting this afternoon?' Martha demanded.

'I thought it'd be time enough to tell you when I knew what line t'union 'ud take.'

'What line have they taken?'

'They want us to carry on workin' while they negotiate.'

'What's the dispute?'

'What it's allus been since they brought in t'weekly wage award.'

'I thought they were in negotiation over piece-work rates.'

'They are. But t'government's just issued some new figures for industry. It seems t'average weekly wage is six pound ten shillin'.'

'Porter gave you lot five pound.'

'Aye. You see how much they think about us,

how important we are to 'em. Well t'men didn't like that an' when there was talk about with-drawin' free home coal as well they had a pit-head meetin' an' voted to strike.'

'It can all be settled while you go on working, if they know how bitter you feel.'

'Martha ...' Ronald said. 'You talk like a woman without experience. They're still dis-cussin' grievances over twelve-month-old now. You know full well they'll not surrender a penny piece till they're made to. They never have an' they never will.'

'It's no bloody time to go on strike, Ronald,' Martha said.

'When will it be time? When there's nowt left to strike over?'

'You know you'll get no public sympathy.'

'We never have had any.'

'You'll get none from me, either.'

'I s'll have to manage without, then.'

'Who backed you more loyally than I did in 1920 and '26?' Martha asked.

'Martha, I can't go against that vote. There's pickets out already and no man'll dare walk past 'em.'

'Don't they know there's men getting shot at and killed so's they can have their bloody meet-ings?' Martha cried. 'Your own lad's out there in the thick of it. What do you think him an' his mates do when they're ordered into battle? D'you think they call a meeting to negotiate a price for it? Eh? With double time for fighting on Sunday? You make me bloody sick with your eternal squab-bles and disputes. You ought to be ashamed of yourselves, every man jack of you. And what are

189

we going to live on? How do you reckon I'll feed your brother's children while you're all out? Am I going to have to scrub a few more floors?'

She made a furious gesture with her arm, as if she would sweep the mantelshelf clean of the trinkets, ornaments and photographs which stood along it. Ronald, with a patient control that surprised Ella, waited until she had relapsed into a sullen silence, then said quietly:

'When I get down t'pit I have to walk three-quarters of an hour underground before I reach me work. An' I don't mean like a country stroll. T'other day we came away leavin' all in order and passed t'next shift goin' in. Before we'd reached t'pit bottom t'other deputy were coming back behind us to catch our man. "What's up wi' that face, Jarvis?" he wants to know. Nowt, Jarvis tells him. It were in good order when we left it. "Well, it's not in good order now," t'other feller tells him. "Tha'd best come back wi' me an' have a look at it, 'cos it's tum'led up from end to end."' Ronald paused. 'There could ha' been a dozen men buried there an' nobody to raise a shout about it. Me among 'em. I didn't tell you because what's good of upsetting you wi' summat 'at didn't happen? There's scores o' things happen in a pit every day 'at could kill or lame a man, if one happened to be just in t'road. What's t'use o' talkin' about 'em? It's the way o' things. In this case there'd have been a dozen involved. Would that have been enough for public sympathy, does tha think?'

Ella was waiting for his voice to harshen and rise to match the intensity of what he was saying; but it remained level and controlled. She was witnessing a Ronald she had never seen before.

190

'I've had thirty-year experience,' he went on when Martha didn't speak, 'an' now they're sending lads down who've drawn t'pits instead o' t'army in a government raffle; lads who don't know one end of a pick an' shovel from t'other – no, nor their arse from their elbow, some of 'em. Lads, what's more, who put everybody round 'em in mortal peril with their lack of experience. And they're taking home as much as me. Meantime, up top, there's fat arses walkin' about factory floors wi' bits o' paper in their hands what get nearly half as much again. "Wait till t'war's over," they say, "then fight for your rights." Aye, while t'owners are drawin' their government subsidies an' grants, refusin' to invest in safety an' modernisation, an' savin' t'best seams for peacetime. If we don't fight for what we're due to now, there'll be nowt left for lads like Arthur to come home to.'

There was another silence. In it Ella became aware of the faint rasp of her brother's breathing and, recognising its cause, was suddenly observing him through an unexpected veil of tenderness. He had dust in his lungs, the scourge of the long-time miner. At fifty, his days at the coal face, in the ranks of the elite, were already numbered.

II

A few days later Ella found herself travelling into Calderford on a bus with her nephew George. He waved to her through the window as she waited at the stop and she got on and took the seat next to him on the lower deck. Before she could say more than hullo he jerked his head and said out of the corner of his mouth 'Listen'. He was eavesdropping

191

on the conversation of the couple sitting behind, whom she had glanced at and taken in as she came along the aisle. They were in their sixties, neat, grey-haired, carefully dressed. It was a wet day and the man wore galoshes. They were talking about the miners . . .

'. . . all of them in jail, John, could they?'

'One in ten should do the trick. That's how the Romans used to deal with soldiers who had failed in battle. They executed one in ten. Decimated them. That's where the word comes from. It doesn't mean annihilation. It means one in ten.'

'They certainly shouldn't be allowed to get away with it scot-free. I just can't believe anybody could have so little patriotic feeling.'

'Oh, they're like that. It's in the breed. They were like that in 1926. Remember how volunteers had to drive buses and lorries.'

'But the miners don't drive lorries and buses, do they?'

'You can't have forgotten, Millie. They brought everybody out with them for a while. It was a general strike. Of course, everybody bar them went back to work when they realised how misplaced their sympathy was.'

'They do get quite well paid, don't they?'

'For what they do, yes. It's mostly unskilled work. Anywhere else it would be called labouring. They were guaranteed a weekly wage not long ago. A guaranteed weekly wage, mark you! We'd have been glad of that when we were running the shop, wouldn't we?'

George couldn't stand it a second longer. He twisted in his seat and spoke over the back of it, his face against Ella's left ear.

192

'D'you mind if I tell you something? The miners' weekly wage award is a third less than the industrial average. In 1938 a survey of wages in one hundred industrial occupations put the miners at eighty-first. If you can tell me what essential job's been stopped for shortage of coal since this dispute started you'll be doing a lot better than others who've tried. As for skills, you need a lot of skill just to stop yourself getting lamed.'

'I didn't know I was addressing you, young man,' the elderly chap said.

'You are now. If you didn't want me to hear you you should have kept your voice down.'

'They shouldn't be on strike. There's a war on.'

'And a lot of 'em have got relatives fighting,' George said. 'You lot seem to think there's never anybody on strike but miners. I happen to know there's others. I happen to know about some air-craft workers who were on strike at the very time our lads were being taken off the beach at Dunkirk. Did anybody make an outcry about that?'

Ella, inclined at first to embarrassment by George's intervention, was now wondering when she might feel obliged to join in. The rumble of the bus's engine was not stopping others from hearing the exchange.

'You can make figures prove owt,' a man said.

'What do scars prove, mister?' another man asked him. He got to his feet as the bus slowed down, his finger pointing to his face where Ella could see the sky-blue tracery of lines high on one cheek; so near the eye, in fact, she suddenly shivered.

The elderly man was on his feet as well, tugging at his wife as the bus stopped. 'Come on . . .' 'But this isn't our—' 'It'll do. Wait a minute,' he called to the conductor. The collier with the scar was on the platform now. He turned and addressed the entire lower deck:

'You all want miners when you need 'em. But when we're buyin' in from abroad and there's coal standing in t'pit yards they can rot as far as you're concerned.'

As he dropped out of sight two or three passengers began to clap. Red in the face, the neat and tidy man stepped down and turned to help his wife. The conductor rang the bell.

'All the same,' George said quietly to Ella as the bus pulled away again, 'they *shouldn't* be out.'

'T'miners?'

'Aye. They shouldn't have stopped work. This war's being fought to defeat Fascism and nowt else matters beside that. If *they* win it'll be the end of strikes. There's no pit strikes in Spain, you can tell 'em.'

They got off the bus together in the middle of town and stood for a minute or two. George was hardly any taller than Ella but had that power and assertiveness you often felt in shortish men. And George added to that the surprising and growing range of his knowledge. The things he knew! He must be the best informed person in the family. His brother Granville could outshine him in some academic subjects, but he didn't know nearly as much about politics and social history. Granville belonged in a library, or perhaps a science laboratory, while George – for all the reading he must do – was part of the everyday world, his place among the people.

'You know I drew t'pits in t'conscription lottery?' he asked Ella.

'Yes, you're going to be a Bevin boy.'

'It's funny, y'know. All me life since I can remember I've heard me dad drummin' on about me an' our Granville not going down t'pit like he had to do; and I've always taken it for granted that I'd find summat else to do.'

'Oh, mebbe this war won't last much longer, then you can get back to summat else.'

'But no,' George said; 'y'see, Ella, I realise now that this might be a blessing in disguise. Happen I was meant for t'pits after all and it took this to show me.'

Ella shrugged. She couldn't quite see what he was driving at.

'I'm going into union work,' George said. 'That's where me future lies. I shall get meself as decent a job as I can underground and do it well. Then I shall go to every union meeting I can get to an' make me voice heard till they take notice of me and recruit me into active branch work. Branch, district, region ... Who knows where it could end?'

Ella smiled. 'We might have a Yorkshire President in t'family afore we've done.'

George gripped her forearm and said, 'Bear in mind when and where you said it, Ella.' She could see no sign of a twinkle.

She watched him as he walked away, curiously uplifted by his conviction of his usefulness and purpose in life. His destiny would acquaint him with heady triumph in 1974, and close his working life in bitter defeat, in 1985.

THIRTEEN

I

First the distant rasp of the trombones was carried to them on a shift of breeze, almost as rhythmic in the march then as the drum; then the unsteady melodic line of the cornets, hardly holding together yet as one air current floated it into earshot and another flicked it momentarily aside. In a gap between the buildings, as the music established itself on a steady tread, the first sight of a banner; maroon, this one, with a great design woven in many colours, swaying between its poles, bellying suddenly as the wind filled it: in a circle of gold a man with a long grey beard grasped the hand of a miner in a helmet.

Ella stood at the roadside with Darby Woodcock. It was the first miners' demonstration she had seen since she was a small child and her throat filled at its impact. Crowds lined the road all the way from the city, where the procession had assembled. She would count thirty-odd banners, half a score of bands: as the double beat on the drum silenced one band before it wheeled into the park, another could be heard approaching. Slowing, half-turning, sidestepping, the men who had the weight of the banners cupped in the sockets suspended from their necks, played their gusting charges like

196

yachtsmen tacking sail. Behind each, the representative body of miners sauntered and strolled in loose formation, soberly suited in weekend best, blue and brown worsted, an occasional stripe, here and there a light grey; a dazzle of white shirts, lots of bare heads, brilliantine on new short-back-and-sides, some trilbies, one or two bowlers. Ella was conscious too of hands swinging: big hands, working hands, hardly a smooth palm to be found. The strikes were over. The government had stepped in and settled the dispute. George Palmer was, as usual, the one with the figures: the miners now had the highest minimum wage in the country, though they came as low as fourteenth in the list of average earnings. 'Bevin says it was all the work of Trotskyite agitators,' George had said. He was incredulous. 'A union man, one of ours. Bevin himself says.' So with increasing talk of an invasion of Europe, a bill had been passed to penalise those who instigated unofficial strikes. Nobody cared. It was another item for the reckoning, but nobody cared now. There might not be any more strikes. When there were would be time enough to worry. The weather was fine. Only the wind marred it and that would drop. It was a big day out, a celebration, a taking stock, a remembering.

The banners gathered in the grassy level of the arena. Looking at them from the rim of the amphitheatre, Ella was put in mind of a film in which Roman legions had come to hear a general, an emperor even; and she recalled the neat and tidy man on the bus with his talk of decimation. There was a fun fair over the far side of a hill. Its mechanical music was carried faintly on the breeze

197

as the assembly fell silent and the instruments of the massed bands were joined in a unison refrain, a wordless hymn for those killed in Yorkshire mines in the past year. Ella wept openly now. She was not alone. A woman nearby spoke as a discordant sliver from the fair cut into the rich harmony of brass: 'Can't they stop it for a while? Have they no respect?' Some of the banners carried the black crepe of mourning. They dipped and stayed down for the two minutes' silence which followed the hymn.

Somewhere in the field were Ella's relatives. Martha had brought Linda and Brian. Ronald and Wilson had walked in the procession. James would have none of that, but he was here with his wife and baby daughter. Florrie had come and George was keeping her company for the time being. Catherine had marched with one of the bands.

There were speeches from the platform. Horace Greenleaf was one of the speakers. It was awkward for him. As a member of the coalition government he could not seem to approve of the miners' way of getting what they wanted; on the other hand, he was a Labour MP and dependent on the miners' votes. A couple of union officials spoke, but one of them was barracked when he rubbed one little knot of men the wrong way. Those standing to listen dwindled as the beer tent opened. Some with families felt the pull of the fun fair. Ella wandered over the hill with Darby. After the probing sexual banter of their first couple of dates, Darby had settled into the kind of loyal attentiveness she fancied some people got from a personal servant. He watched her carefully in order to anticipate her needs and wishes and never laid an improper finger on her person. He seemed possessed of endless patience. So long as she would agree to his company he appeared happy. Happy, she thought, but not satisfied. Among those who saw them together, some who knew his reputation must wonder what she was giving him to keep him so attentive. Oddly enough, Edie Crabtree was not one of them. 'You seem to have got his measure,' she said. 'Keep his tongue hangin' out, till you're ready.' Ready for what, though? If she made any further commitment to Darby it would be thought out, reasoned through, not something she wanted more than anything else.

The fun fair was one result of a policy to encourage holidays at home. Entertain the people, keep their spirits up, ready for the last push – the assault on Fortress Europe. There were two sets of Dodgem cars, the Whip, the Jungle Speedway, half-a-dozen children's rides, a shooting gallery or two, some catchpenny stalls where you might win a handful of small change, or more likely lose one. Though there was an inescapable feeling of a thing not running at full power, of its being damped down by all kinds of shortages and regulations, it was, all the same, the biggest of its kind that Ella had seen since before the war. Daker Feast, 1939. Her first time out with Walter, watching his open-handed spending, his fluctuating mood as she played the line on which she had him hooked. How could you help being cruel when you didn't know your own mind and were faced with someone who wouldn't take no for an answer? Walter might, with justification, have said that he had known her mind better than she knew it herself.

And here she was again, the guarded companion of a man who would dog her while ever 'yes' remained even a distant possibility. She stole a look at Darby's profile while they stood together and watched people laughing and screaming as they were flung about on the Whip. She took him now to be a decent enough man who, if she willed it, she could make happy. Was there, she wondered, any chance at all that she would come to feel for him as she had learned to feel for Walter? Darby glanced at her, smiled and gave a questioning nod at the Whip, which was rapidly slowing down while passengers recovered themselves. Ella pursed her lips and returned a silent 'no'. His smile broadening, Darby extended his neck to indicate the painted horses close by, in their sedate rise and fall. 'All right,' Ella's gesture said.

As they turned to move that way a man hailed Darby, who stopped to speak to him. He was with a woman. Ella vaguely recognised the man from work. He said something she didn't catch and he and Darby had a good laugh. The way it happened it was natural for her to stroll on. She did so, slowly at first, looking at her feet and the crushed grass, then glancing all about her. A stall with glittering knick-knacks took her attention and she went towards it. She thought it must be pre-war stock brought out of storage. Next to it sweets, and tidgy sticks of rock hardly worth the name, were being offered for coupons.

She had drifted into a reverie of comparison with things as she had known them, and as they might one day be again, when the unmistakable resonance of the voice from behind her brought

her back with a start that jerked her limbs like a marionette's. She would have said, if testifying, that nothing again could match the uncontrollable physical measure of her response in the moment when, four years ago, he had stepped back into her life through the heavy doors of Daker Free Library: the man she had no expectation of ever seeing again, who had insinuated into the few days of their first and only acquaintance that haunting hint of a might-have-been which all she had since accepted had denied her for ever. 'Miss Palmer.' No, never: she was older now, wiser in the ways of the world, of the men and women in it, of her own feelings. And she would have been wrong.

'Hullo, Ella.'

Her heartbeat was already pounding through every vein and artery, and she knew that, whatever else she disguised, her breathlessness would surely give her away with the first word she tried to speak.

'I'd an idea you might be here today.'

Heavens! She had thought she might meet him every time she set foot in Calderford, and still her lines were not ready, rehearsed.

'Isn't it a grand day?'

'Lovely.'

'Are you by yourself?' She could only shake her head. 'I wondered . . . I'd hoped you might reply to my letter.'

'Letter?'

'I wrote to you.'

'I never saw a letter.'

'Silly of me but I misplaced your address during my move, so I wrote care of your parents' house.'

She shook her head again. Surely he could see that her puzzlement was genuine.

'When was this?'

'December. Very near Christmas.'

'My father—' she began, when Darby, coming past Howard, said, 'There you are, I'd lost you.' He nodded at Howard. 'You make a better door than a window.'

A number of things happened at once then. The first was that Darby made a move she could have felled him for when, as if with the ease of everyday, he slipped his arm through hers and, directly under Howard's gaze – in as clear a signal, in fact, as a spoken sentence – drew her to his side. Before she could be seen to free herself in resentment of this unwarranted claim, children rushed to her round Howard's legs – young Brian jolting him so that he was nearly knocked off his feet. Then there was Martha and her daughter-in-law and the bundle of Martha's grand-daughter pushed briskly into Ella's arms – 'Go to your Auntie Ella for a minute, doy' – and Ella wondering when the scrap of life she clasped to her breast would take fright at the heart still pounding so relentlessly through its every breath . . .

All in a moment of movement and mix-up that compelled Howard to step back, then let him slip away. Gone. No sign. All too much for him. He was an embarrassment. She had not answered him. How could he impose on her the trouble of explaining him now? Letter seen or not, she had formed another attachment. It had been made plain. But he had written. Just before Christmas. Her father. Her mother's thoughts and emotions too crammed for something as simple as a letter from somebody who apparently didn't even know that Ella had her own house now. There had been something he wanted her to know. It had occurred to her before that he might have seen her in Calderford and taken steps to avoid being seen himself. But he hadn't avoided her today, when he could have done so. 'I thought you might have replied to my letter.' No – he'd *hoped* she would. He was making no claim, assuming no rights. All that might be in the past. But nothing could be settled for him until she replied; nor settled now for her until she knew what he had said.

'Don't look so plagued, Ella: she won't come to pieces while you're just holding her.' Martha nodded over her shoulder to Darby – 'Hullo' – and finished making an emergency repair to her skirt with a safety pin while Avril stood close and gave her a measure of privacy.

Ella bounced Joanna Estelle gently in her arms while Linda and Brian chattered below. Lulling the child gave her an excuse to rotate full circle and look all round.

'Your friend's done a bunk,' Darby said.

He was an irritant now. He saw more than she could abide, with the sensitivity of one who reacted to her every mood and whim. Her resentment flared. 'Yes, Darby, and I'll tell you summat for nowt—' But what was the use now? Darby would pay for his presumption, she'd see to that. Had he recognised Howard? Of course he had. And he'd seen him off.

There was no need to ask where Ronald and James were. They would be in the beer tent or one of the nearby pubs with a special licence to stay open all day.

'Aren't you gaggin' for a pint?' she asked Darby.

'Not 'specially. Not unless you fancy going down.'

203

'You could have half an hour while we give the bairns a ride or two.'

'Oh, I don't mind—'

'You want to watch they don't run out, y'know. There's a lot of dry throats and big thirsts about today.' He made another gesture and Ella, rapidly losing her patience and trying hard not to show it, said, 'You go on down and I'll see you in – what? – three-quarters of an hour, when we've treated the kids.'

Martha said, 'You're quite at liberty, Ella, to—' but changed tack when she felt the nip of Ella's finger and thumb on the soft inside of her forearm. 'You don't see much of 'em at all these days,' she improvised quickly, with hardly a catch of breath. 'And you an' me an' Avril can damage a reputation or two while we're enjoying ourselves.'

Ella turned away from Darby with Joanna Estelle in her arms. 'I'll see you later.' He was dismissed.

Of course, the children knew she was good for some extra rides. They would have held her, one to each hand, had her arms not been full; so they made do with a handful of skirt apiece.

'My goodness, I hope this isn't all cupboard love, because I've just remembered 'at my purse is empty.'

'It isn't!'

'It never is!'

'Oh, it is sometimes.'

'It isn't now!'

'Well, it wasn't, but I gave it all to a little black boy down by the gate. He said he had to catch a bus back to Africa and he hadn't a penny for his fare.' Howard, Howard, why didn't you at least stay in sight?

'We don't believe you.'

'Oh, well then, we'll have to see.' She held out her great-niece. 'Go back to your mam, sweetheart, while I look in me purse. Now let me see. What's this skulking about in this corner? Well, fancy that, it looks like a shilling. Can it be a real one, d'you think? Yes it is. So what are you going on first? Them fly-out chairs? They do fly out high, don't they? Are you sure you'll feel safe on 'em? You won't get scared and want to get off, will you? 'Cos they can't be stopping just for you, y'know. Have you been on 'em before?' No, of course they hadn't. Everything was a first time for them, wasn't it. A part of childhood postponed. Yes, we have no bananas. They might have seen a picture but they couldn't know the taste. Well, Linda might have tasted once, but she can't call it to mind. What else had they never had that they should have had? A mother's love to watch them grow up. But they had something just as good. They were the lucky ones. And the world was full of the other sort. Thank God for where you were born and who among. Poor but caring. 'On you go, then, while I give this man the money. Are you fastened in properly? Good. Off you go, then. Here you are, Martha, take the change and spend it on what they want. I'll see you later.'

No explanation. She was away. They could think she was running to join Darby, if they wanted to. But she wasn't. It was someone a head taller. Tall enough, surely, to be spotted in even this dense throng, which had thickened as noontide turned and the weather set fair. Families strolled, stood, laughed, argued, quarrelled. Children were cuddled, cuffed, sent sprawling, shaken in temper and swung until shoulder joints were at risk. Two held each other up, helpless with laughter; another two – girls – stood four-square and pushed each other in turn, ribboned pigtails swinging; and one little lad spun round and slammed his bigger tormentor straight in the face. A babe-in-arms held over a shoulder effortlessly vomited a stream of creamy mush down the blue serge of the mother's jacket, then rolled its precarious head with popping, unfocused eyes.

Outside the circle of amusements, people were picnicking on the grass all the way back to the arena, where children's games had been organised, donkeys gave rides, a Punch and Judy show waited its turn for best attention and the bands took stints in providing musical selections. But no Howard. He could well have left now. What was there here for a solitary man now that the spectacle was over, the demonstration of unity, of mass feeling done with till another time, in another town. The banners were rolled and removed. The boisterousness that drink would bring to the evening, the brawls and the roistering, the unplanned births that were spring's legacy from summer's abandon, were incidental to the day's real purpose, which had been seen and was now seen to be ended.

She had lost him, and her chance of learning what he had said all those months ago. He had always been wary of her family. He couldn't know for sure how far through it the story of his disgrace had spread. He had been brushed aside. Add the direct message of Darby's action and there was no wonder he hadn't hung around. All those months and she had sent him no word. Because she'd been taking up with somebody else. She had done it before, hadn't she? She was a woman with needs and appetites; why should she bother with a man who showed no sign of being able to satisfy them? Humiliated once, why should she come back for more? That was how she read it for him. But what she knew and he didn't was the emotion strong as a physical blow that she had felt at the first sound of his voice and which had impelled her into this search for him. Frozen now in a moment of stillness, she put that excitement to the test against her knowledge of doubt and her undeniable fear of repeated disappointment. I'd got over it, she told herself. Why open it all up again? Because she wasn't over it and couldn't be until more (how much more?) of what was in waiting for her had been disclosed. She had no choice now but to go with it. It was *meant*.

If she couldn't find him she could write to him, and ask what he had said. He would know from her curiosity that things were not as he must have been imagining. If she went home now and got a letter into the post for Sunday collection he would surely read it on Monday. If, on the other hand, she could get hold of a pencil and paper she might write a note to be delivered to his door within the next hour. 'I couldn't find you' would be all that was needed in that case. She thought with a sudden wry self-awareness what he would make of her haste. She had, as it happened, a short length of pencil in her purse and that general shop opposite the park gate would surely sell her a little pad. If that was what she really wanted to do: give herself away completely.

Turning in urgent purpose, she took no heed of what might be behind her. Had it been a child so close she would have sprawled full length. But it was a man with whom she collided so hard she was thrown backwards, and saved from a fall that way only by the quick arresting reach of his hands.

'I thought I'd never catch up with you,' Howard said as he held her. 'You've quartered this fairground like a frightened rabbit.'

Ella laughed then. She hung at the end of his arms because she couldn't stand by herself, and she laughed and laughed until people looked at her. It was the thought, somehow hilarious beyond words, that all this time she'd been running away from him. But even while people were still smiling in the infection of her laughter she was falling forward against him and all the emotion of the day, the banners and the bands, the hush of silent respects, the impact of this man's voice – more than simply the sum of those parts, the very essence of her life which they seemed to have expressed – rushed up through her and had laughter in tears on the same flood of unstoppable feeling.

And 'Oh, Howard,' she heard herself babbling, 'take me somewhere. Take me with you. Please take me somewhere else. Just take me, take me.'

II

Howard said, 'No, thank you,' and sat straight up in bed beside Ella. He woke her. She was confused for a moment, not only by the novelty of her surroundings but because it seemed at first to be a part of her own dream, which emptied itself completely out of her memory as she realised where she was and with whom. She ran the flat of her

208

and in an arc across his bare back and felt as he
relaxed from bolt upright the still too-prominent
ridge of his spine. He didn't speak again. He
seemed to be considering something very carefully. Then, as abruptly as he had raised himself,
he lay back down, twitched into an acceptably
comfortable position and was still once more. She
heard his breathing lengthen and knew that he
had never wakened up. Turning fully away from
the wall she tucked herself into the curve of his
back and rested one hand lightly on his hip. The
only indication she had of the time was the pale
oblong of the curtained window, which had
appeared out of the darkness since her last time
awake. Resisting the desire to caress him, to confirm and celebrate her victory, she let him sleep
and satisfied herself with the simple pleasure of
having him so close for so long. Their night, once
she had taken him to her, had been like a pro-
longed and carnal extension of that chaste hour they
had spent in Olive's house, the evening before his
unit left Daker. She had been afraid she had
startled him in the park, and remained so until he
had taken her in his arms – not when they had
climbed to his flat, but as soon as the street door
was shut behind them – and, between the small
kisses that followed the first long one, had told
her: 'I really did think I'd lost you this time.'

'I didn't know.'

'I haven't lost you, though, have I? I deserve
to, but please tell me I haven't.'

'Not if you—'

'I wonder you can bring yourself to come here
after last time, but I must know that I haven't
spoilt everything.'

'I hope not—'

'You hope not what? Can't you tell me? You are going to give me another chance, aren't you?'

While ever he was kissing her and holding her so close she simply wanted to say yes to everything. Despite her performance in the park he still craved reassurance.

'I can tell you better upstairs,' she said. 'Not that I want you to break off what you're doing now.'

'Come along,' he said, leading her by the hand. 'How long can you stay?'

She didn't answer him.

There were ways in which a woman could say yes to a man while making love, little things she could do to draw him on to the next stage, or respond to his signs while never for a moment attempting to lead. A man set the pace. His need would start it, his satisfaction fix its length. Ella had never dreamed there could be a man who would require persuasion; not, at any rate, a man who said he loved you and whose kisses were as hungry as any she had known. So there might be some men – as there certainly were many, many women – who kept themselves for marriage. But there were degrees of sexual contact, touching, fondling, caressing, known by many who took virginity to the altar. There were girls who would willingly pleasure a lad by hand; others who could be brought to their own climax by a finger's touch, while keeping fiercely at bay the slightest risk of penetration. Howard wasn't a boy and he had been in the army. He had served abroad in one or two places generally known as hellholes and sinks of iniquity. How much was ignorance; how much a fear of showing what he knew?

Ella had lain beside him in the dark, sick with the knowledge that she had failed a second time to get what she wanted from a man she could sometimes believe she adored, and who swore he loved her.

'I don't know what to do, Howard,' she had confessed into a deep and embarrassed silence.

'No . . . I don't blame you.'

'It must be something about me.'

'I love you. You're the only woman in the world.'

She could feel his frustration. It hung over them like heat. Ella pushed the blanket aside and thought about getting up to make tea. It was too late to go home. She was stuck here for the night. She had intended to be, but not like this.

'What are you doing?'

'It won't do for me, Howard. It's not a full life.'

'I know you'd want children. Of course you would. So would I.'

'Would you?'

'Yes.'

'I wasn't even thinking that far ahead,' Ella said in a minute. 'I was thinking about what's happened just now, and it happening night after night. When I love a man I want him to touch me . . . I don't mean touch . . . I mean . . .' There wasn't a handy single word — not a decent one — which would express her simple need.

'I know.'

'Do you?'

'Yes.'

'Do *you* feel it?'

'Yes.'

'I can't understand that.'

'When I caught sight of you in the park I was almost out of my mind with the fear that you'd reject me, turn me away . . .'

'Didn't you think I had?'

'Not altogether. There was something that made me hold on to hope . . . Then when I knew you'd been looking for me . . .'

'What is it that happens when we lie down together?'

'I can't explain it.'

'Are you scared you'll get me pregnant?'

'Not altogether, no.'

'Because you've no need to worry.'

Not that she could be sure it was safe. She had prepared herself to accept whatever came of their night together; to let life tell her what it required of her. But a man's fear of getting a woman pregnant didn't show itself in that way.

Ella moved again.

'What are you doing?'

'I thought I'd make some tea.'

'Stay where you are for a while.'

'What?'

'I'm going to tell you something.'

'What is it?'

'Will you lie down again?'

'All right.'

When she lay back his arm was across the pillow, ready to enfold her. She put her head into its crook, her hair next to his jaw.

'Can you hear me?'

'Yes.' His voice seemed almost inside her head.

'I'm going to tell you something I've never told anybody else.'

She lay with her weight rolled against him as he

began to talk about the uncle he had gone to live with when his father died. His sister went into the care of an aunt while he and his mother went to live with his mother's unmarried brother, who kept a hardware shop and could give his mother part-time work. Before long this uncle began to touch Howard in ways uneasily different from the friendly contact of an affectionate relative.

'One day he called to me from the bathroom and asked me to take him something. When I went in he was out of the bath and standing there naked. I couldn't help looking at his penis. He meant me to look at it. It was in what I later knew to be the first stage of arousal. He asked me if I'd ever seen a grown man's before and pretended to smile and joke as he told me I'd have one like it myself before long.'

'How old were you?' Ella asked.

'Didn't I say? I was eight, going on nine by that time . . . But he couldn't joke and his smile was fixed. As he talked I saw his penis swell and stiffen to a full erection. I got the distinct impression then that he was going to shut the door properly – I'd left it open a few inches – but instead he opened it and stood behind it while he ushered me out. In another man it could have been mild embarrassment. With my uncle it was a fear of going too far too quickly.

'He used to insist that I leave the bathroom door unlocked when I was in there. He said it was a precaution against me having a fall or a funny turn, and drowning myself. After all, he said, my mother had known me from birth and he and I were only men together. Then he started coming in and sitting there to watch me. He made me let

213

him dry me. He said his rubbing down made sure my circulation was going.'

One night, Howard said then, perhaps it was the apprehension of something further that he couldn't really visualise, only vaguely imagine, he wet his bed, soaking the mattress. His mother was angry and embarrassed for him, his uncle jovial and understanding. But where was he to sleep while the mattress dried? Oh, he was too big a lad to go into his mother's bed, his uncle said. No, he could go in with him. Only men together, eh? And that night wasn't so bad. There was pleasure, in fact, in the warmth of another person, and he could put up with the fondling, the mouth on his neck, his uncle's hand guiding his hand to that enormous erection, the finger moving coaxingly between the cheeks of his behind.

'And that was the beginning of it,' Howard said.

'How long did it go on?'

'Until I was twelve and went away to school.'

'Good heavens! What was your mother doing all that time?'

'Trying to keep her poor wits together. Shutting her mind to the impossible. If it ever occurred to her at all.'

'Was there nobody you could talk to?'

'You can't y'know. You begin to think it's something degrading about you yourself. My uncle always told me it was our secret. If anybody ever got to know they either wouldn't believe it or they would send me into an institution where I'd never be allowed to see my mother again.'

'God! Fancy finding yourself living with a monster.'

'In every other way, in fact, he was a kindly and generous man. I could have loved him. I don't know now that I didn't love him in a way, in spite of it.'

A thought came to Ella. She hardly dared express it, yet she was afraid to let the opportunity pass.

'Can I ask you something, Howard?'

'You've every right.'

'Have I? Did you like anything that went on between you and your uncle? Did you enjoy it?'

'Sometimes the warmth and the closeness ... Just sometimes. And only at first, before ...'

'Before what?'

'I haven't told you what he did later on.'

'Do you want to?'

'No, but I will. I think I've got to. He made me take his penis in my mouth. Other times he bent me over and pushed it into me. I can hear him panting now and pushing, telling me it wouldn't hurt if I relaxed, feeling the cold cream as it—'

'Stop it now, Howard. That's enough.'

She stroked him, her hand moving from hip to armpit, across the corrugation of thinly covered ribs.

'I *don't* want men instead of women,' he said.

'Of course you don't.' She hoped, oh, she hoped, it was the truth.

'But how can a woman want me, after ... when she knows ... ? When *I* know ... ?'

'Women aren't china dolls, y'know, Howard,' Ella said. 'We're the ones who have the babies and help other women have theirs. We're the ones who clean up after them. Women nurse people, not only poorly ones but people who can't

215

control themselves. Muck and mess are part of every woman's life. Every month something happens to a woman that turns some men's stomachs. They make jokes about it because they're scared of it. And then women lay out the dead. Their own and other people's. They wash bodies that were people they knew before the life left them . . .'

'I must have shocked you,' Howard insisted.

'No, you haven't. You've . . . I don't know the word . . . you've disturbed me.'

'Upset you.'

'Don't keep on wanting to make it worse,' Ella told him. 'I shall think you're just looking for another excuse.'

'For what?'

'For not . . .' Again she wanted that single simple word with a single simple meaning.

'I want to,' he said. 'I know what you're offering me and how hurtful it is that I can't take it.'

'You will,' Ella said. 'I know you will in time.'

'How patient are you?'

'We shall see. Can you bear the light on?'

'Where are you going?'

'I'm going to make us some tea.'

'Do you know where everything is?'

'I can ask for what I can't see.' She climbed out over the foot of the divan and fumbled her way to the light switch. 'I wish I'd got some nightclothes here.'

'Use this.'

He took his folded pyjama jacket from under his pillow and held it out to her. While the kettle boiled she went out to the lavatory, one flight down, hoping no one would come out and see her.

216

Howard was sitting on the edge of the bed when she took the tray in. He'd slipped on his shirt and he gave her a quick shy half-smile. He was trailing the backs of his fingernails along the scar on his leg as though trying to relieve an itch too sore to be determinedly scratched.

'How is it these days?'

'Oh, fine.'

'Do you still massage it with your oil?'

'I haven't done for ages.'

'Would you like me to do it?'

'Do you want to?'

'I believe I promised I would.'

'If you want to, then.'

'Drink your tea and tell me where the stuff is.'

'The cupboard over the sink. A tall oval-section bottle, brown in colour, with the words "The Lotion" on a plain white label.'

'Right.' She got it and drank some of her own tea before opening the bottle and sniffing at the contents. 'I thought it might smell of wintergreen, but it doesn't.'

'No.'

'How much do you use?'

'A little more than would cover a half-crown, in the palm of your hand. It goes a long way.'

'Come on, then.'

She went on her knees between his knees, which she had lightly parted, and began to work the lotion into the outside of his thigh with long, firm strokes.

'Tell me if I'm rough.'

'No, that's very soothing.'

Would he, she wondered, if he truly and honestly acknowledged the secrets of his innermost nature

– *would* he have preferred a man to be ministering to him in this intimate way? Or was his plea the truth – that the man who had abused him had shamed him for ever in the sight of women? Suddenly Ella was in possession of a revelation about someone else which Howard's confession and plea had unlocked for her; a revelation of something no more than tantalisingly half-known before he had revealed the things men could do with men; things that, given a different society and no laws for their persecution, some men would willingly, gladly do with each other. That someone else was Arthur Palmer, her nephew, Martha's younger son, lover of the dead Winnie, in whose generous bed he had found refuge from the fear of his own deviance, and, for all Ella knew, in fathering Winnie's unborn child, realised his true and lasting nature. Winnie had seen it and taken pity on him while finding pleasure for herself. And what, Ella thought, was her own likely realisation here? To fail a third time? How often had Winnie needed to tempt Arthur?

Lost in contemplation of this new insight, she had without knowing it slowed the movement of her hand till she rested, poised in thought, with a forearm on each of Howard's thighs. She felt his hand on her hair.

'I think I tire you out.'

What a funny thing to say. As though it was an action she had been considering for some time, she reached without answering to push aside the apron of shirt-lap, and recognised with joy the beginning of tumescence in what she could now see. She put her face forward until her cheek touched, her heart beginning to thump with the daring of what she offered, which she had offered no man before. Turning her face she gave her lips. When she felt him reach for her she took a wrist in each hand to restrain him. As what her lips brushed stirred and held, engorging fast now, she ran her mouth down its length to its root, then back to the purpling helmet of its end which, with another twist of her head, she took in to taste the strange, mild-ammonia flavour of the life it was already leaking on to her tongue.

'Ella,' Howard was saying above her. 'Ella, my darling. Sweet loving girl of mine. Ella, Ella, Ella . . .'

Ella got up and pushed him back on to the bed. Rolling past him she drew him to her.

'Come on, then, Howard. Come to me now, love. We can do it now.'

III

Church bells rang in the square. It was Sunday morning. Howard made scrambled egg from egg powder and served it on toast to Ella, who sat up in bed wearing his pyjama jacket again. Sitting on the side of the bed, he gave her half-shy little glances, his mouth curving in the beginning of a smile. He needed a shave, but all Ella could see was how very, very young he looked now.

'Who were you talking to in your sleep?'

'What was I saying?'

'"No, thank you."'

'I don't remember.'

She thought he did, but didn't insist.

'Does the church get full?' she asked him.

'There's a good congregation. Would you like to go?'

219

'I think I would. Though strictly speaking I'm chapel.'

'It's very austere inside,' Howard told her. 'Hardly any decoration or stained glass. Are you sure you've got time?'

'Yes.'

'Will nobody miss you?'

'No.'

'How long can you stay?'

'I think I ought to sleep at home tonight, because I can't roll into work in the clothes I've got with me.'

'When will you come again?'

'I could stop longer next weekend.'

'And the weekend after that?'

'If you want me to.'

'Can you have any doubt of it, after last night?'

'I hope not.'

'The sooner we get married the sooner we can live together all the time.'

'We've a lot to think about and talk over,' Ella said.

'It's what you want as well, isn't it?'

'In a while, yes.'

'Why are you holding back? You didn't hold back last night. You couldn't be as close as that to somebody and walk away. Could you?'

'No,' Ella said. 'And what I did – you know the part I mean – I've never done with anybody before. So that must prove something.'

'Not with your husband?'

'No. And in case you're wondering, there's only been him and you.'

Howard moved nearer and took her hand.

'As far as I'm concerned I'm your husband now.'

'As long as we know that it doesn't matter about anybody else.'

'I never expected to take up with a woman so keen on living in sin. And I certainly had no idea when I met you that you were that kind of woman.'

'Because I wasn't,' Ella said. 'But this war's changed a lot of people. Women especially.'

'I'm glad you want to go to church,' Howard said. 'I shall go because I want to pray.' It was said with a boyish simplicity to match that extraordinary youthful look. 'Aren't you going to ask me what for?'

'Isn't it unlucky to tell?'

'That's only when you make a wish. When you get the long bit of the wishbone, or see a new moon.'

'And turn your money over,' Ella said.

'Is there nothing you want to pray for?'

'Oh, I don't like Him to think I only go to church when I want something. Besides, it might be as well to give thanks for what we've already got before we ask for anything else.'

'Oh, yes, I haven't forgotten that. I don't know about you, but only yesterday I was floundering, not knowing what life had to offer that was of any value or purpose. Now here we are with a future to share.'

Yes, it had been a bewilderingly swift change of fortune. Ella suspected that with her way of reaching a point where she felt compelled to challenge life to show her what it wanted of her, she might very soon have committed herself to Darby Woodcock. Just in time she had been saved. Though she was a different person from the young girl who had once thought that having this man here – or the man she had perceived him to be – could bring her all she could ever want, she did love him and was intensely aware of the destiny which had brought them together time and time again. After the proofs of the night they had shared, was time to stop thinking around it and accept. They were together because it was meant to be so.

'I wonder', Howard said, 'if you can possibly know how much I love you.'

'I shall let you keep on telling me,' Ella said.

The pyjama jacket was unbuttoned. He opened it and bent to nuzzle his face against her breasts. She rolled her eyes behind closed lids and sighed as desire for him quickened in her again.

'I think I ought to tell you', she said, 'that if you do much more of that, we shan't be going to church or anywhere else.'

But glory, glory, he wanted, and what he wanted he now could take.

PART THREE

FOURTEEN

I

The people who were being made to look at the naked bodies, oh, perhaps ten layers deep, filling this huge open grave, were the kind you could tell one from another on the street. Some of them were even quite well-dressed, as if they had automatically reached for their best clothes when summoned. The ones who watched them from the doorways and crouched along the walls of the huts, all looked alike. They were skulls and sets of bones covered with taut empty skin: you thought they would snap into pieces even as you watched. Don't move, Ella wanted to cry out as one or two feebly changed position, or you'll surely break. Grim-faced British soldiers stood by as the citizens of the nearby town saw what their countrymen had done, had been doing all the time they were mingling with them in the bars, cafés, cinemas, shops – perhaps even the churches. *Arbeit macht frei* it said over the camp gate, which Howard told her meant 'Work is freedom'. A woman among the observers broke down and wept. Ella could hardly believe what she was seeing. On a routine visit to the pictures they had been presented with this horror. Her face burned then cooled as all the blood seemed to run out of her brain. She thought she must faint; the only question was whether to let it happen where she sat or to try to push out to the foyer. The war was nearly over. Everybody said it couldn't last much longer. But look, Ella thought, what we've been fighting for. Here it is, plain to see. What had all those who would have gone on treating with Hitler got to say now? And all those who had recognised the need to fight but thought it was, after all, just another scrap about living-room and who was to be boss?

Howard took her hand.

'Do you want to go?'

'Yes.'

They had already seen the main feature. Outside, Ella took a gulp of cool damp air. Howard put his arm through hers and led her up the street to a little pub. He looked into one room before showing her into a second, a small neat snug with no one else in it for the moment, and a coal fire burning. The man behind the bar told Howard that he hadn't any brandy but he'd recently got hold of a very nice whisky. Howard bought two and put one into Ella's hand. 'You'll feel better for that.' She had no palate for whisky; it all tasted like unpleasant medicine to her; but she dutifully sipped and did indeed, in a minute or two, feel her limbs relax.

It was a chilly evening in April, 1945. There had been some rain. She and Howard had been together for nearly a year now. She spent every Saturday and Sunday night with him, always at his flat, never at her house. Every other weekend he would ask her when they could be married. Every time she started a period Ella wondered why she wasn't pregnant, which would have decided it for her.

'Did you know all that?' she asked Howard, making a movement of her head in the direction of the cinema.

'Not the scale of it.'

She thought she would dream about it for the rest of her life.

'Are there places in this country where that kind of thing could be going on and nobody know about it?'

'Yes,' Howard said. 'And people ready to do it.'

'Oh, surely, Howard . . .'

'They can be found and trained, allowed to let their worst instincts run riot for the good of their country.'

'But it hasn't happened here, has it? I mean, it hasn't, has it?'

'No. Something about us always seems to strike a balance.'

'I should hope so.'

'Do you know any Jews?' Howard asked.

'Is that what they were?'

'Mostly. Some gypsies as well, some Communists, enemies of the regime.'

Ella shook her head. 'I don't think I know any.'

'You go into almost any big city and listen to what people say. Sooner or later you'll come into contact with it.'

'What?'

'Anti-Semitism. Hatred of Jews.'

'I don't think I'd know one if I saw one.'

'Some people think they run everything, secretly: the banks, the businesses, the big shops. They have all the power.'

'Do you think that?'

'They certainly make a mark out of all proportion to their numbers.'

'Good luck to 'em, if they're that clever. It strikes me it's mostly jealousy.'

'They do have a way with money that's against the English grain. And money's the secret of all power, isn't it?'

'I suppose so.'

'Are you serious when you say you wouldn't recognise one?'

'Oh, I don't look.'

'They're not all small and dark with black eyes and big noses, anyway.'

'Aren't they?'

'Take me, for instance.'

'You what?'

'Perhaps that's another thing I should have told you before. My mother's Jewish.'

'You're kidding.'

'I'm not. Do you wish I were?'

'How do I know? I mean no. What does it matter?'

'She married a Gentile and lost her family. I sometimes wonder if that was what affected her mind.'

'Well ...' Ella said. 'I'm sure nobody could have guessed.'

'No,' Howard said. 'Nobody ever has. Perhaps I'm lucky. Or perhaps I shouldn't say that. If you saw my sister you'd think it fairly obvious.'

Ella gulped whisky so fast it made her cough.

'Don't choke. It's not that bad. I eat pork and I go to a Christian church, when I do go.'

'Does it mean', Ella asked, 'that our children will be a quarter Jewish?'

'If we ever have any. Which looks less and less likely.'

Ella knew who he blamed. She said, 'Don't keep calling yourself, love. It could just as well be me. Most men would take it for granted it was.'

'You'd be the first in your family.'

'That's true.'

'It's time we did something about it. Saw a specialist.'

'Yes, perhaps it is.'

'They won't advise us unless we're married.'

'All right.'

'Do you mean it?'

'Yes.'

'What I've told you doesn't make any difference, then?'

'No.' But it was odd looking at him and knowing it. She said, 'If you'd been brought up in Germany you'd probably have been dead by now.'

'Yes, very likely.'

'Except you don't look it, like you say.'

'Oh, there'd always have been somebody ready to inform on me and do their patriotic duty.' He drained his glass. 'Would you like another of those?'

'Yes,' Ella said, 'I think I would.'

II

'Why doesn't he wed you?' Patience wanted to know. She had never met Howard since the one time he had come with Mr Keighley, and wouldn't until he had made an honest woman of her youngest daughter. Not that Ella had ever suggested it. She tried to keep her life with Howard separate from that at Daker.

'Has he got a wife tucked away somewhere else, or what?'

229

'He wants to marry me,' Ella said. 'It's me who's held back.'

'It says summat for him, anyway. Many a man'd be content to take what you're givin' him without obligation. What I can only assume you're givin' him on all these weekends you spend there.'

'Well, we're going to get married now,' Ella said. 'We want to start a family.'

'Are you telling me you've not been running that risk these past twelve months? If you haven't you've let yourself get talked about for nothing.'

For there had been talk, both inside the family and out of it. Her coming off the train every Monday morning with a change of clothes in a case had been enough to spread it at work. Some people who had known her a long time couldn't believe it. Ella Palmer, living over the brush, if only part-time. She was sure that one woman whom she had known all her life had crossed the road to avoid meeting her. Eddie Lindley had been openly offensive. Ella had never cared much for her father-in-law and had seen little of him since Walter's death. She liked Walter's sister Nellie, though, who lived next door to Lindley, and tried to keep in touch with her and her family. She had been sitting talking with Nellie when Eddie walked in. 'I'll come back when your visitor's gone,' he said, turning straight round without a word for Ella. 'Well, I know where I stand with him,' she managed as her colour rose. 'Oh, take no notice,' Nellie told her. 'You know what he's like.'

Ella hadn't, of course, expected it to go on as long as it had done. She told her mother: 'It's not for passing on, but there's something lacking in one of us. We're going to get medical advice, but they'll not entertain us unless we're married.'

The irony of it had only recently struck her. For a year she had been tempting providence and now she was preparing to bind herself before she knew whether what was preventing pregnancy was curable or not. Some might say she was a bigger fool for that than for living with a chap out of wedlock.

'You can't buy a new pair of cotton sheets either unless you're newly wed,' her mother said vaguely, as though the possibility of Ella never bearing children was too remote to even think about.

'Oh, well then,' Ella said. 'We'd best get on with it.'

'Will you be bringing him to live in Temperance Street?'

'Oh, no, I don't think so. No, that was a home for ... for somebody else ... No, we're looking for a house or a bigger flat in Calderford.'

'You might as well give up your home and move in with him now,' Patience said. 'Not that I'm encouraging you in such work, but it's daft paying two rents.'

'Oh, I don't know ...'

Ella couldn't, in fact, do what her mother had so surprisingly suggested. It had come to the ears of the old lady who owned Howard's flat that he was entertaining a woman at weekends and she had spoken to him about it. Ella had not slept at Howard's for three weeks and he was already looking for somewhere else. He had been very patient and now she had caused him acute embarrassment. There were those from whom you might expect that kind of behaviour, the old lady had told him, and she hadn't thought him one of them. It was all Ella's doing. She had made the rules. But he wanted her; she had confirmed him in his manhood; he was afraid of losing her. As for her, she asked herself why she hadn't married him months ago. She loved him. Why saddle herself with this growing reputation for loose-living when she could have settled down with the man she wanted anyway? But the months spent like that had brought to light this other problem. She might never be able to have children with Howard. How important was it? Was there any question that she would not take the risk?

Patience had been cleaning till everything shone. Flames winked in the blackleaded surfaces of the fireplace. Her lace curtains were fresh. There was a velour cloth that she kept for best on the table. She herself was neat and tidy and changed for the rest of the day, her hair arranged with a damp comb and held by two jet clasps. What Ella had predicted had now come to pass: her mother was sleeping in the cottage alone. Whether it was because of pressure put on her by Doris, Ella didn't know. It was never referred to, simply taken for granted.

'Are you expecting visitors?' Ella asked suddenly.

'What makes you ask?'

'I don't know.'

'I like to be tidied up and changed by this time o' day.'

'Yes ...' It was just that little extra something ...

'It's easy when you've only yourself to look

after,' her mother said. 'There's nobody comin' that I know about.' She added after a moment, 'Your Uncle Mauritius might call.'

'How often do you see him?'

'Twice in a week, p'raps. Three times if an errand brings him past door.'

'I didn't know,' Ella said. 'I thought he bobbed in once in a blue moon.' She glanced at her mother. 'He's not comin' courting, is he, Mam?'

Patience moved her legs and pursed her mouth.

'Where did you get that idea from?'

'I only wondered.'

'Your Uncle Mauritius likes his pint too much for my taste. As things stand now that's nobody's business but his own.'

'Well, it was only a thought.'

'It might be a thought to him an' all, but it takes two to make a bargain.'

'One to offer and one to agree,' Ella said. Her mother was looking mildly ill-at-ease.

'There's been no offers,' Patience said. 'When there is I'll let you know.'

'Nay, it's not me he's got his eye on.'

'Me neither, as far as I know.'

'There's summat brings him regular, Mother. Do you bake for him?'

'Bake? Who can bake for anybody these days?'

'By, but if we were back to peacetime supplies you could show him a thing or two. He'd be campin' on your doorstep.'

'Are you makin' gam' o' me, Ella?'

'Heaven forbid. This is a serious matter.'

'What would you say if I did offer to marry again? For a fair question. And it's only a question.'

'It's as well to know, I suppose. Just in case.'

'What d'you think t'others would say?'

'I can't speak for them. But surely a lot'd depend on who you were wanting to wed.'

'Aye. And what do you think they'd say if it were their father's brother, who their father hadn't spoken to for over thirty year?'

'It's a ticklish one, that,' Ella said. 'No doubt about it. I'd say t'only thing you could do would be to run away to Gretna Green.'

III

Victory in Europe. VE Day. A public holiday. People on the streets. Street parties, with tables out on the cobbles and flags strung between the houses. A pity there wasn't more food to celebrate with, but rations were as tight as ever. There was talk that even potatoes could go on ration. What wasn't rationed was either scarce or unobtainable, like cigarettes and facecream. Queueing had become a habit. Two women having a chat near a shop were bound to draw a third and fourth. With the warmer weather women put away their precious stockings – those who had any – and painted their legs. They used a dye now, being too smart to do what some – Olive Sims among them – had once done, which was to use gravy browning and be plagued by swarms of flies. Ella grinned at the memory. As darkness fell light blazed from open doorways and uncurtained windows. Children who had known nothing but blacked-out streets stood thunder-struck as the night sky glowed with the floodlights illuminating public buildings and fireworks burst in stars and streamers of gold above them.

FIFTEEN

I

Two women sitting behind Ella were talking about
a third, whom Ella didn't know.

'I mean, she must think you're dozy, the stuff
she expects you to believe.'

'It's an insult to your intelligence, in't it?'

'Oh, I'd three, she said, at one time – fur coats
we're talkin' about, mind – I'd three, she sez, but
I gave 'em all away.'

'Barmy. I don't know how she does her work.'

'Well, Dick Marshall were listenin' an' when
she'd gone he sez, "It can't be knickers she were
talkin' about, 'cos she's none to give away. That's
how she got her fur coats, if she ever had any."'

They were sitting on chairs arranged in front of
the canteen stage. Though the war in the Far East
wasn't yet over a general election had been called.
Candidates were coming to speak to the workers
in their dinner hour. It was Horace Greenleaf
today. The Conservative and Liberal candidates
had already been and Ella had listened to them
both. But the audience was biggest for Greenleaf.
He was a senior figure in the Labour Party and
had been a member of the War Cabinet. The other
two were nobodies; in politics, at any rate. Ella
had never taken any particular interest before. You

were Labour because of what and who you were; though she did know of some people in little better circumstances who prided themselves on voting Conservative. It was Greenleaf himself who aroused Ella's curiosity. He was defending a good majority and there were places around where it was said that a pig in a muffler could stand and win for Labour. Greenleaf was far from being that. Neither was he a working man risen to represent his own. He was university educated, with a law degree. He came from what Ella – until checked by Howard – had always called the better sort. He had no *need* to be a Labour man. A man who was Labour in spite of his class and education was one worth listening to.

Ella had heard it said that the people would never put Winston Churchill out after the way he had led the country to victory. Others pointed to episodes from his past, like sending troops against the Welsh miners, to show where his real sympathies lay. He had now offended many previously loyal voters by claiming that no socialist government could function without a political police force, and that a Labour victory would mean the introduction into Britain of a kind of Gestapo. Howard said that the forces' vote would be the key, and it wouldn't be registered for the old gang.

The other candidates had been introduced by the deputy Works Manager, but Mr Bascombe had obviously felt it his reluctant duty to present someone as important as Greenleaf himself. Greenleaf began by talking about those who asked why we needed an election; why all men of goodwill couldn't pull together in coalition as they had in the war. Tell them they're advocating socialist policies, Greenleaf said, and they begin to change their tune. Oh, but we've beaten those enemies, they say. Why should we make any more sacrifices? As if the enemies of peacetime weren't equally malignant and just as dangerous to the future of our nation. Unemployment and poverty, poor housing, undernourishment, good education for the few, any old thing for the rest. Sub-standard health care. Industries that were notor-iously under-invested, with poor safety records. 'Haven't you heard them say it?' he asked, pointing over their heads, as if at all the boss class enthroned on high. '*I've* heard them. Let's get back to the good old days when there were ten men at the gate for every job on offer. That's the way they want it again. It's the only way they can see it. To them it's the only way industry can be run.' Never again, said Greenleaf, if he had anything to do with it.

A Labour Government would take into public ownership coal, steel, gas, electricity, the railways, and introduce a National Health Service. It would build five million houses. As Ernest Bevin had rightly said, 'The better the houses, the better the people.' Did they really think that these measures couldn't be accomplished without the backing of a secret police? That we couldn't bring our people the simple justice so long denied them without imposing on them a version of the Gestapo? 'Come, come, let us inject a little common sense into the debate. We weren't all born at Blenheim Palace and educated at Harrow,' Greenleaf said. A twinkle came to his stern eye and the corners of his mouth twitched. Nor, he had to admit, had everybody with the people's interests most closely at heart had the experience of living in a back-to-back and working on a factory floor. But some of them – himself included – could use the imagination and brains God had given them to see what should be done. Ella liked him for that twinkle. She couldn't stand much humbug in anybody.

On the way out she found herself shoulder to shoulder with Darby Woodcock. She had seen him come in, when he had glanced her way without meeting her eye. He never did look directly at her nowadays and they had not exchanged a word for a long time. Ella was on another job and no longer met Darby on the shop floor every day. All the same, his behaviour whenever they were in sight of each other made her feel that she had played some particularly mucky underhand trick on him. Why, she thought – often with impatience – couldn't they have agreed to call it a day and remain friendly? As her way of life became more defiant she seemed to become thinner-skinned, imagining censure where none existed, from people who either didn't know she slept regularly with a man she wasn't married to, or spent little time, if any, thinking about it. But Darby's behaviour was disappointing. She had thought him bigger than that. Realising who was beside him, he pressed forward and started some self-conscious small talk with a man in front.

II

'Our James were right,' Ella said. 'They don't let aunties and nephews marry.'

'I could have told you that,' Martha said.

'I remember he said you'd know.'

'When was all this? Was there ever any likelihood—?'

'They are of an age, Martha,' Florrie put in, 'even though they're of a different generation, so to speak.'

'Don't addle me brains, Florrie, if you don't mind,' Martha said. 'I've enough to think about.'

'Nay, it's not strictly speakin' owt to do wi' thee, Martha,' Wilson said.

'It were Martha's idea for us to get together an' talk it all over,' Ronald said, 'instead of it tittle-tattlin' about t'family.'

'We ought to have told our Ada an' given her a chance to come over, though,' Doris said. 'She'll be blazin' mad if she knows we've decided owt without her.'

'As far as I can see there's nowt to decide,' Martha said. 'It's decided for us. Or *them*. But I want to know what Ella were talkin' about with her and our James.'

Ella held up the Church of England Book of Common Prayer, which had been passed round the room, from hand to hand. It was open at the Table of Kindred and Affinity.

'It says here 'at a woman may not marry her brother's son.'

'And I say,' Martha said, 'it's news to me that you'd ever thought about it.'

'Oh, it were a joke,' Ella said. 'Years ago. We were havin' a laugh in the yard at one of the Boxing Day parties.'

'It must have been years ago,' Florrie said. 'There hasn't been a Boxing Day party for years.'

'1937, it was,' Ella said. 'James had brought a lass. Phyllis, they called her.'

'Oh, I remember her,' Doris said. 'Stuck-up little dolly.'

'Yes. He was afraid she might have found all of us together, in a party mood, a bit hard to swallow.'

'She had two choices, like anybody else,' Doris said. 'She could either take us or leave us.'

'Anyway, James said it was a pity aunties and nephews couldn't get wed, or me an' him could have got together and saved a lot of bother.'

'Did you an' our James ever have a fancy for each other 'at nobody else knew about?' Martha asked.

'I say,' Florrie put in, 'wouldn't it be sad if they had, and then couldn't have ... I mean, there's nothing nasty about that, is there? If they'd been cousins nobody would hardly have bothered.'

'It's just what we're here to talk about, Florrie,' Ronald said, 'only, it's not Ella and our James we're discussin'.'

'For heaven's sake,' Ella said, 'it were a joke. Me and our James couldn't live together for ten minutes.' She would have liked to tell them the sally with which the exchange had ended, when she had said to him, 'Anyway, what makes you think I'd marry into a family like ours?' But while it had made James chuckle, to repeat it now would only feed Doris's rancour.

They were gathered in Martha's front room: Martha herself, Ronald, Wilson and Florrie, Doris and Ella. It had come out of Ella's mentioning to Martha what Patience had asked. Her fair question. What would she and the others say if she did consider marrying again? Especially if it were Uncle Mauritius.

240

Martha waved the Prayer Book, which she had taken from Ella.

'We can talk till we're blue in the face and it'll not make a bit of difference. It says it in here in black an' white: a woman may not marry her husband's brother.'

'It doesn't say whether the husband's dead or only divorced, does it?' Florrie asked.

'It says nothing about divorce, nor about death neither. What it does say is that they can't do it. In plain words, Patience couldn't wed Mauritius if she wanted to.'

'And we still don't know that she does, do we?' Ronald said.

Ella said, 'No, but we'd better make sure she knows she can't before it gets to that stage.'

Doris said, 'Oh, me mother 'ud never marry a man what drinks.'

'Especially one that spent years at odds with your father,' Florrie said.

'How long have you had this book, Martha?' Wilson asked, taking it from her.

'As long as I can remember, nearly,' Martha said. 'Look inside.'

'1913, it says.'

'1913, yes. What difference does it make how long I've had it?'

'Me mam 'ud want to get wed in chapel, y'know,' Doris said. 'If she did get wed again.'

'It applies to Methodists as well as C of E,' Martha said. 'It applies to everybody except blackies an' heathen and they can wed who they like, an' half a dozen at once, if they so mind.'

'Does it apply to Jews?' Ella asked.

'How do I know? They'll have their own rules,

I expect. And what does it matter? It's your mother and your uncle we're concerned with.'

Florrie suddenly giggled. 'Seems like t'only alternative is for 'em to live over t'brush.'

Martha said, 'Florrie . . .' reprovingly, and Doris broke in with a straightening of her back, 'I'd say there's enough wi' one o' them in t'family.' She refused to meet Ella's glare.

Ronald said, 'Well then, are we all agreed 'at me mother should be told what we've decided?'

'We've decided nothing, Ronald,' Martha said. 'It was already decided by somebody else.'

'Found out, then,' Ronald said. 'Discovered.'

'The important thing', Martha said, 'is that we don't want your mother an' Mauritius coming to an agreement an' then being refused by the parson. Your mother would never live that down. It's better they put the whole thing out of their minds now.'

'Who's going to tell her?' Doris asked.

III

Ella would tell her. Who else?

At first she couldn't make Patience see what she was talking about.

'You know there are people who can't marry each other, don't you? Like brothers and sisters.'

'Or father and daughter, come to that,' Patience said. 'It's against the law, not to mention common decency.'

'Well, to marry a brother's wife is against church law. It's here, in this Prayer Book of Martha's.'

Patience waved it away as Ella offered it to her.

242

'You mean I couldn't marry your uncle if I wanted to?'

'You couldn't find a parson to do it.'

Patience now was flabbergasted almost to the point of silence.

'Well, that's a right how d'ye do.'

'I'm surprised meself,' Ella said. 'With all the others there's a blood tie. That's kindred, I suppose. You and me Uncle Mauritius come under the affinity bit.'

'I wonder if your uncle knows.'

'How can anybody speak to him about it without seeming to be . . . ?'

'To be what?'

'Jumping to conclusions. Assumin' summat that might not appertain.'

'I'm sat on,' her mother said. 'It's one thing not wantin' to wed a chap and another being told you can't anyway.'

'*Don't* you want to, Mam?' Ella asked, for the first time addressing the subject directly.

'Oh, I'd have expected him to adjust his ways . . . It's happen just as well . . . On the other hand, he hasn't come anywhere near askin'.'

'No. It makes it a ticklish business stopping him before he does. But if he is working himself round to the idea and getting ready for just the right time to broach the subject, it seems a pity to let him go through it for nothing.'

'So you've had a family conference about it?'

'It was Martha's idea, once I'd mentioned it to her.'

'What did they all think about it?'

'Nay, I don't think anybody said. Once we knew you couldn't there seemed no point.'

'No. Well . . .'

'Would you like me to have a word with Mauritius? Perhaps I can find a tactful way to bring it up. I do get on with him. The others hardly know him.'

Patience rocked as she thought about it. Then she said, 'There's times when you can't beat plain speaking. I'll tell your uncle the next time he calls.' She turned her head. 'Who's that at the door?'

'I don't know.'

'I thought it sounded like Mildred Sadler's knock, but she'd have come in.'

Ella got up. 'I'll look.'

It was her mother's neighbour outside, but she had gone back up the few steps and was looking along the street, while one hand casually scratched at her behind in the worn and faded corduroy trousers.

'Oh, Ella, you're here. That's lucky. I was coming for your mother, but it's you I really wanted. See that suspicious-looking character hanging about by Taylors'? Is he a tramp, d'you think, or something more sinister? Didn't know there were any tramps about these days, what with identity cards and ration books. Perhaps he's a deserter. Better tell your mother to lock her door, just to be on the safe side. There'll be some odd goings-on as the men come home. Not all of them will want to settle back into the old life.'

'It won't be all of them that has the chance,' Ella said, and Mildred said, 'What? No. Beg your pardon. Tactless thing to say.'

'Did you say you wanted me?'

'Chap on the phone did. Couldn't make him out at first because your married name had slipped my mind. Mrs Lindley. I nearly told him he must have a wrong number.'

'Who was he?'

'I don't know. He wouldn't say. Just asked if I could get hold of you. I thought the best I could offer was your mother, to take a message.'

'A good job I am here. She'd have been terrified. But is he hanging on all this time?'

'No, no. I suggested he ring back in half an hour. It'll do if we go round in twenty minutes. I'll just have a word with your mother, if I may. Is she all right?'

'Oh, yes.'

Ella led the way into the cottage. 'It is Miss Sadler, Mother. I'm sorry, I mean Mrs Sadler-Browne.'

'Oh, for God's sake call me Mildred.'

'There's a phone call coming through for me.'

'Oh.' Patience showed no curiosity but kept her gaze fixed on Mildred in kindly interest.

'Are you keeping well, Mrs Palmer?'

'Oh, yes.'

'Good. I expect you'll have got quite used to living alone by now.'

'Well . . .' Patience said.

'She's better at it than she'll admit,' Ella said.

'I have to be.'

'Now, Mother, don't let Mildred think we neglect you.'

'That's one thing I'd never think,' Mrs Sadler-Browne assured her. She took a battered metal cigarette case from a pocket of her wool shirt and waved it at Patience. 'Upset anyone if I smoke?'

'Not a bit.'

'You know we had to get Mother into a nursing home?'

'I didn't know. When was this?'

'A month ago.'

'I seem to know nothing nowadays. Will she be—'

'Away for good? I'm afraid so. She was losing her faculties quite alarmingly. It was that or have someone to live in and care for her. So . . .'

'Oh, dear. Well, there's none of us goes on for ever.'

'You look sound for another good few years, anyway.'

'We shall see.'

'Did the election results cheer you up?'

It had been a curious time of waiting, with three weeks for the forces' vote to be collected. Labour had won with a massive majority. Ella thought it could hardly please Mildred, but once her mother had said cautiously, 'It'll be a change, if nothing else,' she responded with, 'Yes, and perhaps they'll do some things that have needed doing. I'm ready to give them a chance, at any rate. We can always get rid of them if it doesn't work.'

'Is there any news of Mr Browne coming home?' Ella asked Mildred.

'Yes, I'm pleased to say. He's been in America for some time, working on a hush-hush project.'

'What is he exactly? I've forgotten.'

'He's a botanist.'

'Oh, yes.'

'If you're wondering what collecting rare flowers has got to do with the war effort, you'd better not ask me. Except that a botanist's know-how extends over a much wider field than that.'

She was a hearty smoker. She exhaled smoke

from mouth and nostrils together. Ella half-expected to see it come out of her ears.

'And how are things with you? I'm a bit like your mother nowadays. I seem to get to know nothing.'

Ella doubted that very much. Through her work with the WVS Mildred must be one of the best informed people in the district.

'You'll have got quite used to living on your own as well, I expect.'

'Oh, she won't have it to do for ever,' Patience said.

'That sounds intriguing,' Mildred said. 'Are there plans afoot?'

In the second when she might have offered the news that she was going to remarry, Ella held back. Instead she asked, 'Didn't this man give you any idea who he was?'

'He sounded like a serviceman. Somebody with a bit of rank.'

Howard could sound like that. But he would have left his name. And why would he phone her at the Sadlers'? A feeling of unease was creeping over her.

She said, 'Do you think we ought to be going round now?'

'Yes, perhaps so. Be silly to miss him. If he does ring back, that is. We might never hear of him again, of course. She threw her cigarette into the fireplace and stood up. 'Do please let me know if there's anything you want, Mrs Palmer. I meant to say that some time ago. Remember I'm just over the wall. Mr Palmer and I had such good times putting the world to rights down the garden.'

Ella walked with Mildred along the street and through the gate into the courtyard. Along the kitchen passage they came to the front hall, which faced the garden and was on the opposite side of the house from the road. There stood the telephone through which Walter had warned her of his embarkation leave. The last – and only the second – time she had used it.

Her stomach was churning. She sat down on the window seat without being asked and pressed her fist into her middle, while Mildred wandered away. She was still somewhere out of sight when the telephone bell shrilled, making Ella jump. She had got up and was hesitantly approaching the instrument when Mildred suddenly reappeared and picked it up.

'Hullo ... yes ... yes. She's here herself. I'll put her on.' She held out the receiver to Ella.

Ella said, 'Hullo?'

'Mrs Lindley?'

'That's right. Who is this? Do I know you?'

'No, you don't, Mrs Lindley. But I'm ringing you about your husband, Aircraftsman Walter Lindley.'

Ella said, 'There must be some mistake. My husband is dead.'

IV

The house was one of a dozen on a short street only five minutes' walk from the centre of town. Brick. The front door was recessed, leaving a little square porch. A nonsensical strip of soil a couple of feet wide, and a low wall, separated the house from the pavement. Small entries gave access to

248

the back yards. A narrow hallway, with a bend round the staircase, led to a scullery that was stuck on the back of the house like an after-thought. There was a living-room – or dining-room, if you preferred – and a front parlour. The third bedroom had been split to make a bathroom, but there was still space in it, Ella judged, for a single bed, a chest of drawers and a small ward-robe. It was a simple house but pleasant. The sun got into it. It had a welcoming feeling, drawing you in rather than resisting you. Ella thought she could have lived there, but doubted now that she ever would.

Her feet clomped on the bare stairs as she went down. Howard was in the scullery, on his knees, the top half of his body twisted into the cupboard under the sink. She heard his grunt of effort as he strained at something.

'Don't rupture yourself.'

His head appeared. He was grinning.

'You could do your back in at the very least, bent round like that.'

He scrambled up and wiped his hands on a square of dingy towel.

'What do you think of it?'

'It's a nice house. It could be made comfort-able.'

'Could you be happy here?'

'It's not to let, is it?'

'No, it's for sale. There's nothing to let except more furnished flats. We've got to break out of that.'

'How would you buy it? I've got no money.'

'I'm in regular work, on a decent salary. I'd get a mortgage.'

249

'Isn't that a millstone?'

He smiled. 'Endless rent is. You've got some furniture to start us off. We could do the rest little by little.' He took her hand and drew her to him. 'We can't go on as we have been doing.' His arms were round her now. She could hear the resonance of his voice in his chest where her head rested. 'Do you realise how long it is since we even made love? I began to think you might be losing interest.'

'I did explain, Howard.'

'Yes, I know. You hadn't cared who knew before, but once Mrs Limington had spoken to me you thought it became furtive.'

'Underhand, somehow.'

'I still haven't identified her informant. The concerned person who gave her the details.'

'It's not worth worrying about.'

'It would be if I were going to go on living there. But' – he stood back and held her at arms' length – 'here we are with another possibility. What do you say? Shall I take the next step?'

Ella hung her head. 'Howard . . . It's rotten of me to let you run on like this, making plans . . .'

'Why shouldn't you?' When she neither answered nor looked directly at him, he said, 'There's nothing wrong, is there? I've wondered about your mood ever since we met . . . Are those tears? What can be as bad as that so long as we're together? As long as you haven't changed your mind . . . No? . . . Well what?'

'Howard . . . listen . . . I've got something to tell you. I should have told you straight away, but I didn't know how. Howard, I had a telephone call the day before yesterday. Walter's alive, Howard. My husband. He's on his way home.'

250

V

'What are we going to do?'

'I expect you know perfectly well what you're going to do.'

'I have no choice. When I think of what he must have been through, the terrible life he must have led . . .'

'But you're surely glad as well.'

'Glad? Yes, of course, I'm glad he's not dead after all. But I've grieved for him, Howard. I've done my mourning. I can't just switch the feeling back on. All that's been concentrated on you. I just don't know where I am. My head's in a whirl.'

'You must be thankful we didn't get married.'

'We could have done. In all innocence. Who could have blamed us?'

'It's as if you knew.'

'How could I have?'

'Somewhere deep down, subconsciously.'

'Oh, that's all fancy. I've told you, I mourned and I came to terms.'

'All the same . . .'

'The question is, what are we going to do?'

'It's up to me to make it easy for you.'

'Easy? How can it be easy? Nothing will ever be easy again.'

SIXTEEN

I

She had walked past the half-dozen men in hospital blue sitting on the benches along the corridor when the voice from behind halted her. 'Ella.' She knew the voice if not on the instant the man who got up and stood for a moment before taking an almost tentative step towards her. Could this be him, she thought with alarm, this shrunken stranger who had aged ten years in the four and a half since she had seen him? Suddenly he was visible as he smiled, the smile becoming a grin, and her imagination put flesh round bone, taking him astonishingly back to before the man, to the gawky lad with the butcher's delivery bike. Her tears sprang during the few steps it took him to reach her. 'Ella,' he breathed then. 'Lass. You're even bonnier than I remembered.' And then his arms were about her with the most curious delicacy, as though she were the one whose sticks of bones might snap if held too tight.

'Bear with me,' he said as he took her arm. 'I'm not very strong yet. I've got to spend most of me time in bed.'

'They'll soon have you fattened up, Walter, won't they?'

'Aye, but, I've not been well.'

252

'I'm not surprised.'

They walked steadily towards the door.

'Is it warm out?'

'I thought so.'

'Let's go out, then.'

Summer was dying now. A man was raking the shoals of leaves on the lawns. On a bare patch a pile smouldered with a thin thread of smoke. Men stood or strolled about in that startling blue. One strained a girl to him under the canopy of a huge beech, lifting her till her heels came clear of her shoes.

'I don't suppose you've ever been here before,' Walter said.

Always he had had that intuitive way of asking the pertinent – sometimes the awkward – question. And honesty was her best policy. Just enough to be going on with.

'Yes, I have. I came to visit a friend. Oh, some years ago now.' So much that had taken place while he was away. 'I couldn't believe we were so lucky, when I heard you'd be here.' Grasscommon Grange.

'There must have been a slip-up,' Walter said.

'Oh?'

'You don't think they'd knowingly put me three mile from home, when there's places as far away as Southampton, do you? Let's just hope nobody spots it.' He was only half-joking.

'It's all a miracle, Walter. I do want to know what happened to you, but I shan't ask you. You'll tell me what you want to in your own time.'

'It won't be much.' His arm tightened on hers. 'I'd forget it if my dreams 'ud let me.'

'Was it . . . was it really terrible? I mean, we have heard reports . . .'

'Them bombs the Yanks dropped on Hiroshima and Nagasaki . . .'

'Oh, awful, but—'

'They were too good for 'em.'

There was nothing she could say to that.

In a moment he stopped and turned to face her again.

'I can't believe it even now, y'know. That I've come through. That I'm here, and you're with me, flesh and blood, my lovely Ella. Oh, the dreams I had of somehow getting home to you.'

'We all thought you were dead, y'know.'

'Yes. It's queer to think about. Everybody going on living, thinking I was out of it. You could have been married again and a couple of kids.' His hand held her arm above the elbow. There was strength enough there to hurt her. 'You're not, though, are you?'

She shook her head. 'No.'

'No. I think I'd have known straight off if you had been.'

'You know we lost me dad?'

'No. When was that?'

'The Christmas before last.'

'You'd miss him.'

'Oh, yes.'

'Just to touch you,' he said. 'To feel you warm and close.'

'Can't you get out, Walter? Won't they give you some sort of leave?'

'I'm going to ask 'em, have no fear. It's torture having to stand here looking at you.'

'I don't think anybody 'ud object to another little

254

cuddle.' With his arms round her she said into his ear, 'Can you feel how my heart's going?'

'I thought it was mine. You always could make it race. I remember that night, waiting to take you to the feast and wondering if you'd turn up. Then you came towards me with your white gloves and a yellow ribbon in your hair.'

'They always say men don't remember little things like what a lass was wearing.'

'I do,' Walter said. 'You'd be surprised what I remember. There I was with me heart in me mouth till I could hardly speak, and you as cool as a cucumber.'

'"You off to the vicar's garden party?"'

'"You want a slut, Walter Lindley, you go and find one. There'll be plenty about tonight."'

They laughed and stood apart. There was a bench nearby. As a hospital inmate got up and walked away from it, Ella said, 'Perhaps it's warm enough to sit down for a minute.'

'You talk,' Walter said when they were settled. 'I'll listen.' He took out cigarettes and lit one.

'Well ... I left the mill, y'know, and got a job at Daker Forge. I wanted a change. Our James got married. Him and his wife have a baby. You knew our Mary was married. She's got a little lad. James's is a lass. Oh, and Olive Sims got married and had a baby. Surprised us all by marrying a chap quite a bit older than herself.'

'Olive?'

'Thin, fair lass with pop-eyes. I used to work with her. Sex-mad. Allus reckoning to be shocked but keen for all the details.'

'Oh, yes ... What's up with all the fellers in Daker, letting you roam free?'

255

'A lot are away, Walter. There's not been that much choice.'

'And you always were a careful chooser, weren't you?'

'I chose you more carefully than anybody.'

'I used to wonder if you weren't disappointed.'

'But you learned different, didn't you?'

'Oh, yes.' His arm was through hers again, keeping her close. 'Have I any civvies?' he asked all at once.

'I gave what I had to your father. He said he'd wear 'em. You were about the same build.'

'We were then. Have you seen much of him?'

'Not a lot. I kept in touch with Nellie.'

'I don't suppose I'll know her bairns.'

'There is a place for you to come to, y'know. I kept the house in Temperance Street.'

'I'll get on to 'em about a weekend pass. Ask me dad to bring me some civvies, if he hasn't worn 'em all out, then I won't stand out in Daker like a tom-tit on a horse turd.'

Ella laughed. 'Where did you pick that one up?'

'Oh, a chap I knew used it. Londoner. Dead now.' He went quiet. She let him brood, looking herself across the lawns as a military vehicle in camouflage paint came in through the gate and moved along the drive to the front steps, up which, one frosty morning, she had watched Howard swing on his crutches.

'They died like flies sometimes,' Walter said quietly. 'There'd be a spate. Half-a-dozen suddenly not there any longer. But I made my mind up. I told myself I wasn't going to die in that hellhole with them yellow bastards looking on. I'll dance to your tune, I thought, in everything bar that. Before I die I'm going to see my wife and home again.'

'Well, don't be morbid, Walter,' Ella said as lightly as she could manage. 'Let's not be jumping so far ahead. You are home now, and they'll have you fighting fit again in no time.'

He took her hand. 'Ah, but you see, Ella, I've known for some time now.'

'Known what?'

'That I shan't make old bones, lass.'

She glanced at him, startled. There was sweat on his top lip, though, in fact, a chill had sneaked into the air and she had been going to suggest they should move again.

II

The people who knew about her predicament looked on, perplexed. Some were amused. She heard about a woman who had said, 'Well, she's got one for weekdays and another for t'weekend now.' Eddie Lindley was near to gloating: 'I reckon this'll have stopped your caper.'

'You never did like me, did you?' Ella said. 'I could never quite fathom why.'

'Because you never thought our Walter were good enough for you.'

'I made him a good wife, all the same.'

'In t'intervals between running around with soldiers.'

'What d'you mean by that?'

'You know what I mean. You were seen with 'em. You and that Sims lass. She could do what she liked 'cos she was single.'

'There was nothing in that.'

257

'I wouldn't expect you to admit it.'

'There's nothing to admit. I was never unfaithful to Walter, though I don't know why I should try to convince you.'

'You won't convince me, however long you take.'

'Because you don't want the truth, just your own warped mind.'

'Watch your tongue, young woman.'

'Is this all you've got planned for your son's homecoming – lies and scandal?'

'I'll leave the lying to you. You're going to need all your practice.'

'He wants some civilian clothes. Has he got any left?'

'Will they still fit him?'

'Where they touch.'

She was closest to Martha these days.

'What are you going to do?'

'I'm going to stand by him and see him well again.'

'What about . . . this other chap? I thought you were going to wed him.'

'I was. But I can't marry 'em both, can I?'

'What does he think about it?'

'He's heartbroken. He's waited a long time for me.'

'I can hardly ask you which one you really want.'

'No, you can't. I loved Walter. I'd grown to love him. While he was here there was no question what I wanted. I'd helped Howard as well as I could, but that was as a friend. There couldn't have been anything else while I had Walter. And I did grieve for him.'

'I know. I saw you.'

'I grieved and I got through. In due time I turned to this other man. There had to be one, y'know, Martha. I knew I'd never be happy on me own.'

'It's only natural.'

'Then Walter comes back, like somebody risen from the grave. And it's as if there are two of him, one the old Walter, the other one a stranger. You've seen them puzzles, they're shapes on a card. Linda had one at one time. Sometimes all you can see for long enough is a shape with no meaning. Then all at once, when your brain's sort of switched itself over – not your eyesight, but your brain – you see this face. You're wondering how you ever could have missed it and suddenly it's gone again. That's how it is when I look at Walter. Sometimes it'll be him, sometimes it's another chap altogether. Or so it seems.'

'Oh, he'll steadily turn into Walter all the time.'

'That's what I think. We've just got to wait and get him well again.'

'Will you tell him about Howard?'

'I shan't, but somebody else will.'

III

'Me dad says you've been seeing another chap, Ella.'

'A chap, Walter. Not "another chap". He's another chap now, but he wasn't then.'

'It's true, though.'

'Yes. What else did he tell you?'

'He said you'd as good as been living together.'

'That's true as well.'

259

'Why didn't you marry him?'

'Perhaps I didn't want to.'

'You wanted to go to bed with him, evidently.'

'One thing doesn't always lead to the other, though, does it? I thought every man knew that.'

'You're not a man, you're a woman.'

'You'll have to watch out for women, Walter. Some of 'em are not like you remember them.'

'You sound as if you think I'm getting at you.'

'I can't apologise for something that happened while I thought you were dead.'

'I'm not asking you to apologise. I'm just trying to find out whether it was serious.'

'Of course it was serious. I couldn't do something like that casually.'

'Where is he now?'

'He's gone away. He got another job and moved somewhere else.'

'I can't tell you how I dreamed about you. Coming home to you was the only thought that kept me alive.'

'I know, Walter. And I'm here, love. I'm here.'

IV

Mauritius got up out of her father's chair as she led Walter into the cottage.

'I can see I'm about to get under t'feet.'

'Stay where you are, Uncle. We're not stopping long. Walter just wanted to see his mother-in-law.'

There were tears already in Patience's eyes.

'Eh, Walter lad, wherever have you been?'

'Halfway to hell an' back,' Mauritius said, 'if I'm any judge.'

'But he is back,' Ella said. 'This', she went on, 'is me father's brother.'

'I've seen you,' Walter said. 'You lived on Balk Island when I used to deliver meat there. I didn't know who you were, o' course.'

He looked vaguely round, found the chair behind him and sat down. He was tired already. They had walked from the bus-stop and would have to walk to Temperance Street. His sports coat and flannels hung on him. Ella was reminded of Howard in his pre-war made-to-measure, in the Gifford Arms. 'I can't stick around here now,' he had told her. 'But I can't bear to lose touch altogether, either, so I'll write with an address when I'm settled again. I do hope he won't object to that.' She had never solved the mystery of the missing letter, the one he had written to her mother's address, so she had urged him, 'Write, and if I don't answer write again. That way you'll be sure I've got it. But remember you're free. You've got to feel free.' What else could she have said?

'Will you be callin' to see your father and sister?' Patience asked and Walter shook his head.

'They've been to hospital. We shall go straight to Temperance Street.'

'You do right, lad,' Mauritius said. 'What good's con-jugal leave if tha're pestered by every Tom, Dick an' Lucy 'at wants to gawp at thee. Make 'em wait. First things first.'

'Austin,' Patience said, 'you'll make 'em blush. Or me if not them.'

'Speakin' of which,' Mauritius said, 'your mother's summat to tell you, Ella lass.'

'Have I?' Patience said.

261

'Unless you're savin' it for a family gatherin'.'

Patience shifted in her chair. 'Your uncle's asked me to marry him.'

'But, Mother—'

'She hasn't said she will, mind,' Mauritius put in, 'but I have asked, so tha knows where we've got to so far.'

'Mother, I thought I told you – I thought you were going to tell—'

'I know all about it, Ella lass,' Mauritius said. 'I'm fully cognisant with your family deliberations, and I'm delighted to tell you – for you to pass on to all concerned – 'at you were all harbouring a misapprehension, come about from relying on a book some years behindhand. If tha follows me meaning.'

'I didn't know things like that could be out of date.'

'It's nobbut church law we're on about, not t'Holy Bible. It's not engraved on tablets o' stone, lass. T'Church changes its mind about some things and it's changed its mind about that since your sister-in-law come by her Prayer Book. A little knowledge can be a dangerous thing. Another chap, less blessed wi' t'spirit of enquiry than I am, might have slunk off with his tail between his legs an' never darkened your mother's door again. Eh?'

'Yes, you're right,' Ella said. 'If you are right, I mean.'

'O' course I'm right,' Mauritius said. '*I* made sure I were right, unlike a few more I could mention but won't.'

'We were doing it for the best, y'know, Uncle.'

'You were, lass. O' course you were. But as I

262

understand there were no objections on alternative grounds, I've now taken t'liberty o' pushin' for'ard an' leaving your mother in no doubt as to my intentions. Which is where t'matter stands of now.'

Walter had been leaning slightly forward with his elbows on the wooden arms of his chair, a little smile of fascinated wonder on his face, as he listened to Mauritius's flow.

'By,' he said when they were outside again, 'there's a chap who likes to talk.'

'He does that,' Ella said. 'He loves it. Especially when he's showing folk where they're wrong.' She told Walter what it was all about.

'Missing time,' he said, shaking his head. 'Time stood still in one place and galloping in another. I didn't even know your dad were dead, and your mam's ready for getting wed again.'

'Oh, I wouldn't say that. She's not said yes, and she'll make him wait if she intends to.'

'There's got to be moderation in moderation, tha sees, Patience lass,' Mauritius had said. 'Once I can make thee see that we s'll get on wi' no trouble at all.'

Ella laughed at the memory.

When Walter tired again they stopped and he sat on a low wall. His eyes were never still, though. He was pointing out to Ella some difference he had noticed about a house opposite when a couple stopped in front of it. The man crossed over and took Walter's hand, the woman looking both ways before following him.

'Walter Lindley ... By the livin' ... We heard you were—'

'Yes,' Walter said. 'I know. But here I am.'

263

'It *is* him, Ida,' the man said over his shoulder and the woman nodded and smiled. 'I can see that now.'

'She'll soon have you fattened up to full strength again,' the man said, jerking his head at Ella.

'I shall do me best,' she said.

'We won't detain you. Take care from now on, lad. Delighted to see you.'

Ella asked him if he was sure he didn't want to call at his sister's or look in at the shop where he had worked. He was firm in his refusal.

'All that can wait. Let's get to where we're going.'

Everything he saw outside was familiar to him, but he had spent only one night at Temperance Street. It was a home that Ella had made for them entirely herself. She had found the house, painted and decorated the inside, chosen and bought its furnishings. The door she opened to let them in was the one behind which she had found the letter to say Walter was missing, and through which had come the subsequent presumption of his death. It had become hers alone then, the place where she did her mourning, where she fought off loneliness. Where she had come through.

The fire was laid and needed a match only. Since Walter was feeling the cold she switched on a bar of the electric fire until the coals took hold. She was watching him as he sat in silence, smoking and looking at everything; watching Walter emerge, disappear and re-emerge out of the form of the semi-stranger she had known just a few weeks. A small movement, a gesture, the twitch of a finger, the dilation of a nostril would bring him to her, the lad who had so doggedly pursued her, whom she had married and doubted at the altar itself, and had gone on doubting until the undeniable moments of fulfilment and content had overflowed and saturated the uncertain spaces between. She sometimes thought she had loved Howard from the moment she first saw him. With Walter she had had to learn. Now she owed it to him to learn again.

V

She said as she prepared their meal, 'I don't mind going to the pub with you later on, if you fancy that.' He had enjoyed a pint, though he had nothing like the appetite for it of her brothers.

'I've got out of the way of it,' he told her. 'I can't take it. Besides, I've been warned off. The doctors say I shouldn't.'

'You won't want the bottle I've got to go with your meal, then?'

'If you'll share.'

'All right.'

They were going to have their Sunday dinner on Saturday night. Walter had asked for it then. They could finish the meat cold tomorrow. Ella had managed to buy the best joint of beef she had seen in five years. She was going to make Yorkshire puddings with real eggs. They would eat those in the traditional way, to start with. Then the beef, with roast potatoes, carrots and peas. To finish there would be a sponge pudding with chocolate sauce.

When she finally brought it to the table she knew that she had overwhelmed him. He did his best but was disappointed for her as well as himself.

'The first home-cooked dinner I've had in over four years, an' all,' he said when he'd apologised to her.

'Don't worry,' Ella said. 'You'll get your old appetite back. I'd better warn you that you won't get as good a dinner next week, if you come, though. The war might be over but you wouldn't know it from the rations.'

'Perhaps I can try a spot of moral blackmail on somebody at the Co-op,' Walter said. 'Is Jack Tetley still butchering manager?'

'As far as I know.'

'Him spending the war warm in his own bed, well-fed, out of the sound of gunfire, while his old assistant was buried alive in a jungle, living off nuts, bamboo shoots and anything that couldn't run fast enough and the Nips hadn't seen first. Eh?'

'You'd think he'd fall over himself.'

'Well, I can but try.'

He dried the pots as she washed them. Her wireless played quietly. She had tuned it to the American Forces Network, beamed from Germany, and when they heard the music of a big swing band Walter turned up the volume and took hold of her to manage a few steps between the table and the window. As the music stopped he held on to her and kissed her, his hands moving on her back.

'How do you feel about being in bed at nine o'clock on a Saturday night?' he asked her.

'Doctor's orders, might it be?'

'Not what I'm thinking of.'

'Will he mind, though?'

'What's your guess?'

'I don't think he'd have let you come if it weren't part of the treatment.'

'You reckon it is?'

'Essential, I'd say.'

'That's how I look at it.'

He was a mixture of the bold and the shy, his old sexual directness tempered by the gap in his experience of her, of the woman other than his wife which she had become in that time. And how could he put completely out of his mind the other man who had known her as intimately as he had, and for a longer unbroken period?

'Do you know', he said, 'what I remember best, what I used to lie awake at night and picture? When we got up that last morning we ran hot water into the bowl and stood in it on the floor, there, by the sink, and each of us in turn washed from head to foot. I thought how I'd sat and watched you as you stooped and turned, how you rubbed and rinsed, where the water ran, in all the places that had been mine in the night. I'd held you close all night, been given everything a man could desire of a woman he loved, a woman he knew for sure now loved him, and still I couldn't take my eyes off you.'

She hid her face in his shoulder as the colour flamed. She recalled, too, what he had said when, a while after that, they were dressed and she asked him if he was sure he wasn't leaving anything he'd want when he had gone. 'Only you,' he had said. 'Only you.'

Oh, God, she thought, I hope I can carry this through. If he was only intermittently now the Walter of old, her Walter, her husband, her lover, who would he become in the dark?

267

SEVENTEEN

I

'Sicily,' Arthur Palmer said. 'That was the beginning of it all. We were four days at sea from North Africa, in perfect conditions. Imagine a fleet of three thousand ships, barrage balloons, blue skies, and the Italian Navy nowhere to be seen. Then a gale hit us. We were putting in airborne assault troops first, but the gliders were cast off too soon and most of them came down in the sea. Poor buggers. You screw yourself up ready for action, then die like that, because of a cock-up. It was bloody terrible . . .'

Martha flicked a glance at Ella. Arthur's language had never been as free as that before. He was more talkative, too, than any of them remembered. From a straight chair across the room Walter watched Arthur without speaking.

'The enemy never expected us in weather like that and we didn't hit the beaches planned anyway. We were wet through, absolutely sodden. When the sun came out we steamed. And there was Mount Etna in front of us, with snow on its summit in a Mediterranean midsummer.' He shook his head. 'A good job we didn't know what was still waiting for us.'

'A good job you're not telling us all this when we know you've got it to go back to,' Martha said.

268

'No, it's over, thank God. We'll be out of it and back in civvy street soon.' He clasped his hands behind his head and stretched as the friend he had brought home with him came in from the stairs, ready to go out.

'Telling the tale again, is he?' the lad said, with a sardonic look at Arthur.

'How else are they to know that we won the war in spite of the generals?' Arthur said.

'True enough.'

'I'll bet you've got some tales to tell, eh, Walter?'

'He might tell you,' Ella interposed, although Walter made no sign of speaking, while going on looking at Arthur, 'but he lets very little out for me.'

'Most of it's best forgotten about,' Martha said. 'For them that can forget.'

'That's what I say,' Arthur's friend said. He was a fresh-faced boy with full shiny lips and dark hair that stuck out in places. 'Are you ready?'

'Yes.' Arthur sprang up and began to button his battledress blouse.

'You've got a key?'

'Yes, but we shan't be late. We've got an early start back tomorrow.'

'A nice lad, Bill,' Martha said when they had gone. 'I'm pleased Arthur made friends in the army. He was never cut out for a pitman.'

'When you've a father and brother to live up to . . .' Ella said.

'Anyway, he won't have to go back to it. You did make sense of what they were planning, did you?'

'Not altogether, no.'

269

'Arthur's going to work for Bill's father's firm. It's a small engineering concern, Manchester way. Bill says they can train him in no time.'

'He'll have to live away, then?'

'He's going to lodge with Bill. He's got a house an auntie left him. It'll be grand for Arthur till he can find his feet and meet some promising lasses.'

'Don't rush him, Martha. Give him time to enjoy himself. Your grandbairns are mountin' up nicely.'

'Oh, I suppose I just want to see things tidy,' Martha said.

Walter got up and went out to the back.

'He doesn't say much, does he?' Martha said.

'Not in company, no.'

'When will they demobilise him?'

'Not till they've got him fit, and they can't seem to manage that, somehow. And don't ask me what it is. You know how much doctors tell you.'

'They're mebbe thinking about his pension.'

'It's a pity he can't claim off them that got him that way.'

'Hangin' a few war criminals puts nowt in his pocket, does it?'

'No, but I must say it seems to help him to come to terms with it,' Ella said. 'I think he'd string 'em up himself, if they'd let him.'

'He was such a gentle lad, really, behind it all, wasn't he?'

'Not a vicious bone in his body.'

When she knew, from telephoning, that Walter could come out for the weekend Ella preferred to go down on either bus or train and call for him. A vagueness would sometimes settle over him, as if even small things needed more concentration than

270

he could give them, and she didn't like to think of him making the journey alone. His eagerness to show off his memory was less marked now. He more and more accepted things as he found them, without comparison with what he remembered. Again and again she got the impression that he was waiting for something; that often when he was with her he was listening to something that she couldn't hear. He had proved himself by getting home to her and now it was as if another challenge was imminent.

They left the hospital by a back entrance and walked towards the town along a paved path between the high boundary wall and a school playing field where some boys in black- and yellow-striped shirts were running about after a ball. Walter had not spoken much. Now he said, 'I've given 'em me dad's telephone number.'

'Oh.'

'They like to have one if they can.'

Lindley had got promotion at the gasworks and been given a telephone so that he could be called out when needed. He was very proud of the phone. Ella thought he would have liked to keep it under a glass dome on his sideboard.

'You could ring me from there,' Walter said.

'The public phone-box is handy enough.'

'Why don't you an' me dad get on better?'

'You've been known to call him yourself, in time past.'

'Oh, I know he has his awkward side, but as you get older you learn to make allowances.'

'I've enough on me plate making allowances for me own family.'

'I'm not surprised.'

271

'What d'you mean by that?'

'They can be a rum lot.'

'They've never said a wrong word about you, which is more than I can say for your father with me.'

Now, as they walked away from Martha's, Walter said, 'So your Arthur's one o' them, is he?'

'One of what?'

'A brown-hatter. A poof.'

She was surprised at the way it jolted her; as though she had some personal responsibility in the matter.

'I don't know what you mean.'

'You do. You've only to watch him an' his mate together to know. Grandbairns . . . There'll be no grandbairns out of him.'

'I'm sure you're mistaken, Walter.' She realised that she didn't wish to discuss it in these brutal terms.

'We had a couple in with us. One was obvious. We called him Dorothy. Then he took up with this six-foot-two Australian. Sixteen stone. That surprised a lot of us.'

'How did he manage to keep all that weight?'

'He didn't live long enough to lose it like the rest of us. The Nips twigged what him and Dorothy were gettin' up to.'

'Whatever did they do to them?'

'You'd never sleep again if I told you. I didn't meself for a long time, even though I hate the bastards.'

'What's our Arthur ever done to you?'

'Nothing, I just can't stand 'em.'

'He's a nice lad.'

'That's what I'm tellin' you. He's a bum-boy.'

Ella sighed. 'I think Winnie was the first among us to twig it.'

'You did know, then?'

'Only because . . .'

'Because what?'

'Arthur and Winnie were havin' an affair.'

'You're kiddin'.'

'I'm not. I never actually caught 'em in bed together, but I came damn' near a time or two.'

'Winnie and Arthur,' Walter said.

'It's my belief she spotted something different about him an' tried to turn him back.'

'Wonders never cease. Did she get anywhere, d'you think?'

'The post-mortem found she was pregnant when she killed herself.'

'And you're tellin' me that it was Arthur's?'

'I'm convinced it was.'

'Well, well,' Walter said when he had thought about it. 'You have all been enjoying yourselves in my absence.'

'I forget what you knew and what you couldn't have known.'

'Aye. It needs a bit of care.'

'What do you mean?'

'Have you still been seeing that other chap?'

That was the old Walter, the way he could leap a gap and ask the most important question without warning. But the suspicion was new.

'I told you he'd left the district.'

'I've heard he's been seen around.'

'Who by?'

'That doesn't matter.'

'It does to me. Was it your father again?'

'No, somebody else.'

'How many people do you talk to about it?'

'I don't. People come to you with things.'

'Well it's not true. They're mistaken.'

'How do you know he's gone away?'

'He told me he would do.'

'He could have changed his mind.'

'Whether he did or not, I haven't been seeing him. All that stopped as soon as I knew you were coming home.'

'I turned out to be not much cop, though, didn't I?'

'You'll get better.'

'The quicker I do the sooner you can leave me and go back to him. Isn't that the plan?'

'There isn't any plan. The only plan is you and me.'

'Be nice if I could believe it.'

'Walter, I'm getting very tired of this line of talk.'

'I knew you couldn't have been keepin' yourself to yourself all that time. You like it too much.'

'Like what?'

'You know what I'm talkin' about.'

'No, I don't. You'd better tell me.'

'Cock, woman,' he said then. 'You like cock.'

She stopped dead. She felt as if she'd been slapped across the face. A few paces on he waited for her with his head down, his back to her.

'Am I supposed to have refused *you*?' she asked thickly. 'Would that have proved something?' He didn't answer. 'Wasn't it you who taught me to like it? And bloody glad you were to have a real wife, made of flesh and blood, instead of a frozen beanpole such as you might have found yourself saddled with. But some men want it both ways. They take with one hand and throw it back in your face with the other. Well I'm not a whore, Walter, and nobody's going to make me out to be one. I went with another man because I thought you were dead.'

'Nobody's callin' you a whore,' Walter said. 'But you'll have to make a choice.'

'I've made my choice. I'm waiting for you to prove it wasn't the wrong one.' She looked round as she thought she heard someone approaching, but there was, thankfully, nobody in sight. 'If they could see us now.'

'Who?'

'Whoever's been dropping poison into your ear. They'd rub their hands at the job they've done.'

'We've got to get these things out. We can't bury 'em.'

'You could try washin' your mouth out before you start again.'

'If it's settled it's settled. There's no need to bring it up again.'

'I wish I thought we'd heard the last of it, but I'm afraid I'd be proved wrong.'

'Why's that?'

'Because you've only my word for it and you prefer to believe other people.'

'I can't manage without you,' Walter said. 'You're all I came back for.'

'Then stop spoiling it with all this suspicion.'

'Will you swear you haven't gone on seeing him?'

'No, I won't. I'm here with you. Isn't that proof enough? If I'd wanted him instead of you I could have had him. But I chose not to.'

'You couldn't have fashioned to be seen shoving me on one side, not after all I'd been through.

Back from the dead and his missus prefers her fancy man. How would that have looked?'

'Walter, I honestly can't believe this.'

They had not moved for some moments. Ella sat on a low wall and took a small clean folded hankie out of her bag. She wiped her nose, wondering if she was going to cry.

'It might have been better if I'd never come back,' Walter said and Ella, getting up, stepped quickly towards him and put her arm through his.

'Since when did Walter Lindley start feeling sorry for himself?'

'I can't . . .' he said, almost inaudibly. 'I don't seem . . .'

Ella saw with surprise and concern that there were tears on his cheeks.

'Come on,' she said, 'let's get moving. It's too cold to stand about.'

II

He wanted, at that time of year, to go to the seaside. When Ella demurred he reminded her that their honeymoon at Blackpool had been taken during one of the worst winters on record. Blackpool was where he wished to go. He got a three-day pass. Ella took a Friday off work. 'Have you got lodgings?' Patience asked. 'No, we're going on spec.' 'There'll surely nobody be open.' 'Walter says we shall manage.'

They had only a small case each, so were not burdened by heavy luggage while they looked for accommodation. It was a pleasingly warm day. The tide was out and what wind there was blew off the land. They stood on the Promenade, im-

276

pressed as always by the great upward thrust of the Tower.

'Let's not leave it too late,' Ella said. 'It'll get dark quite quickly.' She was thinking about the acres of streets of boarding houses on the other side of the railway station and wondering how many were still taking visitors.

But Walter led her along the seafront for some way before stopping again and pointing across the broad divide of tramtracks and road to a white building with a gravelled forecourt and ornamental chains slung between low concrete posts.

'Remember that place?'

''Course I do.'

They had stumbled across it in the blackout on their first night here. A cocktail bar, a piano. 'It's not officers only, is it?' Walter had asked, nearly as gawky in his new uniform as he looked now in his own clothes, too big for him.

'Let's have a look, then.'

'Don't you think it'd be better if we found digs first?'

'Come on.'

His grip on her arm was that of the old forceful Walter, which was understandable enough with her, but didn't account for the authority with which he approached the desk in the hotel foyer and asked the woman behind it if she had a room available.

'I'll look for you, sir. Just for the one night, would it be?'

'Tomorrow night as well.'

She was looking through a card index.

'With or without private bath?'

'Oh, with.'

277

Ella had heard nothing like it. She dug Walter with her elbow as the woman excused herself to answer the telephone in the office behind her.

'Who's going to pay for all this?'

'I am. I'm loaded with back-pay. I'm bow-legged wi' brass.'

Ella grinned.

Did they want full board, they were asked next, or just bed and breakfast. They plumped for the complete package and were shown upstairs by a uniformed porter who went ahead, unlocked the door and stood aside for them to enter. There was only one thing wrong, which Walter drew her attention to as soon as they went in. He spoke to her in a low voice as the porter went into the little bathroom and switched on the light.

'We can't have a second honeymoon in twin beds.'

'Have we any choice?'

'Have I to ask?'

'If you like. Yes, ask.'

'Will that be all?' The porter put the room key on the dressing table.

'We really wanted a double bed,' Walter said.

'Oh.'

'You must have some.'

'Oh, yes.'

'I'll come down, then, and see.'

'Don't trouble,' the porter said, 'I'll go and ask for you.' He left.

'Nice view,' Ella said.

'We shan't be spending much time looking out there.'

'No.' She turned her back on the Promenade and the sea.

'I've never seen twin beds except in the pictures. Everybody in America sleeps in twin beds.'

'That's only because they're not allowed to show couples in bed together.'

'I never knew that.'

'I thought everybody did.'

'I don't see what's wrong with it, as long as they're not—'

'Neither do I. But it is so.'

'It's luxury, though, isn't it, this?' Ella said. She had wandered to the door of the bathroom.

'It's all right,' Walter said.

'There are people who live like this all the time.'

'All it needs is brass.'

'It gives me the collywobbles, the thought of spending so much.'

'It might not happen again for a long time.'

'I know. That's why you should p'raps be saving your money for something more . . .'

'More what?'

'Well, useful.'

'You've not changed in that, I can see.'

'In what?'

'You're still not the kind to have her hand constantly in a chap's pocket.'

'I never was.'

'That's what I'm saying. I like it. But you should learn to let yourself go when you've got the chance.'

'All right.'

'I can easily pay for this.'

'Well then.'

'And we'll have something nice to remember.'

Walter turned and gazed out of the window. Ella got the impression that he wasn't really seeing anything. He could retreat inside himself in seconds. Once upon a time she had known everything that mattered about Walter, and what she didn't know she could guess. Now when he drew into himself he was looking at all he had experienced which she could never share. Thinking, brooding. Again she had that feeling of him waiting. What, she wondered, did he see for them?

The porter came back and showed them another room. It had no bathroom and it wasn't on the front of the house. But it had a double bed and a washbasin and there was a bathroom along the landing. They looked at each other and nodded and told the man it would be fine.

The next day he gave her a fright. That showing of the old Walter – able, what was more, to handle what the old Walter never could – had lulled her into believing that his recovery had gained new strength. He it was who asked her as she brooded over breakfast, 'Are you all right?'

'Yes.'

'There's nothing wrong, is there?'

'No.'

Nothing, she thought, except the renewed turmoil of her feelings. She had known people – and heard of a lot more – who had gone for novelty or consolation outside their marriages; but who had ever been in the fix she was in? When Walter had drawn her to him in the night it had been as though the clock were turned back five years. For her response had been more than a duty: she had felt the old pleasure in satisfying his need. How could she reconcile that with what she and Howard had grown into together before Walter's return? Was she capable of being blown by any wind, of rooting in any soil she landed on? She missed Howard. There were a dozen occasions in any day when she wanted to draw his attention to something. But how soon would she find him once more relegated to the outskirts of her life, the more quickly it happened the better for all of them? Walter and Howard . . . Howard and Walter . . . They were like two sides of the same desirable coin. I do believe I could manage both of them, she thought at one bold and self-revealing point. But nobody's ever going to let me try.

He tired. She forgot how easily he tired. Stepping out at what she thought a steady pace along the sea-wall beside the crashing high tide, she soon felt the tug of his hand on her arm.

'Take it easy, Ella. We're not walkin' to Fleetwood.'

'I'm sorry. Do you want to sit down?'

'It's a bit parky for that.'

'There's a shelter over there. We could get out of the wind.'

'I'll be all right in a minute. It's just that . . .'

'I know. I'm sorry. I forget. You've so much energy in some—' She stopped and felt herself colour slightly.

Walter was holding his hand to his stomach. He had no colour at all.

'Are you all right?'

'Just a bit . . .' He pulled a face. 'Look, there's a public lavatory over there. You sit in the shelter and wait for me.'

Ella looked back along the Promenade. They must be a mile and a half from their hotel. If Walter's need was urgent . . .

'Has summat upset you?'

'It feels like it.'

'Off you go, then. Have you some change for the slot?'

She sat down in the side of the shelter facing the sea. Where was Howard this minute? What was he doing? How often did he think about her? Had she made it plain that he must consider himself free? Had she really meant it? Did she want him to find somebody else – or hope that he would stay available and within reach indefinitely? Why hadn't he written to her? When would her life settle into normality again? What would normality look, feel, smell and sound like and would she recognise it when it arrived?

The sea rolled in in front of her, hurling spray to within a few yards of her feet. Always grey, this sea; never blue. A northcountry sea. A workingman's sea. Her family had always visited Blackpool. Home from home, people wrote in the boarding-house visitors' books. You came back year after year. Sometimes you would try elsewhere for a change, but if you were really loyal you never missed more than a couple of years running. In a funny way this other place marked the stages of your life more clearly than home did. Because you were different when you came again. You brought the changes of the year with your luggage. Her father and mother had been here in 1915, and her brother Edward had joined the army while their backs were turned. The next time they came he was dead.

Walter was a long time. How long had she been lost in her reverie – ten minutes? A quarter of an hour? She got up and walked round the shelter to where she could see the lavatories. A man came out, nervous fingers fluttering against his flies. There was no one else about. When she went closer she could hear nothing from inside but the faint trickle of water. She paced up and down. It was turning colder. The wind had changed. What could he be doing all this time? A couple crossed the road towards her. She wondered if the man was making for the lavatory. They were the only people about. They would have walked straight by had Ella not stepped out and said, 'Excuse me . . .'

'Why, what you done?' the man said, and Ella thought, I would pick a comic. But he was probably good-natured.

'My husband went in there some while ago and I'm a bit worried about him.'

'Not a back door, is there?' the man said. 'I knew a woman whose husband did that. She got a postcard from Brighton a week later.'

'Leonard,' the woman with him said, 'can't you see this lady's worried?'

'Would you like me to look, dear?' He wasn't a northerner, Ella knew.

'Would you mind?'

'Leave it to me, dearie. What's his name?'

Ella told him. The man went inside. The woman smiled at Ella.

'Can't resist his joke, Len.'

'Better than a long face,' Ella said.

'Oh, yes, every time!'

Ella could hear the man's voice echoing inside the building. She could hear only the one voice. The man came out.

'He's answered me, at any rate.'

'Thanks.'

'Would you like us to wait with you?'

'No, there's no need, thanks. Thanks for your help.'

'I reckon he's fallen into a dream over the sports pages,' the man said. 'If he's not out in five minutes I'd go in and fetch him, decorum or no decorum.'

Ella said goodbye to them and watched them walk away. The woman held the man's arm and trotted to keep up with his jaunty long-legged stride.

Walter appeared in the doorway. He leaned against the frame and dabbed at his face with a balled hankie. He was sweating. Ella put out her hand. His skin was cold. Clammy.

'You got me worried.'

'I wasn't long, was I?'

'Quarter of an hour.'

'So long? I think I must have . . .'

'What?'

'Never mind.'

'Come and sit down out of the wind.' She led him to the shelter.

'I've tried to be a bit too clever,' he said after a time.

'It's easy done.'

'Think you've found your feet and the bastard chops you down again . . .'

'You'll be all right when you've rested.'

'I think . . .'

'What, Walter?'

'I think we'd better go home.'

'If you say so.'

'Aren't you disappointed?'

'Not if you're not up to it.'

'I thought I was.'

'You will be again, soon.' She lifted her head. 'Look, there's a tram coming. It'll take us back to the hotel.'

They walked out and were waiting when the tram stopped to pick up.

III

She awoke thinking she was with Howard, in his flat. But the window was in the wrong place and the bed far too big. As she turned over she rolled into the area of drenched sheet spreading out from under Walter. Her first thought was that he had been incontinent; then as it came to her that he was lying in a pool of his own perspiration, he drew his limbs into his body in a tight ball under her pacifying hands, and she knew that he had been awake some time, his agony real and not that of haunted sleep.

They had come home to a power cut. Her pull on the lazy switch above the bed showed that it was still off. She put on the battery torch that she kept by her in the night and stood it with its beam pointed at the ceiling. Then she knelt beside Walter and clasped his shoulders.

'Whatever is it, love? What can I do? Should I get somebody?'

'Telephone ... hospital ... ambulance ... Hurry, lass ...' He relaxed for a moment as the pain let go. He sighed. She wiped the sweat where it was blinding him. 'Run, Ella ... Run, lass ... I'm badly ...'

It wasn't yet light. With a coat over her nightgown and clutching her purse with pennies in it, she ran to the end of the street. The phone-box from where she usually rang the hospital stood on a corner, but when she had tugged open the door she started back with a cry. A man lay huddled on the floor of the box, sleeping in a stench of something beyond any alcohol she recognised. Willing herself not to panic and go dashing about to no purpose, she stood and concentrated on the question of where the next call-box was located. In a minute she set off towards the High Street and was running again as she turned the corner by the butcher's shop where Walter had been employed.

Someone stepped out of its doorway and she gasped with the frightened surprise of it.

'Where's the fire, young woman?'

He was big. He towered over her, solid in navy blue: a man she disliked intensely but whom she was now deliriously glad to see. Bobby Bainbridge. Behind him she spotted the glow of a cigarette-end he had dropped but not trodden out.

'I must get to a telephone.'

'As bad as that, is it?'

'It's my husband . . .' She paused before adding what was all at once to her no more than plain truth; something she seemed now to have been expecting ever since Walter came back: 'I think he's dying.'

'Come with me.'

In only two or three minutes Bainbridge was opening a door and ushering Ella into what she realised was the telephone exchange. The night-shift man got straight through to the hospital. Then Bainbridge walked her back to the house, asking as they passed the box why she hadn't used the telephone nearest to hand. 'There's a drunk passed out on the floor.' Bainbridge checked in his stride, then carried on. 'I'll deal with him later.'

He said he was qualified in first aid, but Ella knew he could do nothing in this case, and so did he when he'd had a look at Walter. The light came on as he bent over him. Walter had slipped into a coma. Ella put her ear to his chest and heard his heart beating. Not strong, but there all the same.

Bainbridge went to the end of the street to direct the ambulance while she dressed in readiness. But when it came the men wouldn't let her go with them. They carried Walter downstairs on a stretcher and told her, rather offhandedly, she thought, to ring up in three hours' time.

She would have liked then to go to her mother's; anything rather than be alone with her fears. But if they sent a message they wouldn't know where to find her. She put the kettle on for tea. They had brought fish and chips in for supper and the faint smell of them still lingered in the living-room. Ella found the wrapping-paper and used it in lighting the fire. They had made do with the electric fire last night, since Walter went to bed as soon as he had eaten. How close he had lain then. So close, yet without sexual intent. She couldn't help thinking of a boy whom nightmare had driven to the haven of his mother's bed. Another Walter ... So many Walters: the vicious and revenge-seeking, the masterful, the vague and lost, the frightened, looking into the dark at something only he could see ... She played her wireless for distraction. It was still tuned to the American Forces

Network in Munich, and melodies from a new Broadway musical. After a while she made toast. The fire wasn't ready for that yet so she browned the bread under the oven grill. She ate it simply spread with butter, nothing else.

She was trying not to watch the clock, while wondering if the ambulanceman's refusal to take her with them had been because of some military regulation or just his bloody-mindedness. Either way, why should she accept his time of three hours? If they had anything to tell her they could tell her now. She went for her coat.

The drunkard had gone from the phone-box but left dried vomit and a stink that almost stopped her breath. She dialled with one foot holding open the heavy door, her coppers ready on the shelf. The line was engaged. There must, she thought, be another line, but this was the only number she had. The next time she tried, half an hour later, she was dressed for travelling to Calderford and when she got the engaged tone again she walked straight on to the bus-stop in the High Street.

IV

She was looking round the big entrance hall for someone to ask when her gaze fell on the man sitting just inside the opening of a corridor, his elbows on his knees, his hands holding his head. Her heart lurched. He was bad news. She walked slowly across and stood over him.

'Now then.'

Lindley looked up. 'Where have you come from?'

'From outside. What are you doing here?'

'They sent for me.'

'When was that?' He gave her a time. Little more than an hour after they had taken Walter from Temperance Street. 'Couldn't you have got a message to me?' He didn't answer. The question she wanted to ask was screaming inside her head, but would not translate into spoken words. Instead she said, 'Have you seen him?' Lindley nodded. 'How is he?'

Slowly Lindley straightened as his face came round.

'How is he? How do you think he is?'

'How do I know,' she began to say when his brutal declaration covered it.

'He's dead. That's how he is. He's gone.'

Ella sat down beside him but one chair away. The speed of events appalled her. She felt herself begin to tremble.

'I could have been here.'

'Your choice is made for you now, isn't it?' Lindley said. 'If you ask me he didn't want to live.'

'Don't talk ridiculous.'

'What was there here for him when you were thick with somebody else?'

'Talk about something you know.'

'His liver packed up,' Lindley said. 'They say there was nowt to be done about it.' Even in grief he took pleasure in imparting inside information.

'Who can I talk to?' Ella asked him.

'There'll be t'army surgeon along in a minute to talk to me.'

'I'm his next of kin,' Ella said and was ashamed of her petty claim for preference. But the man beside her disgusted her with his groundless dislike

289

of her and his callous disregard in not getting a message to her.

'I could have seen him,' she said. 'I'd have had time, if you'd let me know.'

Lindley suddenly choked, as if his windpipe was blocked. 'Why did he have to come back? Why do we have to go through all this twice?'

EIGHTEEN

I

Why? Nobody knew what to think or how to feel. They had been perplexed when he came back from the grave; now they were bewildered. People liked to think of some great unseen plan behind all things, but they could see no sense in this, no pattern at all. How could he have been taken again, so soon? How could he have died twice? Where was the fairness in it? What was it for?

Ella thought all that too, but she knew that he had achieved something. He had got back, which was a victory in itself. He had died at home and that was his wish – what had kept him alive through his captivity and all he had suffered. He had been happy at the last. She knew it. The sad thing, though, was that he had never known what she had to tell Howard now. Something close to a miracle.

II

It was four months later that she walked along a tree-lined crescent perhaps six or seven minutes from St Luke's Church. The better sort had certainly gathered here, she reflected. The houses were all detached, all different in design, with a variety of embellishments, all big, with seven or eight bedrooms, some of them, and three floors. People on a social level with the Sadlers lived here, with live-in skivvies before the war and perhaps a cook-housekeeper, like Ella's sister Ada. But for all the wealth they signalled there was hardly a one of them that Ella thought she could have lived in without a swift decline into the doldrums. The day, under a sky without light, was no help: it conspired with heavy shrubs and bare trees to increase the gloom, the spirit-lowering melancholy of everything around her.

The address of the house she was looking for had come out of the telephone directory; she had already had a general idea of its whereabouts, and the woman's name wasn't a common one, so she was as sure as she could be that she was heading for the right place. All the same, she had a moment of doubt when the heavy front door opened a couple of feet some two minutes after she had rapped the iron knocker. She had had, she supposed, a vague picture of an imposing woman in twin-set and pearls, her hair handsomely cut and set, and the quite frail old lady in a hat of burgundy felt and an outdoor coat took her aback. Ella guessed at once that she was dressed against the chill inside the house and had not been caught on the point of going out.

'Mrs Limington?'

'Yes. Do you want something?' Her eyes were shrewd. They took all in.

'You are the Mrs Limington who owns property in St Luke's Square?'

'Yes. But there's none vacant.'

'I'm trying to trace one of your previous

292

tenants. Howard Strickland. I wonder if he left a forwarding address.'

Mrs Limington's gaze rested long enough for confirmation on Ella's middle and the burden which enlarged it, as thin rain began to fall.

'Who are you?'

'I'm Mrs Lindley. Ella Lindley. Mr Strickland was going to send me his new address when he got settled.'

'But he hasn't done?'

'No.'

'You'd better stand inside for a minute, er. You did say *Mrs* Lindley?'

'Yes, I'm a widow.' The hall stretched away for ever. Could the old woman possibly live here on her own? 'It's important for me to get in touch with Mr Strickland.'

'I expect so,' Mrs Limington said. 'Not a minute to lose.' Again her quick sidelong glance registered Ella's waistline.

As Ella opened her mouth to speak again, the old lady went on, 'Mr Strickland has been a surprise to me. Such a charming and straightforward man I took him to be.'

'Oh, he is. He's a gentleman.'

'All the same, I don't think it's my place to divulge his whereabouts.'

'It really is important for me to get in touch with him.'

'No doubt. But you must see, Mrs Lindley – and I've no wish to sound offensive – if Mr Strickland had wanted you to know where he was, he'd have told you. Surely. You do see my position. Don't you?'

'*Do* you know where he is, Mrs Limington?'

Ella said. 'Or am I wasting my time talking to you?'

'I do know where he is,' the old woman said.

'Then there can be no harm in asking you to send him this, can there?' She took the envelope out of her bag. 'It's got his name on it and a stamp. All it needs is an address.'

'I'll see that he gets it.'

'Mrs Limington . . .' Ella took a deep breath. All of a sudden her heart was racing. Within twenty-four hours Howard would know it all. 'Please. I'm relying on you not to forget.'

'When I say I'll do a thing I do it,' Mrs Limington said with a spirited edge to her voice. 'Otherwise I shouldn't offer.' She held the door for Ella. 'I hope things turn out for you.'

III

In a little while, as she noted the direction her feet were taking her, she wondered how she could have thought she would leave the neighbourhood without a look at the square. As she walked she ran over yet again the content of what she had entrusted to Mrs Limington. There had been no point at all in writing the letter unless she was perfectly honest and told him everything she felt; no use in keeping anything back, even though she couldn't know for sure what his feelings might be after this interval and the great shock that Walter's return had been to him. How did she know what he had come to terms with, how he had decided his life from then on? All the same, the first thing she wanted him to know was that she would go to him wherever he was. He had only to say the word. But was that now the most important thing she had to tell him? She had thought it through so many times it had flowed easy in the writing, for she had wanted to be ready, as soon as Howard wrote and told her where he was.

She had waited. She had thought. She had pictured him, submerged in that colossal wilderness of streets she always imagined Birmingham as being, and she despaired of ever being able to find him if he didn't write, if he waited until she could bear it no longer, because he thought she was still living her own life, committed to someone else, and no room in it for him.

Again without conscious decision she had walked round two sides of the square and come to the house. It was foolish to wish to mount the steps to the door. There was no point in it. All this should be put behind her until she knew there would be a future to link it to. When she knew what Howard felt and wanted. But she peered closely at the bell-cards to see the name of the present occupier. Lazy of whoever it was not to have changed the card. The ink had faded but 'Strickland' it still said. Her pulse was racing. She felt near to something, some revelation. She started and stepped back as the door was flung open. The girl who came out said 'Sorry' with a grin and would have gone on had Ella not detained her with, 'Excuse me . . .'

'Uh, uh . . .'

'I knew Mr Strickland who used to live in the top flat. Have you any idea where he moved to?'

'He's moved since breakfast if he's moved at all. I saw him go out.' She laughed. 'Hang around. You might catch him coming in.'

She went bounding off. Ella descended to the pavement. The sky had brightened. There was even a little pale sunlight, and a seat directly in it by the church door. From it she could still see Howard's door. She crossed to the bench and sat down.

No wonder Mrs Limington had been cagey, thinking that Howard had tricked her and she was now returning with his child. But it wasn't his child, it was Walter's and it was the most important thing he should know before he decided anything. She was carrying Walter's child and when she went to Howard – if he wanted her to come – it would go with her. If he couldn't bear that there was no future for them together. If he could she would try with all her might and main, with all her heart, to be the wife he had wanted her to be before. She knew that it was meant to be. They were meant to be together. She said it while she still did not know what his feelings were and what they would turn into when he had read her letter. She was going to have to live the rest of her life with a great lingering sadness, but she knew as surely as she knew anything that there could be happiness for them as well.

'Now you know what I feel and what I want,' she had written. 'You know what I can give you. Now it is up to you . . .' And she had added a postscript. 'All we need is to be brave, Howard, and we can have enough. Not all we want or wanted. Life changes everything even as it gives it to us. But we can have plenty. Together we can surely get through.'

Yes, it was a good letter. It said what she wanted it to say and she had missed nothing out. She had

lived through the oddest – perhaps the most painful – months of her life. Now she wanted to know
where she was going.

IV

She didn't see him arrive. One moment there was
no one near, the next he was standing over her
and speaking to her.

'Ella. What are you doing here?'

'Hullo, Howard. I've been waiting for you.'

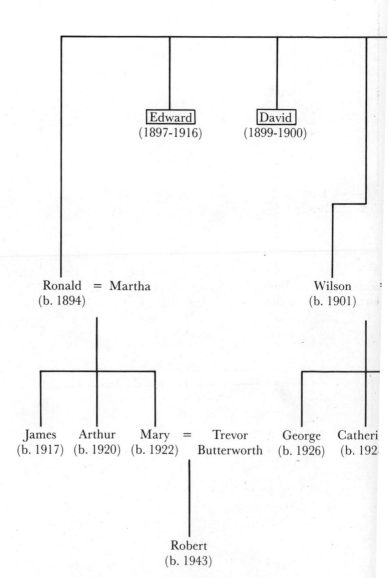

Sugden Palme
(b. 1870)

Edward
(1897-1916)

David
(1899-1900)

Ronald = Martha
(b. 1894)

Wilson
(b. 1901)

James   Arthur   Mary   =   Trevor   George   Catheri
(b. 1917)   (b. 1920)   (b. 1922)   Butterworth   (b. 1926)   (b. 192

Robert
(b. 1943)